CARRION & CO.

Written by Evan Kamriguel
Illustrated by Ella Joyce

ISBN: 979-8-218-35070-3

First edition

Revision five

Cover design by: Ella Joyce

To my Lord Jesus Christ, for blessing me with life and a desire to wrestle with words. May this work glorify Him.

To Mom and Dad, for loving and supporting me unconditionally, no matter what challenges emerge.

To Jacob, for being a great friend and lending an ear to my ramblings.

"Wash me thoroughly from mine iniquity, and cleanse me from my sin."

PSALMS 51:2

CONTENTS

PROLOGUE: DRY SPELL

"*Here be rain,*" misleadingly read a small, crooked sign for an empty, dismal place. It greatly underestimated the torrents of rain everywhere, pelting everything, never ending or ceasing. When, on rare occasions, the rain stopped, trouble and a sort of supernatural dread came hand in hand. Ahead of the sign rested something that resembled a town. It did not have a name, nor did it need one.

Unlike most decent settlements, this town embraced the rain. Other places lived by the clock or the season, but it lived and died drenched in rainfall. At the center, smothered in dripping grey-blue streaks, a gothic church managed to shine amongst the cluttered desolation of cramped, dilapidated buildings that surrounded it. Its jagged spire almost managed to cut the clouds open to free the sun, but it did not.

Lavish weddings took place in the church on the rare occasion that one was needed. Frighteningly, families were becoming an endangered species. Besides ceremonies and sermons, a few town officials met inside the church. They planned to build a proper town hall, but the costs were always too tight. It did not stop them from dreaming their dreams.

The darkened brown-brick market rarely bustled with visitors hungry for overly weighty coats. Stylish yet hefty, they consisted of layers of heavy fabrics, meaning they were only conditioned for a monsoon. Some crafty, often deemed crazy, women tinkered dresses from them to sell. The only buyers, though, remained the townsfolk, desperate to stave away the shame of nakedness. It was downright sinful to let the rain kiss their bare skin, after all.

Near the outskirts of the town was a formerly foreclosed building dedicated to the police force, previously serving as a shoddy convenience store. Despite their best efforts, they could never clear the stench of old rotting food; the little shack cried out for monetary mercy, but none came. Bordering the northern edge of the town, a river called the Cistern occasionally spat up a drop or two of water. It somehow remained shallow despite the rain overhead. Some claimed that the river was cursed, committed eternally to spite them. Perhaps they were right.

Superstitions aside, what little water it provided was funneled through a small plant called the Strayer for treatment. Strangers assumed the torrential downpour eased the load on farmers near the outskirts of the town; however, they were sorely mistaken. The dirt was so wet and muddy that nothing could be planted. So, the town often begrudgingly begged for food from their Northern kin–past the Cistern.

Although if they were being honest, the townspeople saw all outsiders as foreigners. Needless to say, due in part to the environment and equally in part to the people, few visited the town. When some mistakenly stumbled upon it, they were quick to flee, muttering curses for the rain to end. If their dreadful wishes somehow came to pass, the half-aquatic plants would shrivel in despair. The townsfolk had no fear of such irrational things: the rain would surely outlive all of them.

Yet, when one fateful dry spell began, everything fell apart. As drops ceased to streak down roof tiles, clattering all the while, the people, in horror, hid in their homes, drying out. Occasional outsiders, oblivious to the curious lack of townsfolk, continued to roam the streets aimlessly. They had time to do and think about things long neglected, which was not for the best.

As a lost man pursued a nameless thing in an unending search, and some member of the force pondered the news that an outsider would soon arrive at his doorstep, and a starry-eyed coachman found himself preoccupied with the delicate business of saving a soul, and a masked thing, not quite a man, was finally able to set his plan into motion, and a secretary counted his pencils with unprecedented care, and an old polygamist plotted to free himself from prison, and some other doctor set to work on perfecting an abomination passed on to him, and a bartender sighed about another day serving drinks to strangers, and an aging relic of a bygone era polished a display to a shiny gleam, and a wife cried out for her old husband to come home one last time, and a tiny rat scurried about with a pen in its mouth, fate was made. And death came.

Yesterday, today, forevermore...

I

CHAPTER ONE: SALUTATIONS AND SENTIMENTS

A figure, standing still under an awning just beyond the hazy windowsill, held an orange glow in his hand. Occasionally, he twiddled the little light between his fingers, which evidently, was soothing because he had been at it for nearly an hour. The rather large man studying him shook his head; the carriage itself had arrived roughly half an hour prior, already considerably later than expected–so it seemed timeliness meant very little to him. The Deputy had assured him that this particular outsider had his uses and, as such, would be just the right person to accompany him on his case. He was beginning to have his doubts.

Evidently, the scrawny thing decided it was satisfied, so it chucked the tiny torch into the pouring rain ahead. It burnt out far before reaching the ground. Straightening his coat and vomit colored tie, which seemed quite oversized for his frame, the pole-man, or perhaps his shadow, moved away. A few moments later, a knock, followed by a score more for good measure, sounded at his door. If he had put much more force on it, the poor thing would tear free from its hinges. The big man's missus would have plenty to say–she always seemed keen on it.

Deciding he was sick of waiting, the large man made his way over to the door before slowly wedging it open to find the phantom was, in fact, a man. Leading his guest inside, he seated himself comfortably on a shoddy old chair his mother had helped sew. The curious creature before him neglected to wipe the mud off his boots, instead tracking in a brown pile of muck with each step. He awkwardly held a hat, which for some bizarre reason, was filled to the brim with rainwater. Turning it over on the ground, he put the sopping wet thing on the hanger as if it were entirely normal to do so. Grunting, the big man spoke up as the thin man studied him.

"I was beginning to worry you didn't make it, with the short notice and all," boomed the large man with a small little head. It poked off his body like a lantern left on a barrel. Two meaty hands that looked perfect for strangling or breaking, among other things, bobbed on the chair's armrests impatiently. His large, milky, wonky pupil drifted from place to place in the vast ocean of sclera that was his eye. It was rather unpleasant to look at–certainly an eyesore to everyone around him.

A mane, along with years of stress, lay in the intricate folds of his face. They all doubled down through his chin, concentrating bulbously around his neck. Considerable oddities aside, his trunk was stout, and his stomach protruded like a mesa. Veins bulged on his forehead and climbed down his forearms. By all accounts, the large man was quite intimidating.

"Well, the lovely weather here hardly helped. The Fates can certainly be a bitch sometimes, eh?" replied the rail-thin man before snickering. Under better light, he looked more than frail–downright sickly. Two grisly sideburns kissed his cheeks, obviously unkempt for ages. His fingers, bony and brittle, looked as though they were one bad accident away from snapping. Yet, his two glimmering green eyes shined with an unspoken ferocity. Such glittering vitality meant that his ragged appearance could only be so true to form. The large man considered shrugging and jokingly questioning the man's ruined hat but settled on asking something simpler.

"You smoke? Might have trouble with that here," stated the large man as his milky eye, a clouded island, continued to swim around in the cavity in his tiny head. The slim man was clearly one of those types who desperately tried to be an enigma, saying terribly absurd things to get a rise out of others. Studying him briefly with a look of indignation, the thin man shrugged dramatically before answering.

"Of course not. Do I look like some sort of junkie to you, Constable? I do not make a business of answering silly questions," replied the slim man slyly and smugly like a snake. Civility did not suit him either, apparently.

"No... I meant nothing at all. Anyway, there's much to do. Welcome to my home. I'm Constable Brauer, pleased to meet you, although you seemed to presume as much already. I heard..." said the Constable weakly before being cut off before his fatty lips could finish. With a sharp wave of his hand, the thin man interrupted him; he could be the man of the house wherever he so pleased.

"Pleasantries... pleasantries are a waste of sweet, precious time. I did not ride by carriage for six and a half weeks to be bored by a large man with an unhealthily small head in proportion to his *gratuitous* body. If it would satisfy your tremendous need for approval, I would say that judging from your size, your health is certainly well. Dare I say, too well?" replied the pole-man, smirking, causing the Constable to slowly reapportion his weight in a way that his head was leaning towards him.

The big man felt his eye twitch as his face grew flush. A visitor, in his home, had just boldly insulted him—directly to his face, no less. His mother had taught him to stand above such petty things as mothers do. However, his little island seemingly caught on fire, twitching at the realization that this troublemaker would have some witty comeback for whatever he said, however illogical.

Perhaps fancying him as an enigma was too kind; rather, he was not much different from any other "clever" wretch he had met. They were all too common: criminals, other members of the force, and even his wife, had the same edge. He never won against people who carried it as of late. So, naturally, he chose to be quiet. Silence was the only proper defense against a barrage of word-vomit.

The thin man smiled; it seemed the big man tended to zip up easily, which could prove useful. That would be the sort of thing that could help later. A handful of insults was enough to bring him to heel. He continued speaking–someone had to, after all.

"Very well. It seems my rhetoric may have struck you the wrong way and, worse yet, left you with an unfavorable opinion of me already. Judging me this early is hardly a polite way to kick things off... We will sort those kinks out yet. Call me Professor Carrion–nothing else at all. Because, legally, as in every sense of the word, I am a genius. Hold your applause–you have not even seen the papers yet. Would you like to?" asked the professor of an indeterminate subject impatiently as he patted a coat pocket, supposedly housing documentation.

"Sir, I'm sure you're as *educated* as you say, but do you understand the gravity of this situation? Our client is adamant that we get to work quickly," declared the Constable sharply while scratching at the long stretch of fur that coated the bottom of his chin. The rough mess of a beard truly stuck out, especially with the growing silvery bits. The slim man placed his wet umbrella on the lovely mahogany table that had so recently begun to furnish the room. Catching wind of the tension, he continued his tirade, maintaining a sort of righteous umbrage.

"Mind you! You invited me to *your* quaint, little home! I am merely enjoying my right to luxury. But, before you gave me that impudent look, the answer to your silly question is 'yes' because solving murders is my blood sport! Did you catch that or do I need to make things simpler? I'll oblige: there is one thing

I need you to grasp: we work on *my* timing and *my* plans! Do not waste my time or yours," roared the frail little man quite savagely before he plopped himself on the chair with two of his fours resting on the table. His annoying emerald eyes bore into the Constable's good one, neglecting any acknowledgment of his other one. Years of convicts and hardened criminals had not prepared him for a nuisance uniquely like this one, always carrying clever insults and bloated vocabulary–how pathetic.

Horrifically, the Professor was only slightly more tolerable than her, save for their lack of marriage. He presumed she would be here shortly, which caused him to sweat even more. Having to suffer both at the same time would surely be the end of him. Shuddering coldly, the Constable sighed audibly, but it was much louder than he had anticipated. To pass it off as intentional, he highlighted the Professor's largest misconception among a slew of others.

"Look, I have no doubt that we're lucky to be graced with your presence, groveling at your feet. However, as you have already worked out, we didn't ask for your intervention regarding a murder. A murder, as you said, is a 'blood sport,' so look at this as something more exotic–an exception to your usual expertise. But, allow me to set you straight on one simple fact before we continue: I will not have you acting a *fool* in my home. Not when my well-being and lifeblood rest on this case. We will work together as equals, even as partners, if you may. It is in our interest to play nicely together," declared the Constable triumphantly. He had always had a way with words, which was what his mother had told him. She was no longer around to say such things, which made that memory even more precious. It was remarkable just how quickly someone waste away... Shifting nervously, he waited half-eagerly for the onslaught of words that was about to assault him and his poor little home. Yet, none came. The monsoon had relented, even if for the moment, until the Professor spoke up.

"You just put me into a coma. But, when those lips of yours stopped moving and that irrationally irritating voice died out, I awoke. Yes, yes, to every petty thing you just said, partner. Just remember that my reputation rides on this as well. And if, and when, a bullet is hurtling towards your vaguely round person, you will gladly take it for me, okay? Okay. And, as supposed equals, I am sure I could take one or two for you. In theory, of course. After all, there is always someone in this world to take a bullet for someone else–someone lesser than themselves, more deserving of it,"

"Excuse me?"

"You're excused. Anyhow, there's the Bullet Logic for you, aptly named by myself, of course. This whole thing probably went over your tiny head, so think happier thoughts, eh?" asked the self-proclaimed Professor in a semi-joking manner–he was not kidding at all. The Constable stuck out his hand to shake with him reluctantly, knowing his stakes. The rail-man, perhaps more reluctantly, stuck out his hand to meet his. Some dark marking was on his hand... a tattoo?

It almost appeared to be an hourglass, but it was empty on both ends. If that, too, was not odd enough, it seemed to have aged quite poorly. The ink was unnaturally faded, yet it remained strongly sharp around its blackened edges. What an eccentric marking for the quirky little man before him! Eventually, the pair shook hands begrudgingly; both were surprised at how firmly the other shook.

"I suppose we are to begin our little reckoning now that pleasantries are dead?" asked the Professor brashly, brushing his right hand under the table stealthily as a card-player would. He was ashamed of himself for even briefly displaying it–such carelessness could catch up to him.

"Seems like the only natural way to continue at this point. Like I said, this case is not a murder. A man, Franz Herbert, relayed to the force that the most disturbing thing happened to him," replied the Constable as if he echoed a script. Dressing up his petty request might be the only way to convince Carrion, or anyone else, to care. If the force had ever had glory days, they had certainly passed before he had come around.

"'Most disturbing' has a ring to it, doesn't it?"

"Herbert's phrasing, not mine. He reported that a single volume from his two-story library was stolen," finished saying the Constable slowly, attempting to steel himself for the interrogation that would follow.

"What was the book that was stolen?"

"He doesn't remember specifically what book was stolen. However, he is sure that it's missing,"

"You are telling me I waited this long for a case about... a book? Must be a hell of a book. One of a kind, I suppose. Family heirloom or something pretentious–disgustingly personal. Surely, even you question why he does not remember what book it was? If it was so dear to him, would he not bother to remember its name?" asked the Professor, sounding back extra venomously as the Constable shook his head.

Usually, the force stressed a policy of little to no questioning–their donating constituents earned their privacy. Such an overly rigid means of dealing with things often prevented him from going beyond the book. In an attempt to draw yet another half-witted response to tear down, the Professor began to scratch his sideburns, creating an awful scratchy racket. Caving into the pressure, the Constable decided to reemphasize the stakes instead of answering the question.

"Mr. Herbert has offered generous donations to the force rather consistently," said the Constable, cautioning him with a hint of desperation.

"Sellouts, I see! Good to know justice smiles for the dime. You said there would be glory for me? Not just some simple payout. So far, all you have offered me is a foolish test of my incredible, saintly patience,"

"Ah, this case will just be another feather in your cap, if you catch my meaning. Surely you can find some glory in returning a book to a crumbling old man–making his face light up with life, one last time? May I remind you that you've been hired, and so far, your desire to be somebody has only hampered the task at hand? I would venture to say you hate seeing that in others. You know how this world works: a back scratch for a back scratch. I call that the 'Back Scratch Logic.' Help me with this case, and I'll see to it you get some gaudy plaque that commemorates your victory. Right now, though, it's time to play the game," said the Constable furiously, looking as if he were about to make use of those large hands, perhaps even strongly considering it. They had not been set into motion for some time, but times changed.

"Yes! Why yes, of course. I was simply testing your resolve, Constable. Congrats, you passed! 'Back Scratch Logic' sounds clever coming from someone like you. Wonder what could have inspired you? Ah, glory is of no interest to me, and it appears that it is of no interest to you either because there is a curious lack of accolades. I do hope your woman is proud of you," said the Professor callously, causing the Constable to blush as he stared at the barren mantle. Carrion took a mental note of another one of the big man's skin-deep weaknesses: he was missing his right index finger. More precisely, just a chunk of it. Between his peculiar eye and what remained of his finger, this man was strange–though the successful kind. The Constable decided pleading would not get anywhere with him, so surely action would settle him down.

"As I was saying, about that book. Mr. Herbert saw it a week ago, or so he says. He cannot remember the title but figures that the book had something to do with his family. The only detail he remembers is that it had a prominent family crest on the cover. We can…" said the Constable before being interrupted by the Professor.

"What kind of idiot would not organize his knowledge? Hope he gets 'offed,' just for that. We would have already found the bloody thing if he had taken a spare couple of miserable seconds out of his dull life to put his things in order! Dewey is rolling in his grave!" screamed the Professor in a chaotic way that certainly would have caused Dewey to roll in his grave– if he believed in such supernatural things. Staring blankly, the Constable coolly replied.

"He is old, advanced in his age. Not exactly in the prime

of his youth to begin a violent reorganization of a two-story collection if you catch my meaning. I doubt he could sort those books even if he wanted to," finished saying the Constable carefully, pacing his words methodically to have a moment of glorious silence.

"So, we must get this old coot his book back and pressure him to read it with the utmost haste, lest he keel over before doing so?" asked the Professor, allowing a dull ring to echo from his mouth, which some may have called a laugh, although the Constable would not have. Its uninviting nature did little to make anyone want to reciprocate it, even in imitation. The creak of a heavy wooden door, followed by the dull clack of heels down a staircase, alerted them to her arrival.

"Honey, who is sitting there with his hat on my table and a filthy umbrella on *our* new carpet?" screeched a woman, who was midway down the stairway that led to an attic, or what she claimed was an entire second floor when asked. Conveniently, the floor was also perfect for spying on her husband and seeing him sneak out in the dead of night for a "secret" drinking bout. They both studied her, but only the Constable bit deep into his bottom lip.

She was a well-dressed woman with flaming hair that leapt messily over her head. Clenching her strong jawline, she hid the pearly daggers adorning her gum. Her heavy raincoat had been cinched in on the sides, and it had been heavily modified to follow her figure like a dress. Very fashionable indeed, perhaps, even ahead of her time. The Professor shifted his right hand deeper under the table. On a dime, the Constable's demeanor shifted to suit the occasion, contorting his mouth into an awkward smile. He had been a remarkably blank actor for the past few years. Speaking, the big man feigned enthusiasm.

"Honey-lamb! It is our esteemed guest, the venerable Professor Carrion,"

"Tell him to pick that up off my new carpet–right this instant!"

"You have legs of your own, do you not, dear?" challenged

the Professor, still feeling confident from his previous quips. His smirk soon wore off when he received a pleasant slap on the cheek, not from the Constable but rather from his wife. Evidently, she was not easy pickings like her husband. It left a prominent red handprint, something she hoped would remind him of his manners whenever he looked in a mirror.

"Oh, I've dealt with people from your lot before! A little tap is the only thing that gets you acting decently. I got dressed up and everything to meet you," shouted the indignant woman spitefully, clenching her fists. Who was he to enter her place in such a manner? He replied carefully, pure spite underlying each word.

"I did not mean to intrude…"

"Just say sorry,"

"Sorry," replied the Professor emptily, without a hint of sincerity. His skin slowly became a dull reflection of her hair, despite his best intentions.

"Now, let's start over. I'm Red Brauer, his wife, and you are?" asked Red forcefully, half-expecting she would need to give the man more encouragement to behave.

"Professor Carrion. I am not going to do another round of…" said the Professor before cutting himself off for once in his life–the sting of his past mistakes certainly encouraged him to produce more cordial responses. The big man's island braced for the impact of violent waves from twin tsunamis. They were both disappointed by his sudden change of heart.

"I am so *pleased* to meet you!"

CHAPTER TWO: ALMOST THERE

"**S**he is quite the chatter, is she not? Suppose her way of loving you is taking your hearing?" asked the Professor caustically as the Constable made his way to the carriage. Studying the exterior, he was surprised how dilapidated it truly was: the wheels seemed a tad beveled, coated in a thin layer of dust which seemed to penetrate every crevice. As he entered, it was readily apparent that the interior did not fare much better.

The pale lavender cushioning was torn and stained. Barely transparent, the glass appeared tainted by some sort of smoky haze that drowned out every other color. Everything in the cabin smelled like cheap liquor, and if he had elected to try to eat anything, it would have tasted much the same. Taking up a disproportionate amount of room for his size, the Professor reclined comfortably, forcing the Constable to constrict into a corner. To distract himself from the pathetic excuse for private transportation, the big man twiddled his fingers, surprising himself each time with the stub he called his index finger. Every time he fell into its alluring loop, Red was at the forefront of his mind.

Things had not been right with her for a while. In all honesty, he had only accepted the case to put a little distance between them. Distance that, if everything went smoothly, would allow him to reconsider their relationship–to come to the best conclusion for them both. Perhaps putting up with the Professor for a little while would better equip him to deal with her endless prodding and pestering.

Work had been a shoddy distraction from her as of late. Each grey-blue day faded into the next without fail, managing to make comfort feel unbearable. Catching smart-tongued, petty thieves in the market hardly provided any excitement at all– especially when it was the same lot every single time. Such things rarely rewarded trophies or acclaim, meaning Red always lost interest in hearing about them quickly. At least everyone knew each other, except for the folks like Herbert, who evidently found something worthwhile at home.

There had been a time when he had felt like that. Now, he had to settle for the smart-mouthed rail accompanying him on the case, who, at least would not drive him to late-night bar extravaganzas, something that Red had quite a knack for. So, in some small sense, he felt grateful to keep less horrible company. Yet, the Professor was still a nightmarish bastard to contend with, and he certainly could not allow him to criticize Red's name, regardless of how true his statements were. It was, by extension, his name, too, for the time being.

"Don't talk about her like that, you hear? You don't even know her," half-heartily whispered the Constable, attempting to see through the window. With great effort, he made out something familiar: pouring rain. It was a dear, albeit temperamental, mistress. How it thumped in tiny drops, providing such a wonderful sense of time! There was no need for watches; even if such devices were deemed fashionable, the rain, a jealous sort, would lay fury down from the heavens, ruining them in an instant. Thus, people relied fully on the rain, not wholly out of faith but necessity.

Outsiders like the Professor could not understand how

therapeutic the little pitter-patters could be, and he did not fancy himself to explain it. If he made no effort to provide for his comfort, he would do nothing to provide him with thought-provoking, regional insight–marking a truly tremendous retribution. Besides, a joy as simple as rain needed no explanation; it demanded reverence all on its own. Chuckling softly, the Professor playfully clapped the big man's knee.

"Oh, your secret's safe with me and Winston! The secret, of course, being your immeasurable discontentment with your wife. Not much of a secret, eh?" shouted the Professor loudly enough to cause his fellow passenger to glower darkly at him. Opening the window for better visibility, the Constable soon became drenched by the rain, which was still considerably more comfortable than continuing the conversation.

Although he knew it already, the large man took a long gaze outside the open window to see if they had cleared his home. And then, back inside. And then, back outside. Unfortunately, there were only so many interesting things to see. Begrudgingly, the Constable allowed his curiosity to overtake his desire for serene silence, so he devised a simple question, one that he hoped could not possibly find its way back to her.

"Who is this Winston character? Is he the coachman?"

"Hullo, chap! I'm Winston! I've managed this stagecoach for years. Believe it or not, the Professor and I have done quite a lot in this old beauty. She may not look it, but..." shouted Winston from the box before pausing naturally, knowing that he would have been hushed for enthusiasm, something the Professor reviled, anyways. Besides, yelling while in motion was an exercise in futility, despite his enormous enthusiasm.

"Good man, I have taught you well. One day, you will be domesticated yourself, Constable. Anyhow, where were we in our discussion? I appreciate your little diversion, but were we not talking about your wife? Could you find a way to quantify, or rate, just exactly how much you despise her? If numbers are not enough, you could try verbiage," suggested the Professor as the Constable bit deeply into his tongue. This cabin could provide a sort of sanctuary from his home.

Perhaps, with a delicate seasoning of euphemisms, he could express some truth in his feelings about Red. Besides the case, was that not the primary attraction of the excursion anyway? Winston listened in keenly, trying to overhear the conversation past the glass and rain alike. Leaning his head forward to prevent eye contact, the Constable spoke softly.

"Red is difficult sometimes, but... She's the only woman who I've ever loved,"

"I liked the first part of that, so please digress with the difficulties, my perfect little case study. Yes, yes! Your strained relationship teetering on the edge of collapse is fascinating. In other words, it's just right," said the Professor, sneering, with a glint in his eyes as he pocketed his right hand in his coat. He swore to himself that he would be more careful.

"Well, she has always had a certain fire to her, if you catch my meaning. She just used to express it differently. Perhaps in a less destructive and demeaning manner," said the Constable, proud of how delicately he had chosen his words. She would have adored that sentiment. The woman he had loved so long ago had been twisted and warped beyond recognition, save for that lovely spark that drew him in, to begin with. However, it had so quickly grown into a raging fire–one far past controlling.

"Oh! So, that woman was your lass–she must have been swell to keep you around that long," shouted Winston over the rain before falling deathly silent, perhaps realizing that his comment would be insensitive at that time. Yet, more than that, it reminded him of someone he would never forget. Despite transitioning into a new time, he was drawn to such conversations because living vicariously through someone else, even for a moment, seemed awfully appealing.

His hand found a tiny gold pendant hanging around his neck and clutched it tightly. A small set of engraved initials characterized its pearlescent surface alongside fingerprints that made small indentions on it. To some, such an object was just a trinket; to him, it was his last earthly connection to her–everything. The carriage jumped violently over a rock, prompting it to bounce dangerously, breaking him free from his thoughts.

"Keep your eyes on the road, madman!" shouted the Professor, unaware that Winston was already preoccupied. The wheels shouted obscenities through screeches, and the axles groaned under the additional weight. They were not conditioned for such wet, uneven terrain. Neither was Carrion. The rain's pleasant ambiance allowed his mind to drift toward foggy places. Sometimes he thought he made out the subtle cries of disembodied voices–something that Winston strongly suggested he should get help for. His pleadings fell on deaf ears, much like the cries. Fortunately, for both the Professor and the carriage, the unthinkable happened.

The rain stopped.

Shuddering violently, the Constable felt his jaw fall ajar. The thumps had stopped, threatening the very flow of time. This was unprecedented, wild beyond all comprehension. Such a disaster had not happened for decades, much less during his lifetime. His heart sank as he felt the air lose its signature moistness; the end seemed near. Hell should have frozen over far before the rain would leave them to wither away into dust. As much as he prayed Carrion's antics would derail his thoughts again, they could not.

The apocalypse had begun.

"Finally, that blasted rain is gone. Good riddance! Now, back to the pressing matter at hand. What exactly do you mean by 'fire?' I'm assuming you do not mean that she lights up like a firecracker," sarcastically prosed the Professor as his emeralds lit up in interest at the log before him. He continued to stare blankly out of the window, peering through the smoky pane to yet more greyness, stripped clean of any blue.

"Checked out already, are we? Better wake up, my daydreaming dearie; we just arrived," said Carrion snidely as the carriage creaked to a stop before a mansion. With a thump, the Constable jolted back to reality for a moment. The end times would have to wait a while longer. Taking one last nervous glance at the strange terrain, he wedged the carriage door open, stepping out into a new world.

Hands shaking, he pulled his cap off for a moment, surprised at how warm his head somehow felt. Just as quickly, though, it went back on his head. It would surely rain again soon, anyways–it had to, for everyone's sake.

CHAPTER THREE: THE MAN OF THE HOUR

The Constable was mesmerized by the decrepit glory of the mansion before him, which thanks to his eyes, was half murky and half not. It was stunningly grandiose yet horrendously rundown. While the architecture of the manor was beautifully made, with sloping arches and large ornamental columns, it was dated, far past its prime. Crawling up the white serrated edges, dark mosses and lichens pervaded every crack and crevice. The weeds sprouted defiantly, almost seeming to cheer the others on to claim the rest of the home in a violent invasion.

Dead trees, perhaps once great cherry blossoms, rose from the grounds like gnarled hands, twisted into one last shape for eternity. Evidently, the old man had a soft spot for the dried-out husks, unwilling to chop them down. At one point, they must have been imported, suggesting Herbert was somewhat cultured or, at the very least, well-connected. With the general disrepair of everything before him, though, the Constable suspected that some of that influence had slipped from his fingers, perhaps frozen still, too. Smirking, the Professor shook his head. Everything passed away eventually–things and people alike.

As Winston shouted that he would stay on the box, the pair cautiously approached the mansion, stepping over the cracked pavement, peeling like flaky, grey skin. Although the mansion was in pitiful condition, the Constable still respected its size. Such a building could still attract a variety of socialites, should it be played up correctly. It could probably pass as "antique," as opposed to a slum. Feeling his foot caught on a particularly interesting surface, the Professor motioned the Constable to investigate with a wag of his favorite finger.

"You are a constable, are you not? Take a look at whatever this is," commanded the Professor as the Constable bent over, lifting the sole of his shoe carefully. Underneath his shoe, a moldy, leather tome seemed stuck, requiring the big man to wedge his fingers underneath. With a strained grimace, he pried it free, revealing a relatively thick spine with some curious language sprawling on the side of it. Rubbing the muck off the cover gently, revealing a rather ornate crest, the Constable froze instinctively when he heard the Professor screech at the top of his lungs.

"Don't pick that up, you disgusting animal! There are many, many precautions to take before we can even look at it! You could easily taint this evidence with your infectious stupidity," screamed Carrion as he tried to snatch the book from him in vain. Brushing him aside with ease, the Constable felt his island swim over all the vaguely written symbols that somewhat resembled English yet constructed beautifully unfamiliar words. The force would not want him to poke around, but they were not exactly present to stop him–Reiner could chew him out later, per usual, in speech or writing. His expectations for him did not reflect his station.

The markings were just so alluring, each carrying a hint of adventure–escape, even. Perhaps there was a real mystery to unravel? The kind that would tear him away from mundane patrols to something more. Even if it was the book, crest and all, peeking at it could easily be played off as part of the investigation. Furthermore, the old man was far gone, likely unable to distinguish it from any other. To avoid her, he swore to himself that he would continue to make the case as laborious as possible. Puffing his chest up, the Constable spoke.

"Strictly speaking, this is for the case, of course. We need to identify this as a possible candidate for the book in question,"

"Sure. Remember, though, that this is evidence–not a plaything or a dolly. Try not to drool on it, eh?"

"*The Herberts and the...*" read the Constable, unable to make out the remainder of the title. It appeared to have been scratched out rather violently. Such intrigue! Perhaps there was genuine promise for a quest, one that might last longer than the paperwork that followed. This mysterious book was nothing more than freedom, tightly bound in pages–providence in his hands!

Regardless of whether the Professor would entertain his grand ambitions, he would not dare to stand in his way on the eve of change. His mantle could be covered in lovely gold baubles and trinkets, admired by visiting nobles and scores of other important people–the sort of useless knick-knacks and folks that would impress her.

Yet, a scowling grimace from the lying cheat beside him shattered his lovely ponderings. Who was he kidding? It would not be so easy: Carrion would have to be kept well leashed. Yet, the delirious twig was just another challenge to be surmounted, allowing him to seize recognition and respect... even from her. Perhaps she could find it in her blackened heart to love him again, for something real. Then, signaled by the dull croaking of a bullfrog, a golden-orange light approached them.

As it grew larger, the old man clutching its housing, a lantern, became clearer, too. His every step heaved heavy sighs as his body strained to support the massive kimono that wore him, dragging against the pavement in hem strands. Around his neck, a score of necklaces jostled up and down with each flap of his mismatched sandals, tearing leather torn into strips. A near dozen of rings choked his fingers.

"Welcome to my humble abode, esteemed guests!" squawked the old man approaching them as his wrinkles glistened against the ghostly orange light. They carved his face into patches of flesh, which blended it into a mosaic of sorts. His eyes, sharp as a knife, looked equally deadly. The Deputy had made it sound like he was helpless... Yet, his aging body moved with a clear purpose yet unknown.

Carrion could not help but appreciate the old thing's apparent contempt for death despite teetering so close to it. His thoughts were broken by the Constable speaking out of turn. Evidently, scolding, while successful with Winston, would not be as useful with the oaf, who seemed to be a different breed entirely. Eventually, he, too, would be broken in–all things in good time.

"Quite the exotic taste, sir! I'm with the force, and this is my associate who was hired to help with tracking down your book," said the Constable cautiously, half expecting the man to break out into another language from his questionable wardrobe choices. It seemed his eccentricities, however, had not been exaggerated–among other more concerning rumors. Herbert's charity to the church, though, overshadowed them. Biting his tongue, the Professor bode his time for a little while longer; he would have his great prize soon.

"Thank you... At one time, it was much more vibrant. That book is very precious to me–priceless, in fact," said the old man, rasping while intently studying the Constable. As he approached, the big man clumsily hid the book behind his back. While he had never been a ball of instinct, he felt a stirring within that seemed to vindicate his choice. Starved for nearly a decade of any intrigue, he felt singularly consumed by the strange text, which continued to dance in his mind.

The Professor noticed it but said nothing. He was, in fact, quite the thespian, among other things, and played along as he still suspected there was a murder or soon would be. Scoffing, Herbert wondered how long it would take for the pair to give up his goosechase. There was a dead silence before the rail-man shattered it.

"Mr. Herbert, may I have your leave to search your premises for this lost book?" said the Professor in an irrationally calm manner. After a few seconds, he restated the question again but in a painfully mocking voice. The Doctor's fingers began to tighten into fists, contorting more fleshy folds around his many rings. To the Constable's horror, Carrion spoke up again, figuring the third time would certainly be the charm–indeed, it was.

"Oh yes, I nearly forgot! Your faculties are compromised," said the Professor in the terribly demeaning way an adult might speak to a child. Setting the lantern down, Herbert straightened his kimono, rolled up his sleeves, and grabbed Carrion tightly by the throat.

Legs dangling above the ground, the Professor felt the color drain from his face, which rapidly began to sink inwards. His hand fished for something in one of his coat pockets–a usual source of divine intervention. The Constable got his strangling hands ready, preparing to make use of them. The air was tense. The grasshoppers seemed giddy to see what would happen next; perhaps blood would spill again. Shimmering dimly, the lantern's light desperately wanted to extinguished itself. Dr. Herbert spoke up before anyone passed out, to the immense disappointment of the grasshoppers.

"I am not a child, Mr. Carrion, and I refuse for you to speak to me as such. How do you think this life came to me? Sniffing out leads? No, I am not a blithering *simpleton*. I am a doctor! I earned that title... so, you will refer to me as Dr. Herbert, and Dr. Herbert alone!" screamed the angry old frog before he let Carrion go, barely allowing him to catch his feet. Evidently satisfied, the Doctor dusted off his kimono, rolled his sleeves back down, and crossed his arms, pouting like the child he had been treated like. The Constable felt his fists loosen. Carrion was always asking for it: thankfully, the old man could do what he could not. He spoke up, feigning discontent.

"Sir, please excuse my associate! He's recovering from a

nasty blow to the head. Sadly, he's never been quite the same... after the *incident*. No respect for his elders... I mean his fellow man," quickly added the Constable in hopes of defusing the situation. Unsure if it had been enough, he added one clause to his peace treaty, a truly remarkable kiss-up.

"Sir, allow us to be on your grounds for just a while longer. We'll have that book back to you in no time–I'm sure of it," pleaded the Constable, used to dressing up words. It only got easier with time.

The cogs spun in the Doctor's head briefly. He said nothing, instead gesturing some universal sign of approval before sluggishly trotting back to the terrarium he called home with his lantern. The Professor and the Constable locked eyes, each simmering with anger. Their twin glares communicated far more than words could have; they were on thin ice. However, their shared nosiness overpowered any less agreeable feelings, giving way to a shared curiosity that threatened to devour the world. The big man pulled out the book and read from the first page, his island spinning with glee.

"*Preserved for special use by the Herbert family,*" read the Constable aloud, still unsure if such an action constituted meddling. As a "distinguished" agent of justice, reading the book was surely within his jurisdiction. Reiner always had a delicate relationship with the intricacies of rules and laws anyways. Probable cause or something of the sort could cover him. He continued.

"*The Herberts, a long-standing member of the*, that's scratched out, *have upheld the virtues we hold dear. We honor them with the gift of our protection and providence in their times of need. No garden wilts, no stone crumbles. If we,* still can't read that, *draw breath,*" finished reading the Constable as he took it all in slowly. He flipped through the rest of the pages–all blank. Who would promise such protection? More importantly, how could a man so desperately desire a book full of empty pages?

The Professor pulled his right hand back into his coat pocket, sheltering it from the world. That accursed book would suffer before it ever touched the Doctor's gnarled, ring-covered fingers. Herbert had called his bluff in on him; it was his turn, now. A smidge of retaliation always set the mood. The loss of rain, in tandem with the breeze, set the perfect conditions for a lovely little fire. Whether accidental or provoked, it would appear as nature having its own way. A fire burned in Carrion's emeralds, desperate to ignite the book. He snarled before making a bold declaration.

"Sure, the book is what he wants, but after the way he spoke to us, I feel like we ought to deliver it in an... alternative fashion,"

"Professor, our reputation is on the line, here. We have to deliver the book to him as promised. We're already stretching our jurisdiction plenty by even looking at the blasted thing. The force wouldn't be too happy if their generous donations dried up overnight. Work with me," said the Constable firmly. His veins pulsed and seemed to pop, nearly bursting through his hands.

"Oh, I would not have it any other way. Neither you nor your petty feelings are going to stop me from protecting my reputation. We will deliver exactly what was promised–and then some," replied the Professor, smiling with considerable satisfaction as he pulled out a few matches from his coat pocket. With a delicate scratch, sparks charring the air, he lit one and threw it on the nearest bush.

"What in the bloody hell is wrong with you?" shouted the Constable, horrified, as spittle streaked down his lip. He tore off his cap and began frantically trying to put the growing fire out, but to little avail. Feeling quite indecent while doing so, his skin shuddered from the rainfall's caress. If any part of the bush still clung to life, it died its final death when the flames sprouted. Snatching the book from the big man, he ripped a page from its middle.

He struggled to keep his focus; the scene unfolding before him was too much fun. Regaining his composure enough to shove the prize into his pocket, he threw the rest of the book back into the flames with considerable finesse. The Constable wailed all the more but was too preoccupied to do anything about it. Soon enough, Herbert emerged once more as an orange spark in the distance, clutched to the lantern like some earthly coil.

Licking his lips briefly, the Professor began his narrative before Herbert was within ten meters of him, working hard to mask his satisfaction at the old man's obvious suffering.

"I am so terribly sorry, so sorry indeed! A match slipped from my pocket and lit this bush ablaze. How silly of me! Yet, in the burning, I found something of value to you, hidden somewhere in the bush, I suppose. In fact, that was why you contacted the force, to begin with!" exclaimed the Professor, brushing aside the Constable with a dramatic flourish. Retrieving a small handkerchief from his coat, he wrapped his left hand in it before sticking it into the flames.

An unearthly shriek issued from his mouth as what remained of the book came flying free from the flames. He had supposed it would have been more of a mild inconvenience–not something so severe. The Constable, still mourning the lost of his cap, watched him writhe in agony. He assumed that was the least of the pain the twig -man would face: Herbert would see to that.

Unless Carrion humbled himself and asked for help, he was not bound by law to do anything at all. His mother had always told him that pride led to a fall–in Carrion's case, it would be a mess of broken bones. Snatching the book, the Professor, having recovered the best he could from the nasty black burn that peeled his flesh upwards in charred clumps, continued his speech.

"I think I salvaged most of it from the flames, but some of it may have been consumed. You must forgive me, but I do not think that you would have ever found it there. Besides, the book is priceless to you, and this rotting bush is not, I presume," added the Professor quickly as Dr. Herbert's bloodshot eyes pierced through his hand to the book. They had actually found it, after all...

The Constable, fearing that the fire would consume the entirety of the manor, tried the last ace up his sleeve: his beautiful pair of finely sewn and lovingly crafted leather shoes Red had crafted him. The sacrifice was great, but with them, he successfully put out the flames. Now, the Professor would get a little more of what he had coming to him. The old man was so very close now–how very exciting! Carrion, however, delivered a monologue worthy of the greats of old or at least his title.

"I will see to it that *they* pay for it, *all* of it," triumphantly said the Professor to Dr. Herbert. Visibly shaken, the old man recoiled violently, nearly stumbling. This was not the justice the Constable expected or wanted. Nodding slowly, he snatched the book from the Professor's hand before it could be lost again before darting off with it clutched to his chest.

His father's voice echoed; he knew he could not touch him even if every part of him craved to. He had already angered *them* enough. The big man was on the verge of speaking before the Professor retrieved the page from his coat pocket and held it up to the heavens–a great prize in its own right. Less than awestruck, the big man spoke, rather timidly.

"All that for a page, for some petty revenge,"

"That, and watching all his pathetic croaking at his flaming bush almost managed to make me feel something. What a fascinating little man! He would make for a lovely subject. You see, ever-witless Constable, we know of a 'they' now and that *they* are overdue on fixing one Mr. Herbert's house," lectured Carrion with the first real emotion the Constable had ever seen him express. His words carried something more than excessive spite.

"So what? I was nosy, mind you, because he seemed an interesting man. But, you're telling me you burnt down his bush on the suspicion that some nefarious higher power is at play? Are you mad?" asked the Constable, roaring bitterly. From then on, he figured any foothold, any concession given to the Professor, would have dire consequences.

He was far too much to handle. After everything, he set

a bush on fire because he could–just to ruin it for some jollies. What would he torch next? Apparently, he was a thief, too, willing to steal on a whim. This had gone on long enough; some adventures, surely, were not worth pursuing. The grasshoppers scattered off as they usually did because all the fun was over.

"Look, I can tell that you think Herbert is as strange as I do. In my experience, strange men, like him, have secrets. His house is a prime example of an oddity. Where did all the money go? I need these answers... *my* answers," declared the Professor, pursing his lips.

"We had a deal, remember? The damn bullet thing... The plan to give him back his book?" shouted the Constable, fuming bitterly at his increasingly ineffectual words.

"Seeing as the man still has most of his precious book, we are ahead on that count. I merely took a simple finder's fee. This is not about him, though, is it? Deep down, you know you are nothing more than the rules given to you. You can make your silly little report to your higher-ups, but I have a lead to continue my work, here. I did not ride all this way to find a book; I came here for a case–with a bloody murder attached to it. Tell your wife about your trivial victory so that you can sleep well tonight," declared the Professor, scratching his sideburns while clenching the page with his fist. His argument did not fall on empty ears. The Constable wanted to roll the clock back, to see color, again. It was so tantalizing, just nearly in reach. Yet, his injured pride spoke for him.

"Fair enough. Your methods are unconventional, but you have followed through on your promise, mostly. Go right ahead, get this old man thrown away, as I am sure you could. Throw the world in prison while you're at it. The things you made me say about Red are unforgivable! Our partnership is over, done and gone. Stay out of my life–and the hell away from my wife! Do you understand?" asked the Constable forcefully, clenching his fist tightly as the little island looked as if it were about to fly free of the ocean surrounding it. Carrion knew it was time to back off.

The big man would have to find his own way back to him,

being a lousy prodigal son of sorts. So, Carrion raised his right hand to tip his hat to the Constable before realizing he had left it at their miserable home. Smirking instead, he briskly walked off to the carriage. That sorry lump of potatoes would beg to enter his world again. He gestured at the carriage, solemnly shaking his head slowly.

"Suit yourself," said the Professor scornfully, undoubtedly already concocting new schemes, accounting for the big man's absence and return alike. The carriage set off into the night.

The Constable felt his palms sweat, pondering if backing out was the right decision. He wanted to have a new life, but more so, he needed to do something greater. Every part of him desired to do it with anyone besides a snide professor or some quirky coachman. Yet, that future seemed far closer than any vows he had made to himself or anyone else. Clenching his jaw tightly, he realized he was not ready to face Red again so soon. Kneeling downwards in a yard of dead things, sweat dripping from his brow, he had a profound thought.

He could not let his one chance at new life ride off. That bastard, although cruel and nasty, had not been conquered by him yet. If he could rein him in, bringing him to his knees, he could win! If he could come out as the hero of some deep-rooted conspiracy, his mantle would be full! If he got to have dinner with the bloated members of high society, she could love him again, perhaps... All would be as it had been. He still had time.

"Wait!" screamed the Constable, quite unsure how the words found themselves out of his mouth. He bent down to the once-great walkway, a monument to neglect. Giving one last rub to his poor leather shoes, he charged into the night after that carriage, running as his life depended on it–it did. He ran and ran. With every step, he chose to strive forward, seized by a grim determination that grew with motion. Maybe, just maybe, his mother could see him from some distinct place. So, he kept running into the darkness in search of a familiar light. Eventually, shredding asphalt cried out as the carriage slowed to a sudden stop. A familiar voice from the dark reached his hungry ears.

"Hullo again, mate! I thought we lost you! I saw that bush burning from the box... Thought it might have scared you away. Guess you're not a stranger to such things. That is why you married her, isn't it?" cheered Winston. Grunting, the big man knocked three times, per instruction of his mother, and the cabin door opened. The Professor, unable to hide his surprise, anxiously gawked at the large man's frame. The Constable smiled; he had been able to surprise him–and could surely do it again, if necessary. He climbed into the carriage and shut the door with a loud thud.

"Well, I suppose you want some kind of apology? No, I think not. I honestly could care less why you came back, too. However, frankly, it seems the Fates have bound us together. Allow me to delight you with what was on the Doctor's page as I expected," said Carrion as he pulled out a bottle of whiskey and dripped it on the page, expecting a hidden message to be revealed. The page, instead, was ruined instantly, smelling strongly of cheap liquor. The big man sighed, stifling a small giggle. Looking downwards at the crumpled, disintegrating page in his hands, the Professor broke the silence awkwardly.

"In many respects, I am a genius. I have written numerous works of poetry for the arts, and I know my Roman classics. Sometimes it is the small things in life that are perhaps the most threatening," said the Professor dramatically, drawing out his words dramatic effect.

"Chemistry, among a select few other things," mouthed the Professor as he scratched his left hand violently. Theatrics usually came with a lighter cost. Studying his profile, the Constable realized how silly Carrion truly looked. His sideburns, drooping just shy of the bottom of his jawline, violently leapt off his face. What a little clown indeed–how had he been intimidated by him? The Professor, clearly insulted by the turn of events, threw the page out of the window. Winston yelled from the box with a small hint of glee.

"Don't worry, sir, when he starts throwing stuff, he is most sincere. But, perhaps even more importantly, he has a most *stupendous* plan!" finished shouting Winston.

The Professor did not have a plan–yet.

CHAPTER FOUR: A GLORIOUS PLAN

"Yes, I have devised a foolproof plan–glorious even! We shall draw this weasel from his hole. Then, we shall find the rest of the beasties! Disgusting little creatures... We will leave no burrow unturned!" angrily shouted the Professor as he made hand motions to threaten a population of invisible, yet unknown, weasels. He, Winston, and the Brauers sat in what was affectionately called the "living" room–perhaps it was once so. There were not enough chairs since they rarely hosted visitors, so Winston sat on the dirty floor. Red twiddled her red locks with one hand and clamped the Constable's ring finger tightly with the other. With one arm reluctantly around her, he enjoyed his drug of choice: a hearty cup of hard beer.

Sneaking them home from Stanton's was his favorite parlor trick. He had become a frighteningly competent magician as of late. His assumption a few nights ago had certainly proved right–he needed it for the dreadful night of small talk ahead. Foxtrot, the Brauer's dog, sat on the ground, tapping his paw occasionally when the Professor spoke. The little mutt had rejected all the Constable's efforts to tame him–only offering occasional barks of approval. His unique streak of individualism was particularly hard to deal with, often manifesting in the form of droppings on the carpet.

"All right, so you're telling me that my husband is going to become some sort of hero? Perhaps he would have less need to go out looking for attention?" asked Red slowly, letting each word stick her husband painfully, so he would not dare bleed out all at once. He had to say something, anything, after being silent for so long. The big man shifted in his chair nervously, taking yet another gulp of his drink for dear life.

"Whatever you say," replied the Professor dismissively as he got up to pick up his umbrella and hat, which appeared properly dried from their drenching earlier. He put his hat on, and his face felt the cold sting of water droplets. Humorless, he glared at the Constable, who chuckled. Throwing the hat off his head, he pulled a handkerchief from his coat to dab his face dry. All the laughter in the world could not mask the big man's nervousness around her.

Sweat, a little waterfall, poured down the oaf's hands. His wife, clearly impatient, got up and marched straight to the rail-man. Her face, hovering inches before his, caused his cheek to burn faintly. Evidently, she had a fire, after all. Although he could only guess how it roared to life inside her, it was certainly glimmering brightly.

"Mister, I don't feel as though you fully answered my question," said Red, laying on a thick accent as her delicate eyes to bore straight through his head. The Constable's hands trembled, veins pulsing disparately. After recoiling briefly, the Professor softly pressed the spot on his face, still tender, then answered the wretch.

"He will be, without a doubt, the greatest hero that has ever lived, and the force will venerate him like a saint. Maybe, he will get some lovely, marbled statue, where the troubled youths could make offerings! Of course, that might be considered a sore misuse of resources for a man of his considerable stature," sourly said the Professor, unable to play nice any longer.

His limited patience for the woman had completely expired. No one slapped him and asked him to repeat or pick up after himself. Red noticed the glint in his emeralds, allowing them to reach a sort of nonverbal agreement: they would both keep to themselves from then on out, sharing the dubious task of picking at the Constable. She backed off slowly, plopping back down on the couch in an apparently content manner.

Milky eye swirling, the Constable motioned Carrion to get back on track, but the conversation had already derailed horrifically. Giddy, the rail-man was simply having too much fun to stop now. Yet, a hint of restraint crept in when he remembered that the big man was merely a tool. A hardy tool, but one nonetheless susceptible to breaking and blunt trauma.

He was already sort coming apart along the edges, one bad day away from snapping altogether. A busted tool was simply no good at all–possibly far from being able to be repaired. Licking his lips, the Professor took one last glance at the Constable. This big, little man still had a bit more to give him. Grinning as if nothing had happened, Carrion continued.

"Where were we? Ah, yes! The first step of many in our delightful plan is to find out more about the man in question. What makes him tick? We have to find an excuse to talk with dear Mr. Herbert again. I think burning another bush would be…" finished saying the Professor before slowly cutting himself off, taking in the horrified faces of Red and Winston. Their mouths were so wide that just about anything could fit through them–they were famished for answers.

"So… you were the one to set that bush on *fire*? How on earth did that happen, exactly?" carefully asked Winston. Although he had only just barely beaten Red to the punch, her puzzled expression also did the asking. Sitting a tad bit more comfortably, the Constable wondered how he would worm his way out of that one. The Professor uncharacteristically struggled to find his words, making wild gestures in some weak effort to drag them out. A strange feeling swept over the big man, causing him to speak up for the deplorable man-child before him.

"It was by accident, of course. Real stroke of good luck because that's what allowed us to find the book to begin with," lied the Constable, smiling in a weak attempt to mask his deceit. Unconvinced, Winston smelled something on his breath, and it was not from the drink resting in his hand. Red stopped twiddling her hair for a moment, considered his particular choice of words, and then continued as before. Nodding a sharp but subtle thanks in the direction of the big man, Carrion played it off as a cough.

"What nasty business. I don't suppose his missus will have to clean it up?" asked Red, offering concern for a hypothetical woman she had never met. As petty as it was, there had to be some way to take his mind off the heavy drink in his hand...

"I believe he has at least one. However, it could be anywhere from one to eleven. He could be a genuine polygamist– a lucky bastard, to be sure," replied the Professor with a hint of excitement. The large man studied the room around him to gauge their reactions–there was absolutely no way anyone else would buy that. Yet, Winston nodded adamantly as if this was not the first time that he had heard him say something that outlandish. Red still looked confused. Perhaps she was just waiting for him to make sense of it for her... He spoke up.

"Professor, I believe that the rings are more of a status symbol. In this fine day and age, having more than one wife seems to be quite difficult. One can *certainly* be enough," stated the Constable slowly, indifferent to Red's glaring eyes and flaring nostrils. Eye twitching for a moment, the rail-man calculated the punishment he would deal out before settling on something to shut him down.

"Let me remind you of something, guppy: I'm the professional here. Your abilities were probably perfectly adequate for your petty squabbles but nothing more. Need I clarify again that I'm a genius? Next time you doubt me, remind yourself that your strengths end at your fists," said the Professor, quite venomously, causing the Constable to shake his head wildly. His supposed "genius pass" barely covered half the stupid things that left his mouth.

Chances were, he was not even a professor, of any sort. He was, after all, little more than a moron, playing pretend, who had nearly cost them everything with a fiery, in all senses of the word, temper tantrum. Dr. Herbert would certainly not be clambering to spill anything now, thanks to his antics.

For someone so allegedly educated, he carried himself like a complete jackass–perhaps that was the fine fruit of academia. Biting deeply into his lips, creasing the dry patches all the more, the Constable sighed, which the Professor took as a sign to continue his tirade.

"Remember, we cannot allow our feelings to intervene in any serious matter. We must be above such things, eh?" asked the Professor mockingly, aiming his words straight at the heart of his prey. In-kind, the Constable decided it was time to deal out a proper verbal lashing, so his gnashing jaw could be put into real motion. He spoke, one leading question into the next.

"The mansion, how many rooms does it have?"

"I fail to see how…"

"I asked you a question?"

"Eight observable bedrooms,"

"How many wives did you suppose he had?"

"Eleven,"

"Okay, if we are putting two and two together, I think it is a reasonable assumption that his wives did not share a room,"

"I think it is rather obvious from history that concubines were not particularly picky with their accommodations,"

"Dr. Herbert was wealthy at some point, right?"

"Yes, that is what we have observed thus far,"

"If he was rich, surely he would have constructed an addition to his house for his wives? To show he cared about them?"

"Perhaps the wives came to him after he lost his fortune? Do you reckon they are hookers with a heart of gold?"

"Those rings are ancient, decades old at least, and they

appear valuable. Not just some gaudy fleeting vow of love,"

"Have you ever heard of rustic taste, simpleton?"

They continued for ages like a pair of quarreling children. Winston fell asleep, soundly, midway through. Although she did not do much to show it, Red felt something close to pride for her husband defending himself against a self-declared *genius.* At least something beyond a grunt left his lips. She stopped twiddling her hair and listened intently.

After a long while, the conversation came to an increasingly violent climax. With all the vicious scratching, the Carrion was beginning to seriously thin his sideburns. The Constable, island throbbing violently as his face sunk in, delivered an ultimatum.

"This could go on for centuries! For a man above relishing in glory, you do not relent. We shall see for ourselves when we visit Dr. Herbert again! But, before that, I have a bet. You're daring, aren't you? Do you see that carpet, yes–the one you trampled all over with mud? If you're right about him having eleven wives, then it's yours. Brandish it about as a little trophy for all I care! However, if I'm right, then I have the luxury of revealing to this room something 'most disturbing' about yourself–a gap in your precious amor. Do we have a deal?" roared the Constable as he sat back down, feeling his weight suffocate the couch. The Professor considered the deal carefully, realizing he had nothing to lose and everything to gain. Their thoughts of him, besides Winston's occasional useful nuggets, were completely irrelevant. Smirking, he replied emptily.

"Yes, Brauer: you have a deal. I assure you that carpet will have a place of honor in my home, hung above my mantle, which, by the way, is rife with trinkets. Rest easy, for you will be bested by nothing less than the best," declared the Professor with a rare, upturned smile.

As silence claimed the room, Foxtrot's racket, in the form of raucous barks, slowly stirred the room back to life. Jolting awake, Winston shook his head at the little thing–what a crazed beastie it was. At one point, the Constable intended to sell it to some other poor sap, but he just could not do it. The dog felt more like family than her than she did sometimes. Carrion, setting aside the gnawing desire to be right for a moment, spoke up. There would be more time for that later.

"Does that thing ever shut up? Put the poor thing out of its misery. Where were we? To find out more about Herbert's lineage, I will do some schmoozing with the locals. I propose that you, Brauer, should make your way back to his shack and find a clever way inside. Kiss his ass more if you must. I know counting is not your strong suit, but get an accurate count on those wives–fingers and a pair of toes should suffice. Winston, ride as if your life depends on it, like the Fates are nipping at your heel. Oh, and Red–stay dainty. Overall, I would say this fabulous plan is special, even for one of mine. One more thing..." said the Professor before pausing for dramatic effect. He waited to make sure he had all their attention. With a deep breath, in and out, he offered one last bout of theatrics.

"We can assume that *they* most likely have a bloody history. When you find a corpse, take some form of identification off of it. Rings or fingers work very well. I will leave you to sort it out. I do not say this often but rely upon your gut. In fact, guts work very well for identification purposes," said the Professor, darkly laughing, as Red chimed in for good measure.

"Doubt my husband could even pick up the knife. Mushy blood and guts would bring him to his knees. Too squeamish to do anything except drink. That's all my *honey-lamb* is good..." said Red, covering her mouth as her cheeks inflated, growing green. Leaping from her chair, she made a mad dash for the bathroom. Gurgling intensely, her stomach gave way when she was over the carpet. The carpet, already wet, was now properly ruined. Winston seeing this, promptly began gagging before darting off. If the carpet could have become sick, it would have done so.

The Constable went to comfort his wife, but she brushed him off with a wag of her favorite finger and rushed frantically to the bathroom. Winston came back in, clearly very disappointed in himself. Carrion had one thing to say about the entire ghastly display. He disclosed it loud enough for the entire home to hear.

"Only the strong survive," shouted the Professor as he heard a few knuckles crack through the thin drywall. A small phantom pain kissed his cheek, so he silenced himself before he could continue. The Constable stared longingly out the window and back at the carpet. Standing there, still as stone, he further realized he had made the right choice. His island dripped one single drop, rolling down his cheek into his scratching post. Why was he crying? Adventure awaited him, now.

She could throw up her intestines for all he cared.

CHAPTER FIVE: ON THE COUNT OF WIVES

"So, how exactly was the Professor going to search for locals?" shouted the Constable ahead to Winston, who was focused on calming down a rather unsettled horse–advanced in his years and named Honeysuckle. The stench emanating from the bushes must have bothered it. The big man enjoyed getting the entire compartment to himself, stretching out his thick legs like a king. Even little bouts of autonomy were worth savoring. Similarly, Winston enjoyed his newfound, albeit fleeting, freedom of speech. He planned on making good use of it.

"Hullo! I don't know. He can be quite resourceful, ya know! I'm sure he found someone to take him about. I do wonder where he went? He didn't say I don't think although I was out for a good portion of his spiel. A solid nap, indeed. Had a dream that I drove him around. From here to there and all around! Not much of a departure from reality but nice, nonetheless. Where was I? I'm spewing... Oh yes, the Professor! He won't tell what his *Professorship* is in. Prodding does little to change his mind, unfortunately. We met a while after I had been a priest... Well, almost that is," said Winston enthusiastically, continuing on and on about their history.

While the Constable stopped listening, it was still nice to hear the boy expressing his thoughts. He tried humming to replicate the forgotten rhythm of the rain. Unable to focus, he eventually slipped into sleep. Rest was usually scarce, but Winston's almost melodic ramblings could have been a sorrier substitute for the rain. Awoken by a shrill whistle, he lurched forwards, allowing his eyes to readjust.

"We made it! Kind of a nice place, if you ask me. Little paint here and there, and it would be good as new!" cheered Winston as the house was better lit by the red-orange morning son. He was unsure if he had slept for an hour or a whole day; time had truly departed with the rain. Peering out the window, the Constable realized elegant candles had been set around the grounds, but they paled in comparision to one triumphant light.

The lantern, which now hung on the porch, held a reinvigorated flame, burning with an intensity that threatened its casing. It lit a nearby gleaming black tombstone. How had he missed it the last time? It was almost a monolith to the decrepit ruin surrounding it. He leapt out the carriage door, making his way to the monument to read the inscription.

"*Here lies Franz Herbert,*" read the Constable aloud as his island thrashed about to and fro. His heart almost skipped a beat as he realized it was already too late. The man was dead–a little after a day that they had last seen him. Something inside dared him to read how such a dreadful thing came to pass.

"*Senior,* here lies Franz Herbert Senior," clarified the Constable quickly, relieved that Dr. Herbert was still alive. As long as the old coot lived, his adventure did too–on borrowed time but time nonetheless. Somewhere, the good doctor would be lounging in filth with his one, single wife, content as a pig at a trough.

"I can see that you, too, have reverence for the dead. Shame they feel nothing for us," whispered Dr. Herbert, who seemingly appeared out of thin air. A moldy tricorn hat, drooping down the side of his head, was a delightfully strange addition to his already peculiar wardrobe. It somehow managed to look more ridiculous than the kimono, which still hung below his ankles. The old man certainly had a presence to him—an enchanting sort. It compelled him to finish reading the inscription.

"*Poisoned from the inside, no antidote in sight,*" read the Constable solemnly, face as stone-like as the pillar before him. He paused, overcome with chill as the apparition floated closer. The Doctor's black robes swayed against the wind as orange light peeked through the cracks with an ethereal glee. Shuddering coldly, he heard words enter his ear one by one, all marching to die, to find final rest. Reflexively, his hands tightened.

"He made me what I am and look at me now! All his secrets, buried with him to rot forever, along with everything else *they* gifted him–all from Hell! I had no chance to fill his shoes. I wasn't what *they* wanted, but I earned *their* attention! That book was supposed to mean something, but *they* don't give a rat's ass about my father's legacy. Just another pawn in *their* sick game... He left me nothing. Now, I'm a broken man, reminiscing on nothing. Yet, still drawing breath... Come with me while I still do. There is much to discuss," said Dr. Herbert before grunting weakly as his guise of strength further melted away under the light. Lines of purple wrinkles tightened in folds around his bulging eyes. His chin drooped, saggy and weak, like a sac. Unsteady, his left leg hobbled behind his right, failing to fully support the strain. It had long since given out, just like many other things.

Leading him up the cracked tile steps, past the lantern, and into his home, Dr. Herbert cursed under his breath. With each step, the floorboards creaked desperate confessions, crying for small mercies. It was a mess. Hundreds of little, yellow paper cranes dotted the floor en masse, making it a minefield to traverse. Most of the tiles had been stripped from the floor altogether, sitting in piles in the corners of the room, leaving more room for the broken bottles.

The fireplace rested desolate and empty, age-old cinders and ash smeared on the grate. Most hazardous of all, a few planks stuck up like a rib cage, exposing a massive hole in the ground. But these details paled in comparison to one particularly jarring aspect of the home, causing the Constable to nearly fall over. There it was: an hourglass, empty on each side, carved into the wall. It was exactly like the tattoo on the Professor's right hand, just slightly more defined.

"Ah, I see you're familiar with *their* accursed mark?" asked Dr. Herbert, noticing how long the big man's one good eye lingered on it. Shifting uncomfortably, he carefully reclined on a tearing, velvet sofa. Moments of comfort, however temporary, felt miraculous now. Mind swimming with questions, the Constable decided to further curtail formalities and asked a simple yet complicated question.

"Who are *they*?"

"*They* are not the past nor the future,"

"That is not…"

"You cannot understand what *they* are until you understand why *they* are,"

"Why *they* are? What on earth do you mean?"

"The past is dead, and the future is ever coming–*they* live by that doctrine! It shapes who *they* are. But the present…"

"Why do you speak of the present this way?"

"Don't you understand? *They* are the present; *they* are the change!" roared the Doctor. His bloodshot eyes twitched as his body was swallowed up by the sofa. Chattering uncontrollably, his teeth clanked in shrill squeaks, which slowly devolved to hiccups. The surrounding wine bottles, nearly all empty, served as an audience for the unfolding drama. The Constable bent over the old man. This pretentious nut would not deny him his answers.

"How do you know all of this if you failed? It seems to me that all you know is what *they're* not! I will ask you plainly as I can one more time: who are *they*?" asked the Constable as his island sunk beneath the heavy waves. Recoiling sharply, Dr. Herbert saw a glint of insanity and violence hidden behind his eyes. Below his brow, that milky moon, so pure, cast judgment on him for his sins. Looking downwards at his rings, he saw how their silvery glint had all but vanished.

They looked good from a healthy distance, just like him. Yet, they were merely a shoddy façade for his poor choices. His whole life had sunken into disrepair, everything was in shambles, and his possessions were merely the weakest expression of that reality. His waning eyes, laden with tears, drifted up to *their* insignia one last time. All the secrets would not die with him.

"Listen, and I'll tell you everything. From a young age, my father, Franz Herbert the first, entrusted me with certain responsibilities for *them*. He was exceptionally gifted as a boy with chemistry, perhaps a prodigy. Soon enough, *their* research consumed him. Some man kept coming by the house–insisting his talent would no longer be wasted. I wasn't allowed to see him. Yet, he funded and believed in my father enough to bankroll everything–before it started drying up,"

"So, this place came from your father's money?"

"No, let me finish. You see, I was supposed to be next in line; he practically bred me to take up that burden. He left me thousands of notes, hand-scrawled and marked. Soon enough, they started becoming nonsense. I saw him less and less–he slunk away into isolation. The work had driven him mad... One night, I heard a stirring. Creeping through the dark, I lit a candle and found his body. The light flickered off his glazed-over eyes. That was it. The force never succeeded in identifying what happened. Once, I foolishly believed it was an accident... But, I cannot any longer," declared Dr. Herbert as he stopped wiping his eyes. There was no point: the pretense of youth was long gone, tears or not. Backing away, the Constable remembered his dear mother and her last days. The old man's weak, slinking frame was an all-to-familiar sight: the mind clung to life while the flesh gave way. Sniffling, the big man took the old man by his hand, clenching it tightly. It felt like rough sandpaper, but a softness seemed to lay beneath the surface.

"I know what that feels like," replied the Constable

knowingly, unable to prevent a tear from slinking down his face. Soon, another joined, creating a streak. Soon enough, they both wept, each drip threatening to color the room. As their sniffles gave way to silence, they had newfound understanding. With a final snort of his nose, Dr. Herbert drew himself upwards. Motioning to the only bottle with any liquor left, the Constable presented it to him. Taking a hearty final swig, he continued.

"My mother passed away soon after. By then, I was a rather somber youth of fifteen. The man that represented *them* came back. He asked a few questions, but I could not force myself to look into his eyes, soulless pits... my wife thought he was an oni,"

"An oni?"

"A demon from her land. Deeming me unworthy of my father's legacy, he said I had nothing to offer him, nothing at all. He took my hands, clenching them tightly. Made me swear I would burn all the research–the last thing I had to remember my father by. Piece by piece, I sent each scrap of parchment to the abyss. Yet, I could not bring myself to destroy one book. Some small part of me clung to the idea that *they* would return to fix my world. That's why when your associate claimed that *they* could fix everything, I was a bit taken aback. No one had invoked *their* name in a long time..."

"I'm sorry to dredge up all of this..."

"Don't be. I am far too old for such trivial concerns as 'politeness.' You're welcome in my home, you know. I don't resent you for your company. As much as I wanted to strangle him, though, it was not a risk I was willing to take. Not with *them* involved..." finished saying Dr. Herbert, darkly laughing as he clenched his stomach tightly. Laughter, of any kind, had become foreign to him–a stranger knocking from within. It struggled to clear his throat. Eventually, it felt more like an old friend again, causing him to wipe the spittle from his lips on the sleeve of his kimono. Wheezing painfully, he continued unloading heavy words from his heart.

"Where was I? Aimless, destitute, adrift. Alone in an

uncaring, indifferent world. Yet, a local pharmacist took a small liking to me. He taught me everything, medical or not, I know today. When he passed away, I went around the world, met many women, and lived many lives. Some were fortunate enough to come back with me here–for a time," said the Doctor painfully. Fists tightening, the Constable remembered his formerly prized rug, so he quickly mustered the courage to ask a very important, albeit largely trivial, question. At this point, it was far more than a rug to him: that silly thing was retribution in physical form–puke stains and all.

"I'm sorry to interrupt... How many wives do you or did you have, if I may ask?"

"Over the course of my long life, eleven. Currently, one, Iitoyo; the others left me a long time ago, some in death. Every time it hurt... *every* time. I wear these old things, so I won't forget them," croaked Dr. Herbert, brandishing his tarnished rings, shimmering against the pale orange light. Chuckling gently, the Constable was amused. They had both been right in a strange sense. He wondered how they would reconcile this–perhaps they could find a compromise? Past tearing it down the middle? Red might manage to pretend to be impressed, per usual, yet the silliness of their competition did little to ease his concerns about the rail-man. The tattoo, the symbol, had to mean something bigger was at play. The old man continued speaking.

"Soon enough, surrounded by loving arms, I forgot all about *them*. Yet, that book continued staring at me on the shelf. When hard times came, snatching many of my loves from me, *their* promises echoed in my ears. As my world continued to crumble around me, I started looking for it again. Unfortunately, I did it all horribly drunk, of course, as you can see by the bottles. All my searching was for naught. In all honesty, half the reason I contacted the force was to spite them with a hopeless task. Yet, here we are, with you returning for answers. I suppose you peeked at the book, then?" asked the Doctor tactfully yet kindly. Reaching behind the sofa, he pulled what was left of the book free, holding it up. The Constable's white eye twitched before he answered him as honestly and succinctly as he could.

"Yes,"

"I don't blame you. It's not every day you see a man in a kimono and tricorn hat asking for a book damn-near full of empty pages... and promises, for that matter," replied the Doctor, shaking his head slowly. Straining his arm, he chucked the book into the hole.

"What good it did for me, or anyone else,"

"Still, as a member of the force, I shouldn't have meddled..."

"I frankly don't give a damn who you're with or not. I cannot stand the thought of this all dying with me... You would think that I would have had a child at some point–one that would have been around to listen to me... I guess some things are not in the cards of life," replied Dr. Herbert, yearning for what he knew he would never have. The Constable, moved that his secret was safe, gently repeated his question. The thoughts of a child of his own never departed him.

"I guess things aren't always that simple for our lot. If you don't mind me repeating myself, could you make a gander about who *they* are?" softly asked the Constable to the wizened mirror before him.

"Suppose I was bound to break the Code at some point if I hadn't already. Perhaps they are aristocrats, royals, kings–people of power? Men who are not happy with the way our current world is governed? Evil? Good? I do not know. But, I beg you; please tell me anything you discover, so I can die with some semblance of peace, knowing what happened to my father,"

"Yes, of course,"

"Good... This house is a prison. I thought I wanted to fix it up again, but the sins in these walls cannot be tiled over so easily. You know, all those cranes were my doing? They were supposed to bring me peace. A thousand of them later, and all I have are stiffer hands and clutter. A lavish and ornate cage remains a prison... And I am *doomed* to be its prisoner," declared Dr. Herbert sorrowfully, staring blankly at the filth before him.

The truth seemed more real to him as it left his lips. No book could ever have the power to bring them back. Some things were destined to remain out of reach forever. Locking eyes with the pale phantom one last time, the Constable swore to himself that his future would be better–it had to be. Perhaps the Professor's little quest would be as fruitful as his... if he told the complete truth.

"I promise I'll tell you everything I find. Thanks for your hospitality, Dr. Herbert, and I'm sorry for..."

"No need to apologize, son. Go out: find answers. I do not trust your friend, and I would watch his matches, carefully," advised the old man weakly, sinking deeper into the cushion. Starting to doze off, the old man felt his arms slowly slump into the tearing red armrests. He almost looked at peace, but his furrowed brow betrayed the illusion of comfort.

"Went through the bush, found the charred remains of a match. I knew a man of the force would never do such a thing, yet that curious reptile that you call your partner would. No hard feelings: the blossoms are dead, too. Perhaps it is time for rest... In my dreams, I can still find them there, to garden. I bid you a good day, Mr. Brauer," mumbled Dr. Herbert as his eyes shut tightly.

"Indeed, take care, sir," replied the Constable, leaving delicately in hopes that the old man could find rest. The hourglass towered above the big man until he made it to the doorway. He would question him more diligently the next time they met, perhaps under nicer terms. Winston, like a madman with a loaded gun, immediately began firing words off in the big man's general direction.

"Hullo, sir! Did you learn anything?" shouted Winston gleefully as his face shone off the now fully golden-orange sun.

"Yes. A good deal, to be precise," carefully said the Constable, skeptically pondering one small word that vexed him–something peculiar that would not put itself to rest. He had called him by his name, which while refreshing to hear again, the old man should not have known it at all. Palms growing sweaty, he put his hands together for his fingers to touch before remembering he was missing one. With this new sense of dread, the Constable entered the carriage with purpose beyond adventure, answering a question seemingly without an answer.

Did the Doctor know more than he had let on?

CHAPTER SIX:
THE TRUTH AND
A FEW LIES

"**S**o, just to spell this out clearly, you haven't learned anything about Herbert? Nothing at all? What happened to the agreement that we were peers in this case?" angrily asked the Constable to the Professor, now standing outside his home. Resting his arm on the rough, dry brick, he felt strangely surreal: slick surfaces had become a thing of the past. His island was submerged in liquid magma, and his flushed cheeks were strawberry red. He could just feel her on the other side of the wall, eavesdropping on their conservation, just waiting for an opportune time to strike.

Perhaps she had finally emptied all her innards, which would only be a humble start at cleansing the rot within. Plenty of her was broken; her womanly machinery certainly was. Years of trying... for naught.

Winston sat still against the wall, taking in his surroundings. The sky was overcast since the still clouds repressed their teary-blue drops. A certain rainy day had provided a lovely date for him ages ago. Now, it seemed as though she was now as distant as the clouds, floating in some secret place among the stars. A tad overwhelmed, he walked into the Brauer home, rather hurriedly. Sneering, Carrion replied cooly.

"No. I merely wanted to give you cause for my absence; I had something more important to investigate than some silly doctor. His mark... There is something of greater importance than your play date with Herbert," finished saying the Professor before being cut off by a curt wave from the large man, who merely shook his head slowly.

Staring deeply at the palms of his hands, the Constable saw calluses and the light etchings of wrinkles. Small imperfections and scars kissed his knuckles, and certain clumps of skin had begun to cinch tightly around them. A delicate, white hair protruded from a mess of stringy black ones. Time had rendered his fists useless–what else would it take? His wife? All the labor of his hands, for all his life, had been for naught.

Eye filled with bloodlust and hatred, he furiously slammed his meaty hands against the bricks of his home. Howling profanities at the sky, he slammed again in sheer defiance of every visible and unseen opponent before him. Bones sounded their protest in violent cracks, yet he persevered until his hands were a mess of blood and flesh. Every contact cut deeper, straight to his soul. Fluids, red and the like, seeped out of his ruined fingers.

The wall grew a shade more crimson in splattered blots, to his immeasurable dismay. He could not escape her, even here! Eventually, he stopped, crumpling down silently on one knee in the wet grass. Its greenness taunted him. The Professor brought himself a little lower to put his right hand on the big man's shoulder. His hammer had already broken itself so soon–serious mending would have to be done. But, there was something else, altogether foreign: a twinge of pity.

Red had indeed heard the racket, but she likely decided her husband had deserved whatever punishment he had received.

Perhaps Reiner had finally caught wind of his drinking–he might be more like his old self again. Mumbling with clattering teeth like a cold child, the Constable stared blankly as he spoke. His own raspy words disgusted him.

"You were supposed to be my way out, my escape, my freedom. Yet, turn after turn, you've been in my way! Made a fool out of me, blunder after blunder. Would you like to know why I was so quick to put everything on the line–so nosy about Herbert? I have *nothing* to lose and everything to gain. Separation of any kind from her would be liberating. Doing something, no matter how meager, could make me feel alive! I would settle for anything at this point. Our endless arguments are insufferable. Take the damn carpet! Have the bloody thing. Might as well nab the keys to the house while you're at it. Just give me a *cause*," cried the Constable into the Professor's ear, clutching at the tufts of grass. What remained of his hands tightened over each other, barely able to clasp at all. The railman remained still before regaining enough composure to reply.

"I refuse to waste my precious time speculating about what claws at you from inside. However, I am clearly not the problem nor the cause of your... sorry state. I will not apologize; instead, I will give you something that has value: the truth. For an oaf, you are astute: I am sure that you noticed my tattoo immediately, despite my best efforts. It is remarkably odd, is it not? While it is true that I came here for triumph and glory, I was also drawn to this dismal place to find the origin of this very marking. As far back as I can remember, I have had this accursed thing. I *need* to know why... Now, with the scent, my pilgrimage, my journey, has begun. That night, you came crawling back to me to escape, and fortunately for you, I intend to deliver it in spades. You can leave your shackles in that hut–so long as you help me get what I want. There is no force in the world that can stop me from finding my truth. I neglected to tell you this because your insipid questioning would have drawn this case into the gutter. Now, things have been set into motion that cannot so easily be neglected," declared the Professor while reaching deep into his pockets, withdrawing a small handkerchief and a flask of alcohol.

Pouring it on the open wounds, he tore the handkerchief into two, wrapping them tightly around each of the big man's hands. Spasming, the Constable's island appeared as if it had risen from the ocean in pure shock. He studied the Professor's handiwork: he had actually done a good job. Feeling repulsed by his admiration, Carrion quickly spoke up.

"Do not think anything about it! This was merely to stop the bleeding. Nothing more, nothing less. As I was saying, this mark has some meaning. It represents *their* philosophy, if you will. You have noted the hourglass: empty on both sides. *They* believe that the past and future are meaningless, intangible. Instead, *they* seek some mumbo-jumbo salvation through the present. Did Mr. Herbert's statements agree with my findings, Brauer?" carefully asked the Professor, attempting in vain to mask his interest in the conversation.

A partial truth would have to suffice for the big man; the larger truth was certainly complicated at best. Looking up sheepishly, the Constable reluctantly stared into his emeralds to find a sliver of truth. The slithering, uncaring snake before him still offered him a means of escape. Gradually, he could break his tether to her, one tug at a time. Hands still shaking, the big man replied simply.

"Yes,"

"Then we have proven something simple yet important. Whoever *they* are clearly hates all forms of causality and time—sounds cultish. I do wonder who hurt *them*,"

"Where did you hear all of this?"

"Based on what Winston told you, I presume you believe that I just stumbled into pleasant company? I know I'm charming and all, but…"

"No, of course not. Don't be ridiculous,"

"Brauer, save the lying for the rest of us. To satisfy your curiosity, I stole a ride in a carriage. He looked like a jolly sort—a bit tipsy. A bit, being a good deal, of course. With a twinge of clever storytelling, I convinced him that I was a specter, warning him of calamities to come,"

"How am I not surprised?"

"Finally, you are starting to get how this game is played. I told him I was bound for the local tavern, but a quick glance at his grizzled paw gave me pause,"

"He had it, didn't he?"

"Yes. Realizing this could be my chance, I immediately insisted on riding for a while longer–to his initial dismay. Surprisingly, he was not terribly fond of riding with a man he presumed was Death. A whiskey quickly changed his mind, sourced as fresh as something could be from a coat pocket. That got him talking a bit more, so I asked him about the lovely tattoo on his hand. I learned a good deal about his sister Erma before the old coot mentioned the mark. Apparently, it is rather important to his family–even a part of their coat of arms," recounted the Professor while the Constable further found his footing. The weighting of his body felt strangely unbalanced; his fists hung too loosely from his wrists. Perhaps they were down and out for good. The big man sighed before speaking, hoarsely.

"Did he start sputtering nonsense about the past, present, and future?"

"Precisely, just as I am sure you heard from everyone's favorite doctor,"

"He didn't bear *their* mark,"

"Excuse me?"

"Dr. Herbert didn't have your hourglass marking. I spent a too much time staring at his rings, and there was nothing of note on his hands. He claimed *they* didn't believe he could advance their movement. Yet, how could this ruined man, this drunkard, have been accepted by *them*?" proposed the Constable, pulling his coat sleeves over his ruined hands. He was not in the mood to be chewed out by her again so soon. So many useless conversations to placate her... Carrion's emeralds squinted, almost as if he was confused. His hands flailed as he ran an arithmetic calculation in his head, grasping at an unknown conclusion.

"My newfound companion swore he was a doctor of sorts. Perhaps it was the whiskey speaking?"

"Dr. Herbert swore *they* wanted him to be a chemist like his father.

"So, that does not exclude the idea *they* recruit scientists, but there might be a rigid structure to how they choose successors. What was his name?"

"Olmsted Guess. What a name for a pretentious bastard,"

"Guess... That name almost sounds familiar. He's from around here, but he hasn't been here for long. As for Herbert, perhaps he wasn't chosen because *they* disapproved of his father. He was found dead in his chair with no clear cause," said the Constable, enjoying hearing his voice again. He had figured he would get to use it more after his promotion nearly a decade ago, but that had been wishful thinking. The Professor was already sick of his yammering, but the tool needed to mend itself.

"Typically, complacency does kill people," replied the Professor unemotionally. The big man's hands still ached painfully, or he would have given his face some color. His lack of regard for anyone besides himself was truly disgusting. Perhaps no one had ever cared for him... Leaning against the bloodied wall, the Constable stayed silent in thought. Bothered, the Professor spoke up again.

"Have you put the pieces together, in there, yet?"

"That there's foul play? Suppose so. You're saying Herbert's father was murdered? As much as you hate him, his son actually thinks so, too. If *they* have such influence with these wealthy families, procuring some poison would have been child's play," skeptically declared the Constable, noting the Professor's widening grin. His misaligned, yellowing teeth looked like a disorderly row of sick canaries. Beaming happily, he playfully patted the big man on the back.

"Indeed! You impress me, for once. As I have said, there is *always* a murder. Where it stops will be for us to decide, now. Is there anything else I should know about our dear friend?"

"He might be sick–he insisted that we find the truth about his father quickly. Most strangely, he knew my name. We had never met,"

"Curious–strange, even. Based on the words of your wife, you are not notable, even in the homeliest sense. You must have met him before in passing!"

"Never, not once," replied the Constable before letting out a suppressed laugh. Carrion had sadly cut too close to home, quite literally. Perhaps, in a strange sense, he was a genius, one unusually capable of peering into the lives of others. His emerald eyes could pierce something hidden away in flesh and muscle, just like hers. Even if she did not see his hands, she would know something was wrong. He would have to have an explanation–something particularly humiliating would have to do. Breathing heavily with anticipation, the Professor continued.

"Clearly, he knows more than he lets on. He must have done his homework on you after the first time he saw you. All the hallmarks of dysfunction are there: a dead father, rejection, and obsession. Goodness, I have heard it all before. *They* killed his father, burying secrets with him," said the Professor before being cut off by the Constable, of all people. His island swelled up as he spoke.

"Why did *they* not cut off all loose ends?"

"That is irrelevant. I will speak to Herbert myself, and you can have the luxury of speaking with a hungover Mr. Guess,"

"No, it is not irrelevant. Big powerful organization could have snuffed him out like a candle. He must be living on borrowed time. Dr. Herbert said he fell on hard times–somebody must have brought him down. Yet, *they* still spared him. Why? This is the question we should be asking," pressured the Constable impatiently. Leary of his newfound confidence, the Professor quickly worked to snuff out the spark shining in his good eye. Restoration was more than enough for his purposes.

"Yes. All things will be in good time. One small matter, how many wives did Mr. Herbert have?" asked the Professor, working overtime to divert the conversation at hand. The Constable stared blankly at him. What a petty little man he was. With a distinct lack of energy remaining, he answered honestly.

"Many at one point. All but one left him or died. We were both right in a sense. You can keep your clutches off what is left of my carpet, and the gash in your armor is safe from the world's judgement," said the Constable as the Professor, apparently satisfied, smirked. Breathing in deeply, the big man strained his face into a contented grimace–their little arrangement would continue for the time being. They shook hands. Looking down at the coppery-red blood patch on his hand, Carrion wiped it on the Constable's jacket before making a declaration.

"Well, partner. We have work to do."

CHAPTER SEVEN: A HANDFUL OF EXCUSES

"Yes, he was quite furious. Told me I had utterly failed at picking at Dr. Herbert," lied the Constable to his wife, her face glowing nearly as red as her hair. Clearly, his condition was the result of another night of drinking; his drunken stupors always carried a strong scent of alcohol and mistruth. He kept pulling his sleeves down over his dwarfish fingers. What was he hiding? Curious, Red decided to play along, wondering what he could possibly fabricate next.

Prodding, no matter how blatant, had proved remarkably inefficient in making him act in any respect. She stared deeply into her husband's good eye–that always seemed to work. Shifting away from her, the Constable grabbed his drink from earlier, disappointedly flipping it over as his eye reflected in the empty bottom.

"I suppose you got a few good knocks back on him?" replied Red, convinced that she would be unable to get a rise out of him. Her husband never seemed to feel anything anymore, far more taken with cheap ladies on bottles than her. She wondered how far she could take this before he would finally say something, anything at all.

"What do you think, *honey-lamb*?" asked the Constable forcibly, with a hint of volume carrying his speech. He caught Red's eyes flicker before they moved past him to the corner of the room. There was Winston, sitting completely oblivious to their spirited conversation. He was such an empty boy, always lost to his surroundings. No one in the world ever seemed to touch a precious lamb like him. His baffling innocence was unearthly.

"Oh, sorry there, folks. I think I should go now. The Professor probably needs me–I'm sure of it!" shouted Winston without much confidence in what he had just said. Floating through the door with ease, he was gone in an instant. The heavy, wooden door remained awkwardly open, swinging back and forth, albeit more slowly each time. Impatient, the Constable arose and slammed it shut–the violent crack almost sounding like one that left his fingers earlier. Shivering slightly, Red felt like she had struck a chord: a golden opportunity to drive out the man she loved, at long last.

"I think you got what you deserved, as always," smugly replied Red, displaying her brilliant, white teeth. They had been finely doctored to perfection early in their marriage. Sadly, not all things were so easily fixed. The big man felt the raw sinews in his knuckles cry for vengeance, for retribution; they wanted to be heard. Teetering dangerously, he was about to snap. The honesty from his last conversation welled up inside him, threatening to release itself. And then, it did, spewing out from his lips without a care in the world.

"You used to be content with the fact that I was with the force. That's not enough now, though, is it? Even the damn promotion couldn't satisfy you,"

"Excuse me? Honey..." said Red stammering, unsure of what she had unleashed upon herself. His enraged eyes caused her to back away slowly from him. She clutched the edge of the sofa tightly, tearing a hole in the fabric with her talons.

Lumbering forwards, the Constable began to boil over in a violent explosion.

"How have I failed you? I certainly know how you failed me," shouted the Constable, throat beginning to seize up. Red's eyes blinked quickly and emptily, beckoning him to claw deeper. He expected her to release an outburst of tears, silencing him in an instant. Instead, her face glistened against the dim light of the nearby window.

Her husband was still broken–no amount of force could coax him out of this rut. But now... There was no going back. Swallowing deeply, she tried to find her words. Shaking his head at such a weak attempt at mimicking empathy, the Constable laughed: no calculated display could reel him back in. Seized with hatred for the wretch before him, the big man raised his voice again.

"I asked you a question, and I *deserve* an answer. No more smoke or mirrors. Answer me! Now!" roared the Constable, tapping on his newfound rage. His face was significantly redder than the horrified face in front of him. Growing deathly pale, she felt the color drain from her face. The gash grew deeper into the couch, breaking one of her delicate nails.

"Get out..." pleaded Red softly, almost in a whisper.

"Of my own home! The one I paid for all with my blood! What have you given to me? Not one child! I'll die alone like Herbert! But you'll leave me beforehand, won't you? You horrid *bitch*,"

"Leave..." whimpered Red, tears down her face in long streaks.

Trudging to the door with clenched fists, the Constable spat on the ground. His feet carried him toward the door and away from the monster. The sound of tears breaking delicately on the coarse ground was soon lost to a tremendous crash sounding from the door.

His crimson rose could writhe and wither into dust.

CHAPTER EIGHT: DRINKS AND CONFESSIONS

"So, she gave you the boot from your own house?" asked the Professor, eagerly awaiting to hear the complete story with every minute detail. He heard a dull clink issue from the ground of the cabin. Lying near the pole-man's feet, a large golden ring rattled before settling against the ground, glinting from what little light entered the carriage. The Constable looked down at his shaking broken hands, straining to relax them over the seat cushion. At some point, he figured he should cut his losses and lop the remaining nine fingers off. What good they did him.

"Life is far too short for this," said the Constable before sighing heavily. He did not bother to sit forward–they could think what they wanted of him. When he had first entered the carriage, the Professor had wisely kept his mouth shut. Clearly, that luxury was fleeting. Despite his seeming disregard for the big man's condition, he was very much concerned with how frequently he got busted up. Red had played the game much more roughly than he had anticipated.

In such a drained stupor, he would be no good for any more tasks, or anything else, for that matter. So, he quickly proposed an idea–one he suspected would be to the big man's liking. He was in no place to protest.

"I'll take that cryptic answer as a 'yes.' My friend, would you be interested in taking a small detour? Take your mind off a few things," proposed the Professor, fully aware of what the answer would be. Surely enough, the Constable shook his head affirmatively before cobbling together a few words.

"Yes, I think that is the first thing I have ever heard from you that isn't complete horseshit," muttered the Constable, slackened against the seat. He grimaced tightly, feeling phantom liquor lap on his tongue. It would drain down his throat like a fiery snake, but it was worth it. Perhaps that was the real escape he was craving, all along... He knew Carrion's plan before he had even finished articulating it. The little man actually thought it would improve his condition... what an idiot.

Glancing at him, the Professor was pleasantly surprised about how well his plan was going. The Constable would be exactly the sort to drown himself in beer. Hopefully, he would wake up more like his old self–a lovely, blunt object for smashing that did not bother thinking. The tool spoke.

"Perhaps a drink at the... um, I have not..."

"Bobo's or Stanton's... Any other place that's still open. Really your choice if you catch my meaning,"

"Which would lift your spirits the most, my good man?" questioned the Professor, unsurprised by how well-versed the big man was with beer. He probably knew it better than his wife. Oh, how his little island bobbed with excitement at the mere thought of drinking!

Yet, something invisible seemed to tug at his fatty throat, making his breathing harsh. This was not his first detour, and they always came with a cost. At least the big man felt at home in the cruddy little bar–the only place where he was valued as a regular. He answered him.

"Stanton's. Oh, it's about time that I teach you something, you pretentious prick,"

"Sounds like the perfect medicine to cure you of your affliction," replied the Professor to an apparently indifferent Constable, who lifted his head to stare blankly out the window. The road was surrounded by withered plants. The loss of rain had already claimed its first victims. Patches of greenness seemed to stretch far from the road as if they were migrating along it to an unknown future. They might die, perhaps, or thrive. He felt a tiny warmth grow inside him.

Carrion, too, saw the plants; they threatened him with their wilting frames. Nothing he could do in his lifetime could save him from that Fate. Those plants were surely going to die as he would. The only thing that kept him from shriveling away was his glorious purpose–the quest for truth. He dared not to think of a future without it. Feeling a sharp chill cut from inside, he shrugged it off before shouting a command to the box.

"Winston! Find a pub called Stanton's or something of that sort. We need a drink or two, or perhaps a few. This is, of course, the only way that we may have the fervor to pursue this case," finished yelling the Professor, knowing full well that Winston would not join them inside. He was a teetotaler, after all–how pathetic.

"Will do, boss!" replied Winston, excited to drive a tad bit more. After a long journey of silence, they arrived at the pub. Due to the convenient timing of their arrival, the only thing to greet them was the rising moon. Hearing the crackle of gravel, a well-dressed bartender creaked the door open to a familiar sight.

"Mr. Brauer! You sure are early tonight!" cheered Karina exuberantly, expecting him to arrive hours later. Her mind was already racing with the imports they had just gotten in yesterday until she saw an unfamiliar man standing next to the Constable. He was tall and lanky, with striking sideburns and brilliant green eyes.

"Hello Karina, this is…" said the Constable before being cut short by young woman, who was already quite fearful of losing a moment that had not even happened yet. New patrons were always exciting.

"Oh, I am so pleased to meet you! My name is Karina, and I'm the bartender at Stanton's, as you can well see. Who might you be?"

"The first thing that you should know of me is the fact that I am not one for pleasantries, my dear," replied the Professor, slightly masking his savageness with an upturned grin. It was hardly a cordial introduction, but Karina was undeterred. Difficult as he seemed, there was something captivating about him that propelled her to dig a bit deeper.

"*Of course*! But, I will need just a simple name for the drinks, of course, nothing more. It's just protocol, something I am sure you can understand," replied the dauntless woman, waving them inside politely. The Constable watched this bizarre scene unfold, staying silent in hopes it would continue to get weirder. He was, after all, just in it for the drinks. However, he would happily enjoy the free show attached to them with glee. The rail-man introduced himself.

"Professor Carrion: legendary detective and certified genius, at your service. That should be sufficient information for your purposes, my dear," sharply said the Professor, causing poor Karina to blush redly. Distracting them with another grandiose swing of her arm, she ushered them inside again, this time more vigorously. Tailing the back of the group anxiously, Winston carefully passed through the wooden frame. Carrion snarled as he caught a glance of the boy before whispering into the Constable's ear.

"He *always* ruins it," whined the Professor. Shrugging, the Constable studied the spacious pub. Empty, of course. It was nearly the middle of the night, after all. For being such a loyal patron, he had hardly made the time to actually look around. The stools were peeling and tattered, clearly well-loved. The tables had several etchings cut into them, some more or less appropriate. One, in particular, consisted of two names and a heart encircling it—surely, a lovely declaration of lies!

On the mantle of the fireless fireplace sat a large skull from an indeterminate animal–perhaps Leviathan itself. Newspapers were strewn about on the walls, recognizing the pub for various superb drinks, unsurprisingly all imports. The group sat down as Karina moved behind the bar counter to begin serving them.

"I just thought I could sit in," said Winston cautiously, fully aware of the glaring green lights directed through his head.

"Oh, hello there, what is your name?" asked Karina to Winston. She was giddy to have this many customers at such an absurd hour when she had not even expected one. Business had been slow lately. Despite the acclaim they had received from the local news, the bar had too few denizens. She just supposed that drunks did not usually make much effort to read the morning paper.

"Winston! Sorry, that was terribly abrupt. The name's Winston!" replied the man who was certainly Winston before shifting uncomfortably. Karina felt awful; after all, she had not intended to make him feel embarrassed. However, something larger than idle conversation clearly tugged his heart downwards. It had a name: Amelia. She had given him grey-white streaks in his dark hair and small wrinkles in his wide-set eyes. For being absent, she remained ever-present yet out of reach.

"Anyways, Professor! That is quite the title you have there. I'm a chemist in my spare time myself. I suppose that was bound to happen, working with drinks and all, every day. Lot of time to think... Sometimes too much. Anyways, what drink will you have tonight–a fine whiskey, perhaps?" asked Karina, somewhat cautiously.

"Sure! I suppose it does not matter how I permanently disfigure my innards!"

"Excellent! Constable, I know what you like by now! A large craft beer?"

"Yes, of course–you know me too well,"

"Ok, and you, Winston?"

"I don't drink. Not anymore," replied Winston, further

drawn to thoughts of her. Karina caught a glimpse of something burrowed inside him–the very same something that the Professor had neglected to tend for years. She did not want to sour the drinks with sorrow but suspected it would find its way out, all on its own, anyways. The Constable studied Winston more carefully; the cheery optimism he projected was beginning to give way to something else altogether: sorrow. Karina bit her tongue before asking simply.

"You lost someone, didn't you, Winston?"

"Oh, I wouldn't dwell on that. Goodness knows I do enough for all of us... Her name was Amelia. Always called her Milly, though. She's been gone for some time now. Could I tell you about her, though?" softly pressured Winston to the group. They all solemnly nodded, even Carrion, albeit begrudgingly. Despite being terribly sick of mushy "love," the big man wondered what misfortune could have touched such a happy man. Karina began preparing the drinks, but her ears perked up like that of a cat's. The Professor, clenching his teeth, was not nearly rude enough to interrupt.

"Ah, she was my woman! Didn't even have to try to convince her to marry me. It took change, but we both just felt it was right from the get-go. A year or so passed, and when we were married, we did everything we could together, being stuck on the road. She was my only passenger that stuck around... Every night, we'd sit up on the box and just talk about anything that came to mind–just to talk. It was extraordinary! A sort of magic, I suppose, but real. I had hoped it would last forever. But, that part of my life ended when she..." said Winston before pausing and tightly clutching a pendant wrapped around his neck. The Constable knew where this story would lead: she would leave him to rot in misery. What gall! Karina brushed her hair behind her ear, bracing herself to hear what she dared not to think.

"Died," finished saying Winston slowly, wincing from the pain that cast deep wrinkles on his otherwise youthful face. The Constable felt something about his wife–at least she was still alive. For once, that felt more like a blessing than a curse.

Perhaps he had taken that for granted, among other things.

Karina bit deep into her lip to prevent her eyes from harming the drinks. Misfortune had a way of taking from everyone. Twitching, Carrion felt a twinge of disappointment creep up on him. Something so simple, so exploitable, had eluded him. But, there was another feeling, too, more than pity: pain. Not his, no...yet it stung. They had been together for so long... Perhaps he owed him more? Winston continued speaking.

"I don't drink to honor her–a sort of last rite. I know that somewhere, up there in the clouds, she is waiting for me. When I finish passing through, I'll see her again," preached Winston from the heart, with faith in his eyes. The Professor could not believe in such things. Although the Constable could not either, he still appreciated the sentiment. Smiling warmly, Karina set the drinks on the table. By that point, no one was too thirsty. Winston, unusually observant, brightly remarked.

"Cheer up, lads! I have you all now. Drink to your heart's content," cheered Winston, exchanging his sadness for fleeting joy. He could afford to cease battle with that great beast for a few more moments. Excluding him, they all took a long drink, along with Karina herself, who took it directly from the pitcher.

"Now that 'that' is finished, I believe that we need to work through all the mushy stuff that is clogging your clockwork, Brauer. I take no joy in stitching you back together, but in your current state, you are just pathetic. Your wife seems to embody your suffering, and it seems she is hell-bent on the destruction of all things you hold dear, including your home, your job, and your feelings. Quit sitting around and doing nothing!"

"Just let me drink in peace!"

"As you wish. Go on, then, drink yourself to sleep tonight and cry the tears. Slink back to your favorite mistress. Empty your system and start again tomorrow," said the Professor to the Constable, whose hands rattled frantically. Every part of him wanted to slam the meaty things into the wooden table, except the silly little heart etched into the table made him think about Winston instead. Raising his cracked hands upwards, he carefully brought them downwards to clasp around the cup of beer, instead.

He drank heartily. It never made anything better... But, tomorrow would be a new day. The Professor smiled sourly; he had pegged the big man perfectly—so gooey, so sentimental. He would never muster the courage to take from her as she did from him. Karina stared somewhat longingly at the broken men before her; her heart thumped impatiently for an unknown cure.

"Karina, now that the Constable is mollified, I have a few questions for you," proposed the Professor, looking Karina in her brown-orange eyes for the first time. With a small, pointed chin, her sloping nose supported a heavy pair of gold-rimmed glasses. Black strings of hair were begrudgingly held upwards in a seemingly indestructible bun. Her resoundingly unladylike attire was threateningly interesting to him. Clearing her throat, she replied.

"Oh... me? Sure, by all means. What may I help you with?"

"Have you ever heard of a man by the name Olmsted Guess? I met him briefly the other day before he darted away,"

"Yes, like Mr. Brauer, he is a regular here—one of the few I have left," replied Karina honestly with a hint of disappointment carrying her words.

"One hell of a doctor. Would you not agree?" tactfully asked the Professor, catching a puzzled glance from Karina. She scratched wildly at the dark, messy hair on her head, attempting to make sense of what he had asked. What was he really asking? The conversation felt more strategic than polite. Her head turned sideways like a locked cog; she answered the only way she could.

"No, I can't think so. He always talks about his bricklaying business... Why do you ask? Is something wrong?"

"Oh, nothing at all! Just curious. I will have to trust that you are not mistaken. Truthfully, I am unsure of how observant you are. However, by chance, did you catch any strange markings on his wrist?"

"Yes, some sort of hourglass. One must keep her eye on her patrons," replied Karina kindly yet forcefully. She was very observant, and no one would tell her otherwise. Patrons would have dropped dead many times over if it was not for her keen sense of attention. Many times, the Constable had been on the other end of her all-seeing gaze. He always paid, but there nights it seemed the sales carried a greater human cost. She vowed to be even more watchful, yet.

"That filthy liar!" roared the Professor, storming out of the bar to the dingy grey alleyway. He screamed in defiance at the heavens so loudly that a nearby flock of birds flew to the sky for haven. Karina frowned deeply before pursuing the crazed thing out of the door that had been flung open. Lips pursing, she scowled at the tantrum before her–such behavior was not fitting of a man. Eyes darting wildly, the Professor shouted in a nearly unintelligible manner in her general direction.

"No, not you! *Mr. Guess!*" screeched the Professor while kicking a small waste basket, causing him to wail all the more about his ankle. Backing into the pub, Karina shook her head slowly before returning inside. Surely, somewhere in that raging beast was something dignified. Winston looked over to her, mouthing that was always what he did when he found out he was wrong. Regaining his composure, a flush, exasperated Professor returned inside, clutching at the door frame weakly. He spoke in between labored breaths.

"That behavior was a bit unexpected. Thank you, Mrs...."

"*Ms.* Flores. But, I insist that you call me Karina,"

"Fair enough, Mrs. Flores. Your insight, though rather unsettling, has given me some food for thought. The drinks, though all the same, seem to be adequate here," said the Professor, weaving around any sort of apology. Her eyes lingered on the living enigma before her–they would meet again. Curtsying playfully, Karina grinned before replying.

"Thank you all for coming, although I wish you could stay a while longer... Do come back soon! I'm honored to serve such an educated man and member of the force at this humble establishment! Oh, and of course you, Winston... Goodness, I do believe Mr. Brauer has passed out!"

She was correct. Poor Mr. Brauer had taken the pitcher and downed it in its entirety. A small stream dribbled down his chin. His barrel was bloated full while his arms sprawled weakly over the table. Winston attempted to help him over his shoulder, along with the Professor. Crumpling underneath the poorly distributed weight, the near-sighted man grunted painfully. With ease, Carrion tipped his cap to Karina as she called out to them one last time. Winston could carry his own weight, at least according to the Professor–he likely disagreed.

"I hope to see you again soon! I would like to hear of whatever comes of the business with Mr. Guess as well. Please look after Mr. Brauer," said Karina softly, feeling somewhat guilty her eyes had failed her–or perhaps, her heart. She had no idea things were so bad. The Constable would inevitably be back, but she vowed to herself it would be under a far more restricted pretense.

"Of course! I will be happy to straighten out Mr. Guess myself..." replied the Professor, rubbing his favorite pocket of his coat.

The one with his fine collection of matches.

CHAPTER NINE: THRESHOLD

"**C**onstable, are you with us currently? Took my suggestion to heart, didn't you?" asked the Professor in a rhetorical manner to entertain himself. His voice echoed in the empty cabin, forcing him to hear himself far more than he would have liked. Eventually, as it issued out the cracked cabin panels, newfound silence emerged, giving him ample time to reflect. A stabbing sensation consumed his side, causing him to shift nervously. Sweating icy bullets, his hands clutched over one another for dear life. One question stood above the pain, echoing much louder than his own shrill voice could have.

Who had he become?

He was not always like the way he was. Yet, he could not remember when he was someone different. His head drifted down to a pocket that was not meant to be opened. Its contents were far more dangerous than simple matches. Pulling a single corroded coin from it, he took a harmless look at it. Flooding dangerously, the memories came in as a torrent that could not hope to be stopped. Lines became curves, and darkness erupted into a searing light.

Sinking...

    Sinking...

        Sinking...

            Sinking...

"Thad! Come over here and play! You silly, little thing," shouted the young girl before his mind's eye. She was about five, standing near a wooded area. He took in his surroundings: tall, defiant trees engulfed by a serene blue sky. Birds were singing their songs. Everything was peaceful. All was calm. Save for the bickering pair of two children–their cries deafened by the clamor of an indifferent world. Thad replied to his sister, chirping.

"No! You know what Mother and Father said!"

"Thady's a *scaredy* cat!" sounded the freckled girl back, gleefully running into the forest with her arms flailing with the wind.

He took one last glance at the small wooden sign that read countless warnings he could not read yet. Those ugly, swooping letters could mean nothing good. Regardless, Thad gave chase with reckless abandon, valuing his sister over his fear of the forest. Perhaps less nobly, his legs carried him so that he would suffer no mockery from her. He nearly tripped over a root, then a spiked branch. Bare feet passed over stone and bramble alike, charting their own path. Jagged things tore into his tiny toes.

Yet, something particularly special caught his foot through the muddy-brown earth. Bending over, he felt his little hands pour through the dirt, but he already knew what Thad would find. They both held up a coin, an alluring prize for the young boy. Thad studied the glimmering coin, smiled at the sky, and pocketed it.

Carrion stared longingly into the coin for meaning. Its reflection was empty. In an instant, the memory passed back into the wind–away.

            Hurtling back...

        Hurtling back...

Hurtling back...

Hurtling back...

He knew that was not all: it could not be. The pain became acute, sharper than any hungry razor blade. His brittle nails dug into its green-metallic surface.

Clink!

That pretty little face was no longer spotless. He was not finished.

Clink!

Its face was still recognizable but had two deep scratches carved into it.

Clink! Clink! Clink!

The face of the coin was ruined. Carrion threw it out the window, laughing bitterly. Such a weak attempt... Normally, they were far more convincing. No more memories of some pathetic boy could hurt him. Only strength from fear could provide for his passage, his truth. He would play his part dutifully, as would the others. His vows were now theirs, too– inextricably bound by the Fates. They filled his weak lungs before spilling out into the empty air.

"For the Constable. For Winston. For Thad."

CHAPTER TEN: ON THE COLOR SCARLET

R ed sat silently, sinking into her chair. It was unbearably uncomfortable. The room seemed so much emptier, even incomplete, with her husband gone. How long had it been since she thought about herself–truly? That would be truly uncomfortable.

Her fingers danced on the armrests, trying to work motion into the rest of her languid body. After a good long while, she decided to peer out the window. Perhaps it was the last time she would ever see the man that she had loved so long ago. At least he had finally done something, even if it was an outburst.

Already weary of lounging at the window, she opened the door and began to walk aimlessly. The pavement was curiously rough–perhaps in part to her distinct lack of shoes. She turned briskly around, marching back through the door. Sliding the first heel on, she felt her ankle reject any advances it made. With a slight dismay, she noticed a crumpled note in the base of the second heel. Folding it open, she read it.

"*To my dearest–may these remind you forever of but a fraction of my love for you,*" finished saying Red, tucking the note back into her shoe carefully. He had bought them for her on their honeymoon a long time ago, which had actually been in town. Grunting all the while, she worked her heels on. Not all things fit like they used to. Sighing about her general aimlessness, she grabbed a list of groceries and made for the market. Early in their marriage, they had always gone together.

There he was again: back in her mind, with such ease. Though he had stormed out without any money, or much else, for that matter, he lingered. With some loose calculations, she figured she would be able to eat for the next week or so, comfortably. The force's grand bounty was living paycheck-to-paycheck. Whatever came next was not worth thinking about... yet. Perhaps it was time to reconsider starting the dress shop, which might no longer be immaterial.

The walk itself faded into a dream. Without the rain, one step blurred into the next and the next. Eventually, she stumbled into the now barren market to buy some bread. Living on bread alone would soon be reality.

A wrinkled old thing sat before a small stand of bread–by herself, in a once-alive place. The muddy browns of abandoned, empty stands stared hauntingly at her: they were thirsty for water. Carefully pulling a morsel of bread from the stand, she was surprised to find the old woman smiling at her. Crinkles of white-grey flesh clung to her cheekbones, exposing a kindness that permeated beneath the surface. The old woman spoke.

"Take it; I think you need this bread today more than I do."

"No, I'm happy to pay..."

"I insist, dear,"

"Thank you," replied Red, unsure of what else to even say. Some people really seemed to understand others without understanding their hardship at all. He used to have that gift many moons ago.

Shuffling away, she clutched her blessing tightly. She had never known a time without rain or darkness–it did not surprise her that everyone had hidden themselves away. Nothing short of the moon crashing down from the heavens to the earth could have been more disturbing. Passing the pointed tower of the church, Red saw a faint light creeping through one of its windows. Reverend Sharp... He would help her, should she need it.

They had been married there, of course. His mother, Reiner, and some of the folks from the force had attended. Her own parents had... declined to make an appearance, just happening to be out of town. She had not thought of them for some time. Perhaps that would have to change soon. They would love nothing more than to tell her they had been right.

Looking downwards, she was surprised by how many weeds still poked out bravely from cracks. Not everything had died. Something in particular caught her eye: an envelope with a decorated knife pinned through to the inside of the pavement. Its red-wrapped hilt called her by name. With great effort, she managed to peel the little Excalibur out from the crack, opening the envelope. Shaking profusely, Red realized it was addressed to her. It must have been some sick joke from him... Instead, it was something far more interesting–even sinister.

"*Good evening, Ms. Loxley*," read Red slowly, confused as to how someone would know her maiden name. She had not used that name in nearly a decade, despite it sounding much more pleasant than "Brauer." The silvery blade of the knife reflected eerily against the green-grey weeds as she cautiously read on.

"*Ms. Loxley. We respect your contributions to this grave world. In eagerness, we wish to reward you. The changes we will make together are shattering. We carve this world into pieces and put it back together again. You cast aside your past and future for the one thing we can change–the present. Take our knowledge and find the real change you desire. Prepare: you will meet the Councilman soon*," finished saying Ms. Loxley; her voice wavered in tandem with the swaying weeds.

Could the sender of the letter be the very same group her husband was rambling about? Who was the Councilman? The letter made it sound as if there was little choice for her to decline their invitation. Her legs started carrying her home. One hand clenched the knife for dear life; the other crumpled the letter in tight squeezes. At this rate, it would soon reduce itself back to fibers.

Panting heavily, she nearly yanked her door off its hinges. Inside, she locked the door. Feeling the softness of her palm, she realized the letter was gone. Tugging viciously at the blinds, she struggled to reach and pull them down.

The door was still locked. She was safe. Safe enough because the door was locked–tight. Collapsing into the chair, she studied the gleaming hilt of the dagger. It was an hourglass carved as deeply as the growing lines in her husband's face. An ornate inscription in beaming gold letters invited her deeper into this strange new world.

"*Putrescat praeteritum et futurum. Et nunc colligit in palmam,*" murmured Red, attempting to sound out the alien words that barely resembled a language. Somewhere among the mess of books were answers. Typically, she abstained from such lowly endeavors as drinking. Yet, for a special night like this… she could make an exception. Fetching a bottle, she took a swig.

It burned down her throat violently, causing her to gasp in vain for air. Nerves made everything worse. But, it had some serious kick to it. It barely made him squirm–though he had plenty of practice drinking. Swallowing, she tore through the books until a promising one came to light. It was particularly musty, but with the same sort of strange, swooping letters that were on the hilt. It was apparently some form of Latin. Piecing the inscription together, letter by letter, she scrawled the words out on the page.

"Let the *Past and Future rot, the Present gleams in our palms,*"

A severe migraine crept inside her head. She supposed something was bouncing around in there–hopefully not because it was empty. Foxtrot barked softly from another room, causing her to shudder coldly. One moment later, the door was still locked. Her armrest… She could talk freely with it. Perhaps more accurately, to it. Surely, no one could hear her. Her lips struggled to make words come out.

"*They* know who I am. So, they've got to know my husband

and that professor who brought all of this upon us. Who else do *they* know? If *they* left that for me, surely, they knew when I left my home... and when I came back," cried Red, gnashing her teeth as realizations compounded. While the letter was not explicitly threatening, *their* knowledge was more than enough to drive her deeper into the cushion's warm embrace. To tear the world apart required, among other things, violence. What if she found a way to anger whoever *they* were? Food would then be the least of her problems...

She continued rambling, struggling to keep her thoughts in motion with her roaring mind. The armrest continued to listen, albeit silently.

"How do I keep *them* at bay until someone, anyone, comes back? The door's locked, but how long can I trust it? There must be something within this house already–some way that *they* can hear me," said Red quietly, slowly cupping her hand over her mouth.

They could probably hear everything she was spewing at that moment. As she looked around, her gaze lingered on something most peculiar: the entrance to the attic was open. A small tracking of dirt smothered the edges of the beams of the ladder. Grabbing the knife, she held it as close to her heart as she could without cutting it. Pulling herself up the ladder, she found strained breathing greeted her own. Drowsiness overtook her as a figure emerged in the dark.

Not quite a man–no. He was not entirely of anything. His face was hidden away by a mask of jade, perhaps stolen from a ziggurat. Two slits cut out his eyes, and one pushed his lips outward. Small reading spectacles failed to cover the soulless grey pits which rested behind them. A sort of grotesque flesh clung to the edges of the mask, which bled onto his face. An hourglass was carved into its forehead.

As the light flicked on, she saw his coat, which was a curious sort of animal fur. He was not from the town–the usual dampness would ruin such a thing. Such class for something that did not seem human. Dangling talismans on his neck failed to hide the molting skin beneath. His drooping hands were similarly scarred, burned, and covered in blemishes, all hidden beneath layers of bandages and wrappings. The mummy's hand rested on the top of a cane while the other raised upwards to gesture her forwards. She finished climbing up, instinctually pointing the knife at the intruder threateningly. Her efforts yielded a shrill cackle: this must have been the thing called the Councilman.

"*Our foolish child. We are pleased to see that you put down the weapon, and of course, your posture in that chair is most commendable. Please, find yourself seated. You need not fear us,*" mouthed the thing emptily, almost inviting her to disagree. Red felt her fingers release the knife to the ground as she sat down in an antique chair, which should have been sold moons ago. They were surrounded by fabrics and looms, all of which had not been touched for years. Now, she would never have the chance again.

She was entranced, ensnared by an invisible thing that crept into her mind. Yet, she was still aware she was trapped–powerless to do anything about it. Like a fly caught in a web, left to the mercy of the spider. The mask continued to wheeze exaltations.

"*We note your predicament. You are free now to find your own path, your own fate. Your friends are dead in the past, bound by loss and regret. You foolishly hold onto your husband, who thinks past deeds or future promises can curry favor with you. The past cannot save anyone, as with a begotten future. We are old–so much older than a good many things. But, we bring about true change, real change. Change can set this world on a different course. You must agree that this world is surely doomed in this never-ending, never-ceasing cycle? Do you not?*"

"Yes, I believe so,"

"*Good. I expect that your husband and the snake are searching for us? That old freak does not know us–such foolishness. We always come for them, to them. We await their company eagerly and with open arms. Ms. Loxley, are you willing to put aside your silly pretenses and help change the world? Put aside the worthless man you call your husband? Will you help us find him?*" asked the mask with a hint of sincerity. Red found herself unusually lost for words. He was not worthless. She would not have tried to fight so hard for something without value as much as his damn antics and tantrums made it really difficult to keep that sentiment. Shifting nervously, she bit her tongue. Her words would not be as kind as her thoughts.

"*Ah, you need not answer us now. Mull over what we promise you: a better world for a simple answer. Go ahead and tell them about this meeting. They cannot stop us all. We are everywhere; just look around. The days of empty promises are over! No more secrets or riddles… no choice,*" stated the thing dryly, stressing each word to allow them to float in the air longer. One singular thought found its way through the searing pain in her head. It was louder than the whirring in her ears, making it through the tightening channel that had once been her throat.

"Who are you?"

"*We are the Councilman. We speak for them,*"

"Who are *they*?"

"*You already possess the means to that answer—enjoy your evening, Ms. Loxley. Welcome to a brave new world,*" echoed disembodied words as the figure grabbed his cane and leapt out of the open window with ease. The curtains flew against his movement, avoiding his touch. Red was rendered speechless, paralyzed. With what little courage and strength she had left, she stumbled towards the window. There was nothing there: he had simply vanished.

Clambering back to the knife, she stared at it once more. Its edge was so seamless and sharp. How could her husband hope to prevail? He was out of his league. That thing seemed omniscient, hell-bent on achieving some new vision of the world. She nearly fell off the ladder when she heard a familiar barking; the drumming in her head did not relent. Falling to her knees, she found a way to use her hands. Quickly lifting the floorboard, she started to tuck the knife to rest. If she ever saw her husband again, she would tell him. If not, it was his loss.

He had abandoned her, after all. Years of trying to reach him had been for nothing. So much of her life was spent... wasted on him. Now, he was entirely out of reach–just like the rain. There was a time she would have settled for bickering with him one last time. Now, she was not so sure. In the process of sealing the board, she found one last surprise. The knife grew heavier in her hand; the inscription along the side of the blade called her by name to read it.

"*Quod sapientes iungere nostra causa,*" whispered Red quietly, eyes darting back to the book. It translated loosely as "the wise join our cause." Was she foolish not to join *them*? *They* offered security in a way he no longer could.

Perhaps it was time for new things. Terrifying as he was, the masked man could offer safety, which was more than she currently had... perhaps, at the cost of her husband's, if he would even like to be referred to as such. Though safety paled in comparison to freedom–no more time would be wasted pouring into an empty, leaky vessel.

Yet, as tempting as it seemed, she had absolutely no idea what she would do with it. With him gone, what would she possibly spend her time thinking about now? Some happy little dress shop could only keep her moving for so long. Would she grow used to silence? Surely, not telling her husband about the stranger was not the same as selling him out. Even if it was, would that even be so bad?

She would sleep on it.

CHAPTER ELEVEN: LIKE FATHER, LIKE SON

After passing the pale-white marble gate that guarded the walkway to Guess' manor, the Professor and Winston were led to the patio by a rather timid butler. It, like everything else, was lavishly gaudy. The house was all just too clean, too spotless; it looked like it had never been lived in. Carrion was already tired of seeing Guess' head etched, painted, or sculpted outside the manor. Although he could appreciate the care that the manor received, particularly in comparison to Herbert's place; the other doctor's leering faces turned his stomach in a unique way.

Those statues were not true immortality–such a thing could not exist. While they would certainly outlast the frail man they depicted, they, too, would crumble into dust. Eventually, every legacy ended, only managing to produce cheaper imitations and echoes of what had come before. Once he had his truth, seizing it with strength alone, he would no longer have to make a song and dance out of everything. A dirt nap would suit him just fine, should the Fates deem it so.

Leading them inside, the butler scurried off to find Guess, currently lending his likeness to another sculpture. Reclining comfortably on the royal-red sofa, the Professor studied the room carefully. Such an elaborate mezzanine; he could just imagine him peering over it. No markings were present, only conceited reflections of an even more arrogant man; they could only be so true to form. Yellow nightshades hung from the story above–such dismal things. Eventually, the man of the manor emerged, continuing to shake the rail-man's hand. Poor Winston was neglected entirely, carefully withdrawing his hand from the open air. Carrion sparked the conversation, much to Guess' dismay.

"Ah, the famed Olmsted Guess! I can see that you are a tad soberer than the first time we met," said the Professor snarkily, drawing Winston closer to his side. He was a far more reliable tool than the Constable, as of late, who was still out of commission. Which reminded him of a terribly important question–where was the alcohol? No drinks of any kind were visible within the home. Why was Guess so hungover that night? If appearance was so important to him, then he should be ashamed of seeing his drinking "buddy" again so soon. Guess' butler motioned Winston away to speak with him, fancying him to be another servant scared of the wrath of his master.

Feverishly scratching his sideburns, Carrion continued to display his rancorous, yellow teeth in an apparently friendly manner. Hopefully, such niceties would crack the conceited little man before him. Unfortunately, Guess' sleeve covered the edge of his hand. He would have to find a way to draw it out. Staring awkwardly, Guess tried to calculate a proper response to such an impolite greeting. It was *his* home, after all, as much as *they* allowed it to be. He replied, curtly.

"Professor Carrion, pleased to see you again so soon, under better terms, as you have noted. Please, call me Olmsted,"

"How is the brick-laying, Mr. Guess?" asked the Professor, nearly sneering, figuring there would be no harm in going right for the jugular. Guess' face should have contorted into a different shape, but it remained stone, no more alive than the statues that littered the house. Sighing, he awkwardly raised his hand to scratch what little hair he had left. There it was: the mark. It betrayed far more than his face possibly could have. Tired of the charade of formalities they were playing, the balding man grimaced to form an awkward half-smile before replying bluntly.

"I believe you may be mistaken. I am a doctor–a neurologist, to be exact. Perhaps I misled you last time we met… I don't quite remember what nonsense came out of my mouth! Well, it's water under the bridge now, I suppose. I must insist you call me Olmsted, alone. So, what leads you to *my* home today?" asked Mr. Guess forcefully, growing increasingly antsy to make him leave. Undeterred, the Professor was unimpressed by his little façade of strength. Nothing could cover that mark now–the cat was out of the bag. He had no more statues to hide behind.

"Oh, just pure happenstance, like our first meeting. Tell me, Mr. Guess, what was all the talk of *them*? Sounded shady… I was merely concerned for your well-being,"

"My client? I only meant that they have strange beliefs, nothing more. Those are private matters, though. For the last time, please call me Olmsted,"

"Excuse me, Olmsted, if you do not mind me asking further…" said the Professor slowly, well prepared to finish his thought, regardless of any protest. Flattery was sometimes the only way to get answers although he took no great pleasure in it.

"What sort of work do you do for *them*?"

"Anatomical reports on the brain, mainly. I don't know why that would concern you, my friend… I've been retired from my professional career for some time," replied Mr. Guess with a slight dagger underlying his words. The bricklayer ruse had failed; now, a partial truth would have to suffice. *They* were already growing impatient. The Professor took a step closer towards him, raising his nose upwards like him. Bluffing was so much more fun than flattery.

"My apologies. I only ask because I am seeking to meet with your client for some work of my own. I have a unique skillset myself, being a professor and all," lied the Professor, forked tongue dangling out from his mouth. Mr. Guess smiled, baring his own fangs. Skin struggled and stretched around his eyes, threatening to pop them out of their sockets. They had appeared around the time of *their* advent into his life; fortunately, the sculptures still captured his true visage–or at least what he figured it used to be. He could barely remember. Unfortunately, they were not capable of speaking for him, so he forced himself to speak one last time.

"Professor, *they* demand a specialized, elite selection of thinkers. If you don't mind me asking, what are you even a professor in? What are your credentials? We need chemists and biological minds... What am I even saying? Enough of this! Have you come with any other business?" asked Mr. Guess rhetorically, leaving little room for Carrion to respond. However, he had already said more than enough. Smirking, the Professor felt his mouth stretch into a smile, allowing his yellow nubs to glisten against the light.

"None of your business, but shall we not have a drink first?"

"No, I should think not," sourly declared Mr. Guess, realizing that if he were in a drunken state again, all the secrets would be lost. *They* would have his head–and perhaps more than that. He had to get Carrion out of his home in one piece. He could not be disposed of yet.

"Well, I have a large estate to manage, and this has been a glorious waste of my time! Come along, Winston, we have places to be!" taunted the Professor before pausing to whisper directly into Mr. Guess' ear.

"And, frauds to uncover, brick-layer," muttered the Professor, scurrying towards the door with Winston. Mr. Guess grimaced, barking at his servant to fetch the artist before his precious beauty was lost. Past the patio, the pair heard the loud thud of the door being sharply shut behind them.

However, the Professor would not leave without leaving his own artistic mark on something first. Vandalizing had a strangely therapeutic effect on him. Pulling the Constable's nightstick from his pocket, he tested its weight across his fingers. It had been so easy to nab it from his seemingly lifeless body. Looking around, Carrion felt the cheap imitations of Guess mock him. Summing up all his strength, what little it was, Carrion struck the nearest bust of Mr. Guess right off its ornate pedestal.

It shattered into a million shards of nothing–one image, swept away for good. A match danced between his fingers, which could surely burn the rest of them away, too. Winston was horrified, and, unable to keep quiet any longer, spoke up.

"Professor, you can't do this again so soon, mate. There is no need to make a repeat of this. On top of being pointless, it only complicated our case. Please, it won't even have the same kick if you do it over and over again," pleaded Winston, trying to snuff out the fire within the man. It was not as easy as blowing out a match. The Professor laughed weakly before feeling the warmth drain from his body.

This was why he needed the Constable more than ever–someone incapable of tempering him with far less opinions. If the large man had reasoned with him, the air would have been choked with flames and ash. But, with Winston… He had not known about Amelia. While the boy's words had very, very little sway over him, he would humor him, just this once. He did have a dead wife, after all–which almost made him pitiable.

"Enough of that nonsense! The only sensible reason not to burn this place down is that we're going to take the whole bloody house, casting him down to the streets. Let's save a little fun for later, eh?" replied the Professor while his green eyes lingered on some distant, unknowable thing. Shaking his head, Winston realized he was still unwilling to meet his eyes. They walked the rest of the way silently before arriving at the carriage. Carrion spoke, feigning enthusiasm.

"Winston. Check on that lazy 'member of the force,' would

you?"

"All bright and wakey, sir! You've been out for some time," cheered Winston, causing the Constable to jolt upwards. His slumber had done little to stave the liquid rage in his liver. Indignantly, he shouted, words half-slurred.

"You came to the house without me? This was *my* job if you catch my meaning! You were supposed to go to Dr. Herbert, picking at him. Did you learn anything?" roared the big man, island drifting lazily in his head. Pointing his stub accusingly at the Professor, he burped loudly, watching his arm fall back downwards, seemingly on its own. Carrion grinned at the Constable's sorry state before speaking.

"He referred to *them* as his client. Immediately dismissed the notion of being any sort of brick-layer. Brick-laying must be a ruse in order to cover up that he is still in practice, just for a shadowy organization. Too bad he decided to reveal his hand early: he claimed *they* were only interested in chemists and researchers specifically. This fits with why little Herbert Junior was never adopted, but... if *they* killed his papa, why? He likely yielded valuable research–perhaps he outstayed his welcome," said the Professor passionately. The Constable would have no part of it, furiously raising his arm and failing voice again in vain.

"He was mine! My scoop! Dr. Herbert was your chore. Damn you! I needed that!" shouted the Constable before wheezing loud enough to cause Winston's feet to leave the ground from the box.

"I see that you have not recovered fully. Next time we will ensure you stay out a bit longer. Dr. Herbert is yours; besides, you made a 'connection' with him anyways. Go cry with him again, big man," commanded the Professor, sneering as he barged into the carriage. The Constable was in no proper shape to fight the irritating little man right now, and he knew it. So, he sourly looked out the window with a stubborn pout as a child would after not getting their way.

"Winston, to that wretched shack that Mr. Herbert *calls* a home!" shouted the Professor as the carriage sped off again.

After a short while that felt considerably longer, they arrived at their destination. It appeared as before: lantern, headstone, and all. Except something seemed wrong–very wrong. Even from far away, the lantern had been very clearly snuffed out. There was no light. The setting darkness had seized what little color remained in the building, denying any attempt for any orangeness to shine through it. The door creaked open, seemingly on its own, to beckon them inside. Dr. Herbert was nowhere to be seen. Perhaps the desolation had finally swallowed him up for good.

"Constable, make use of your 'force' status, and go check on him! We need him alive," commanded the Professor as the Constable tried to pull himself out of his drunken stupor to wedge the cabin door open. As he forced it open, he felt a less-than-subtle tap on his side. Withdrawing the nightstick from his pocket, the Professor dropped it in the big man's hand. He did not have the time or energy to berate him. Panting heavily, he tumbled towards the open door.

"Be careful!" jeered the Professor, smiling as he pondered just how he might finally have his murder. Moving through the doorway, the Constable felt his milky pupil spin like a top with reckless abandon. The room was as cold as death. The empty bottles, torn pages, wooden spikes, cranes, and Dr. Herbert greeted him–what was left of him. His husk was an ashy grey; rings lay strewn around his body without care. Split and torn at the seams beyond recognition, his tricorn hat sat far away, shielding itself from the head it once sat on. The big man knelt solemnly before putting his fingers to the man's neck.

He was dead.

Everything he knew died with him. The Constable's lumbering frame almost made a second tombstone, unvisited and without mourners. Reaching downwards, he sealed the old man's eyelids, twin slabs guarding mausoleums for the rest of time. The body had no readily apparent abrasions–he had died without much of a struggle. Searching the surrounding rooms, the Constable realized that the dead man's last wife was nowhere to be seen. She must have fled. The Professor strode in the gaping door, barely containing his excitement.

"Oh, what a shame indeed, dead! Soon enough, he'll be six feet under with dirt thrown over his face. Constable, remember one thing. Some day, we will all face the same fate; our days are numbered. Herbert, for all his supposed accomplishments, could not escape Death. So, fight until your very last breath. The Fates will have their corpse eventually, but deny them while you still can," proclaimed the Professor as his emeralds glistened slightly, almost emotionally. Still as a towering obelisk, the Constable pondered if he would see his mother again one day. Pulling a small scalpel from his coat of seemingly boundless resources, Carrion made his way to the corpse, causing the big man to speak up, loudly.

"What are you doing?"

"We need evidence! Remember what I told you? That was rhetorical; I am sure you forgot. Go ahead, turn away. Cover your precious eyes,"

"No, I will not,"

"Excuse me, assistant?"

"You and I both know damn well that you don't need to defile his body any further. You animal! We are not going to add more to the scene of the crime. As a member of the force..."

"Fine. Too squeamish to even look at it? We will never know what killed him. Guess the only one that cannot live with that is him, eh?"

"Professor, it's time for you to leave. No doubt the force will be here soon. I will answer their questions about this mess... and explain that I found him this way. This is no place for you. Leave, now,"

"Fair enough, Constable, make use of yourself for once. Meet me at my place,"

"You have a place to stay! You came by my home–just to ruin it?"

"Ah, that is not your concern now. Not really your home anymore, is it? Oh, make sure your buddies cannot tell that you had a little blackout at the bar!"

"Go, now,"

"Have fun!" replied the Professor, cackling, leaving the Constable without solace or direction. He moved to the window to see the rail-man gleefully hop into the carriage, soaring off without any care in the world. What a broken man! Carrion could never understand why he cared for the Doctor... They had both suffered when they lost someone special to them, rejected in matters of love, leaving them adrift and aimless, and wanted something more, just beyond the reach of their cells.

They were two of a kind. But, now, one of them was dead— and the other was not. He would not make the same mistake the old man had: dying alone, locked in a vacant home, separated from the one he loved... drinking himself to death. Surely, he could fall in love with her again: the Red he once knew must still live. His crimson rose could surely bloom again. Time alone stood in their way. The man he used to be had to be alive, too. When he had given chase to the carriage, blood pumping in tandem with every step, the years seemed to wash off him. In that singular moment, everything felt right as it once was... before his mother's death. Life would not end longing for what he had lost.

He would have it all again. And perhaps more.

II

CHAPTER TWELVE:
A GRAVE MATTER

"Constable Brauer, under exactly what circumstances was Dr. Herbert found dead in his home?" slowly asked Deputy Reiner inside what little remained of the Herbert home. He was an older man of considerable stature—though a good head shorter than his underling, not counting his custodian helmet. It nearly covered his beady, black eyes, which rested on thick, droopy eyelids. A rather impressive silver-white beard, the proud culmination of a decade of careful grooming, just nearly reached his belly. His coat, old enough to be considered a proper antique, was in immaculate condition, except for a hole, likely from a stray bullet, in the collar. Hanging from his belt, a service revolver, perhaps the only one commissioned from the force, jostled. It commanded authority as he did. The only way death could take him was in his sleep.

Earlier that day, a rather anguished woman had darted by his carriage, shrieking about her dead husband–no, murdered husband. The Deputy, well on his way to arriving at Herbert's place, turned around to try and catch her, but she was lost to the night. Soon enough, he arrived at the scene. Murder, or really serious crime of any kind, was certainly a uncommonly gruesome occurrence in the town. Particularly troublesome, the donations to the force would surely dry up as quickly as the corpse before him, which could prove quite problematic.

"I came to check on him, and found his door wide open. Naturally, I went inside to investigate and found his body on the ground surrounded by his rings. His wife was nowhere to be seen. I looked closely over his body, and there were no signs of trauma. My best guess is that he died of old age; his wife couldn't cope and fled," carefully answered the Constable under oath, sweat dripping down his palms. He had not lied, of course, but he also had not given the complete truth–the part concerning the Professor's influence on the whole ordeal.

"So, allow me to clarify. You, and the man we hired, found him his book, meeting our agreement. Then, he died of a completely unrelated cause. Doesn't quite add up, huh?" asked the Deputy, looking at the absurdly large hands before him. Cut and bruised, such clumsy things were not built for thinking. He knew the formal paperwork for an incident like this one–even lousy Beckett could see to that. Most of the time, he was not terribly fond of protocol, but there was something resoundingly disingenuous about the Constable's answers.

"Yes, we were able to return the book before his untimely departure. The Professor is still in town although I am not sure why. I swear he's a nasty sort," said the Constable honestly, fearing that his own hide would be lashed if he caught wind of their activities. Licking his lips, the Deputy asked a simple question that he suspected would yield a complicated answer.

"Do you trust him?"

"What do you mean? You hired him?"

"You know *exactly* what I mean,"

"There is no chance he killed Dr. Herbert,"

"You didn't answer my question, darting around it. You're not being straight with me with your eye spinning about. If something's wrong, just tell me. Do you trust Mr. Carrion? Seeing as how his arrival seemingly brought Armageddon to *our* little town," said the Deputy forcibly, stressing each syllable. Their little game had gone on long enough. Sniffing out dishonesty was a chore for bloodhounds, or in a matter of speaking, his lackeys–if any of them grew a pair to leave their homes. It was just rain, no paltry god to bow down before. The Constable's island welled up as he struggled to keep it as straight as his answer, which teetered dangerously closer toward mistruth, despite his best efforts. The big man replied.

"No, that is why I have continued to follow him. He seems to have an unusual interest in our town. To put it plainly, he's here with ulterior motives... Whether they're good or bad for us, I'm not sure,"

"C'mon, was that so hard, Mr. Brauer? Good, yes... good. I agree that we need to keep a closer eye on him. It wasn't exactly within your purview to decide that was the best course of action, but seeing as how you already did it, consider this my official blessing, But, there's something you should know: something foul has come up near the Cistern..." murmured the Deputy as if speaking aloud would invite a ghostly apparition to join their conversation.

He supposed it was close enough anyways. Unfortunately, it would lend more credence to the fears of the superstitious folks holed up within their homes. The Constable slowly backed up, clutching his nightstick more tightly. His mother had always said that some things were better left unsaid. Swallowing, the Deputy continued speaking.

"With the absence of rain, we uncovered something near the shoreline. Without the rain, the Cistern spat it out, dryer than it's ever been,"

"What on earth was it?"

"A body, fresh, too. We cannot identify who it was. Hacked into pieces and then diced again for good measure. No one has even picked it up yet. We don't know what happened, but it's mighty strange that Dr. Herbert's demise was on the same night.

Two deaths in our little town, eh? No less, within the Professor's visit... Is that what I think I smell on your breath, Brauer?" asked the Deputy angrily, scrunching his nose at the oaf before him. His voice had grown dangerously high, smoke nearly pouring out from his ears. The Constable shuddered, snapping his mouth shut to no avail. It was too late: Reiner had caught the scent.

"I... Yes, sir, of course,"

"Again? This is the last time this stays between us, you hear? Next time I catch you like this... You know I could have you turned in?"

"Yes, sir,"

"Keep away from drinking, especially when you're on the job–your station deserves better. Don't make me take you away like some sick son of a bitch. You're not like the others here–keep it that way. They don't even deserve a uniform... Not that we have any to spare since the lords of town hall don't think we deserve a dime. You have been given more; act like it. I expect more from you,"

"It won't happen again, I swear," promised the Constable in an earnest manner. The oath was beginning to feel a bit too heavy on his shoulders. The force had grown rigid, inflexible, stale. The lack of a steady source of crime had reduced them to little more than secretaries. Papers had replaced criminals. He had not signed on for such duties all those years ago...

Relaxing slightly, the Deputy took one last look at the overgrown toddler before him. Scolding worked when he was a child, and little changed: old tools remained the best. Yet, it did not even reach his ears. The big man's mind floated past the empty words to a crumpled body in a wheelbarrow. *They*, whoever *they* might be, had to be responsible. As for that washed-up body... it could not be a coincidence. The Deputy, evidently satisfied with himself, continued.

"All right, well, the body was *all* apart. Kind of grisly for our town. It's been so long since anyone has been hurt, much less put to rest. I thought my time would be up before that ever happened again. So, just keep an eye on that Professor and report back to me if he does anything suspicious. You hear? Men like us always must resort to the scraps left by freaks like him, carrying around some fancy title to beat us over the head with. If I had known what he was like, he never would have set foot here, but Herbert demanded it. You know how outsiders are,"

"Yes, sir," sounded back the Constable, beginning to take a distinct liking to the skillful art of lying. The Deputy shook his hand as his men lifted Dr. Herbert into a wheelbarrow. They draped something vaguely purple over his head and carted him out the front door. Perhaps he would be buried with his father, reunited in whatever, if anything, came next.

With the tip of his hat, the Deputy walked out, leaving the big man to sink into the melancholy of the empty house. He took one last long look at the hourglass carved into the wall. As he stepped out, his foot slipped. He bent down, allowing his island to study the floor's viscous surface for meaning.

"The Professor will have to see this."

CHAPTER THIRTEEN: MR. CHEESE

"**Y**ou found a large stain just splattered near the body, untouched and unnoticed by the force's buffoons, including you? Color me surprised," prosed the Professor thoughtfully as he studied the marking on his hand. It was so much of a relief not to conceal it around him anymore. Under the dusty, dim light, the tattoo appeared even deeper within his skin–somehow darker than its surroundings.

They were now at his place, if it could even be called that. It was nothing more than mud-brown bricks crudely stacked upon one another, precariously challenging the laws of nature. The less-than-lovely little shack had one thing going for it: it had been abandoned a long time ago. When the Deputy had offered the big man a ride home, his eye lingered on the shoddy thing, which drew him closer. Swearing he could make it home from there, the big man stumbled into the strange little place and, surely enough, found Carrion. Winston was there, too, of course. It seemed those two were inseparable; he still had not the foggiest idea why. Wetting his lips carefully, the Constable began to retrieve something from his coat before speaking.

"Yes. What's more is that it looks like nothing I've

ever seen. It almost seems to glow," finished answering the Constable, studying a small swab he had taken of the substance. He had never expected to make use of them for anything beyond ear wax. Deeper in the same pocket rested a small tube containing a sample of what he expected was the very same stuff. The tube, liquid and glass alike, writhed and wiggled in his pocket, almost fighting to break free from its casing. Something that volatile could easily be flammable. For that reason alone, he was skeptical about handing it to a proven pyromaniac. Yet, his green eyes pierced through his pocket, forcing the Constable to bring it to the light. Even under the weak light, it glowed with defiance.

"That must have been how *they* killed him. It must be a poison of some sort–nasty stuff. We can certainly test that. One moment!" cheered the Professor as he scurried away to find an old friend. Winston reclined on the dirty sofa, just happy to have a place to sit for once. This comfort could only be transitory: Carrion's episodes were beginning to resurface, after all. When they did, he would be there for him in whatever capacity he allowed.

The Constable studied the messy floor, trying to picture where his carpet would have ended up. No doubt, in vermin–the whole place was infested. The Professor came back in, twiddling a rat in a circle by its tail. Although to the big man, the pair were barely distinguishable–particularly under such dingy lighting. Cocking his head, he decided to rock the boat with the rail-man.

"How long have you been holed up here for? Starting to feel like you've been here longer than I thought,"

"A few days. Your boss was 'kind' enough to throw in this shithole, too,"

"I see,"

"Sure… Well, gentlemen, back to the pressing matter at hand. We have a very fortunate test subject today: Mr. Cheese. I have affectionately dubbed him as such for his vicious raids on my pantry. I intend to repay him in full. I am a man of my word, of course,"

"That isn't very humane of you,"

"Oh. I am deeply sorry for offending your delicate sensibilities, Brauer. Here, let me drink this, and we'll see what color I will turn. In fact, since you are the righteous defender of this *vermin*, why will you not take the first swig of it? I am sure Mr. Cheese will be relieved as you and I are flopping on the ground like beached fish,"

"I catch your meaning; I'm not an idiot,"

"Sure, if saying that makes you feel any better. Give me the vial now. I am growing weary of asking nicely," demanded the Professor as he struggled to free the vial from the large man's iron grip. Mr. Cheese was moments away from having the vial's contents forced down his narrow throat. Winston, ever the peacemaker, spoke up.

"Mate, I don't think that should be necessary. Do you remember Karina?" said Winston weakly, staring into the horrified eyes of the defenseless thing before him. Quite frankly, the rat was as entitled to the house as they were–they were both squatters, after all. The Professor put the vial down, almost spilling it in the process. He pulled out a pocket watch with his spare hand, dangling it before putting it in the boy's lap. It started ticking ferociously, clanking in mechanical grunts.

"When that thing sounds, Mr. Cheese is getting his medicine. Give me one reason not to cure him of his gravest affliction: being alive,"

"Karina was our bartender last night. I don't know if you were paying attention or not, but she mentioned being a skilled chemist. That sample you've got there is far too good to waste on some... rat. There are many other ways you could dispose of it, *humanely*, I must stress, but we need that sample for testing," pleaded Winston before recoiling as the watch chimed suddenly. The Professor grimaced, delicately weighing the vial in his hand. The liquid sloshed from one side to another, demanding release. It would have to wait for just a while longer. Sighing, Carrion rolled his eyes dramatically before replying, begrudgingly.

"Okay, Karina would be an adequate choice. I suppose Mr.

Cheese deserves a yet more spectacular death," finished saying the Professor before flinging the rat into the garbage can as hard as his weak arm could. He blamed the sorry throw on his poorer hand, which was itching terribly today, developing a splotchy-red rash all over. That damn burning bush meant Herbert had the last laugh on him. Except, of course, in the sense he was still breathing, and the good doctor was not.

Wrapping several bandages did not make the itching any better; the scurrying rats beneath his skin kept clawing from the inside. However, something as trivial as pain would not keep him from what was his–only death held such power. He did not plan on giving in to it any time soon. Tucking the vial into his coat pocket, the Professor noticed the milky thing following it intently. His emeralds narrowed into the Constable's good eye until it relented, finding something more appropriate to gaze at longingly. Eventually, he sighed, deciding it was time for something a bit different–good, clean fun.

"Well, now that we have sorted out our little plan: would anyone care to fling some knives?" asked the Professor as he withdrew a set of knives from his coat. Each looked razor-sharp, appearing to have dried blood, among other things, coating them. The Constable looked down at his missing finger, shrugged, and walked over to the rail-man, taking the longest one from him. Winston, rather nervously, joined them. The Professor jeered.

"Oh, aren't you daring today? Come to win the favor of Ms. Loxley? Like a real man? She's hard to please–though I'm sure you've heard as much from her,"

"Enough talk. What are we aiming for?"

"Oh, come on. Let us make this fun. That vase, you see? The one on that shelf? Winston? Pick one before it slips from my fingers,"

"Professor, I don't think…"

"Nonsense, nonsense. Show us how this is done!"

"If you insist," replied Winston sheepishly, reluctantly wrestling a rather ordinary-looking knife from Carrion's enflamed hand. Raising it back gently, he threw it, watching it soar through the air like a drunken eagle, before, surely enough, missing the mark. The Professor cackled darkly, patting him on the back. The disorienting scream he had produced moments earlier had probably deterred the boy from doing any better. Life was never fair, and this game would be no different.

"Weakness, imagine that?" whispered the Professor into Winston's ear. Steeling himself, he took his marked hand, licked his index finger, and smeared the saliva on the face of the blade with a dramatic flourish. Readying the knife, he flung it about like he had Mr. Cheese. It flew, hungering to shatter the vase. However ravenous it was, however, it narrowly missed its target, rebounding to almost catch the Professor's foot, instead.

"Guess the Fates were not on my side this time," said the Professor slowly, grimacing darkly as Winston,who snickered. He plopped himself down on the sofa, pushing the boy to move over with little civility. The Constable straightened his back with a cacophony of pops, eventually reaching down to retrieve the now-dinged knife, setting aside the other one. He knew better than most that damaged things still had their uses.

"My turn,"

"Oh, those big hands are far too clumsy to throw that blade. Your vision is not exactly up to snuff, either, is it? You really are a freak of nature. Better hope fortune smiles upon you because nothing else will,"

"Coming from the twig-man who waxes poetic about bullets," sourly replied the Constable before delicately allowing the blade to float free from his hand and into the air. It spun in mid-air, starving, nearly famished, for the vase. He did it as if she was there. Surely enough, it found its mark, exploding into brilliantly dismal green shards. The Professor stared emptily as his jaw fell ajar, much to his own chagrin. He muttered.

"Guess those big hands are finally good for something,"

"Bravo! Bravo, you're a natural mate!" cheered Winston as his hands clapping furiously. Even though the Professor's hands found themselves colliding, each clap pained them immensely.

The big man felt his island bask in the glory, content to rest in slow waters; however, the rail-man had loftier challenges in mind. Patting the big man on the back, Carrion exclaimed.

"Yes, yes, bravo! You deserve a bonus round,"

"I'm listening," replied the Constable enthusiastically. Such a trivial victory was a victory, nonetheless. In some strange sense, it felt more real than his promotion, more tangible than some phantom title. Sometimes he forgot he had a name. "Constable" was merely a title, another word that failed to capture him. The Professor's hand rummaged in the can, pulling out the now notorious rat. Clenching it by the throat, he continued his show.

"We have a very special guest tonight. All the way from one pit, just to get sent to another. Please clap for... Mr. Cheese!" said the Professor, cheering as he spun it like a top. Winston slowly turned white, a shade away from that of those departing the mortal plane. Wrapping a small rope around its tiny waist, the pole-man tied the rat to a random pin in the wall, watching it squirm in vain with glee. Unease washed over the Constable as sweat climbed down his forearm to the hilt. Smirking, Carrion poked fun at him.

"Oh, too much of a conscience, eh? What can that little thing do to you? It deserves death. Scampering about without a care in the world. Throw the damn knife,"

"It's... a rat. Don't you think this is a tad excessive if you catch my meaning?"

"Did I stutter? Do you think we get to choose what happens to us? Of course not. Yet, here, we have the power to choose. We hold the gun, the bullets. It is subject to our wishes!"

"Enough!" declared Winston with a hint of anger bubbling beneath the surface of his glasses. Carrion had to be reined back in and restored to something better. This outburst was simply inexcusable. The case had been a promising effort to soothe something inside him that was still broken. Yet, it only seemed to make him slip deeper into... he knew not what–something like the fire that danced in his bloodshot eyes.

The Professor backed away slightly before roaring with laughter even more. If he were ever to reach his answers... he could not afford to cave in now. Without a healthy sense of fear, all his strength would so easily slip from his fingers. Winston's incessant nagging was becoming all too tiresome, yet it would be a bothersome waste of energy to humble him. Although he was not quite the workhorse the Constable was, the boy still had some good in him. Sighing, he relented, dropping the rat to run free to live the rest of its miserable life out.

"Since you are so taken with this rat-thing, I will spare it. I should never have named that blasted thing. Such a silly name convinced you it had value. Winston, find yourself some real friends, will you? One that cannot so easily be chopped up by a knife," said the Professor, snarling as he pocketed his knives with disappointment. The Constable sighed gently before his mind rumbled at the thought of another hacked-up thing. Sadly, it had not been spared like Mr. Cheese.

"Professor, I forgot to tell you about something else the Deputy mentioned. Some rather dismembered remains washed up near the Cistern. He said it was hacked to pieces," said the Constable emphatically, expecting full well that the pole-man was still far too concerned with a rat to hear him. However, it seemed that Carrion actually picked up on the seriousness of his tone.

"Interesting. Besides the fact they are both dead, Herbert may share more similarities with this body,"

"He said it was fresh. But clearly, we 'force buffoons' know nothing. Would you care to go see it? Perhaps you could identify it from its ear?"

"Shut it. Why would I not want to see a corpse? Winston, ready the carriage. We can fetch Karina later if we must," commanded Carrion as Winston grunted in reply. Wedging the door open, they stepped out. The clouds still hung heavily, crying no tears. Sitting in the back of the carriage, the Constable stared pensively at the shack. The poor thing was nearly abandoned, and yet, Carrion still called it home.

How would it feel to have such a place?

CHAPTER FOURTEEN: CRIMSON ROSES

T oday was a very special day. As Red forced herself out of bed, she felt something odd. It was stirring inside her, beyond reach and yet so intimately close. Perhaps it was just food poisoning or payback from her gut wrenched from a sleepless night of contemplation. No... It was a thing. Something that was causing an excess amount of cramping–almost reliably. Red stared in pure disbelief, reckoning with the truth that was so clearly before her. In her? Could that be a foot? A kick? It had to be.

She must have been pregnant.

Red had given up hope on conceiving long ago. Her husband, however, insisted that she still had it in her. Every time, he promised it would be the one, but slowly, his patience eroded away, and so too, their intimacy. Yet, at the end of their chain, the miracle finally arrived, one she enjoyed entirely alone within her home. The pitter-patter within her began to race in tandem with her heart, thumping together as one. If she could ever hold her husband close again, he would have felt it, too.

Dragging the sheets away, she found her way to the fraying sofa. Arching her back, she attempted to support her belly teeming with something new. Looking at that all-too-familiar armrest, she talked to it, herself, and him.

"Ah, Red. Where have you gotten yourself? All alone with a baby!" cried Red as the air sucked the words in, spitting them back at her. They condemned her. Cool tears sizzled down her steaming, flush face. They were different than the ones that leaked out when he left to drink. More painful than the streaking drops that urged him to come back to her. They kept pouring and pouring. The masked thing could have done something to them... In an instant, it all could have ended. Her miracle would have been lost–snuffed out far too early.

She could not put her faith in a stranger to take care of her own. As faithless as he was, her husband had once been family. He did not deserve to ever hear from her again, but this was far bigger than either of them now. So, she had to find him and tell him everything–even if it went against everything she wanted for herself. Perhaps, that was what being a mother felt like. Yet, that did not make it any easier. Doubling over, Red wailed.

"I hate how he is now! Everything became just another excuse to drink–a chance to be 'somebody.' When I first met him, he was just content with loving me; he truly cared for me. Then came that blasted promotion, giving him a fancy new title. I knew it wouldn't be enough for him. But at that moment, I was so proud of him. Everything was fine until his mother passed," finished saying Red, recoiling as dark realization slapped her across the face.

His eye, though always white, had lost more and more of what little color it had every day after she died. It grew paler, releasing so many tears that the blueness drained out with them. Until all that was left was a milky white. Yet, it somehow found a way to become emptier with her passing... Studying the tears climbing down her delicately thin fingers, she saw his face peering back, pleading with her to save him. She pointed accusingly at the armrest, defending herself.

"Just because you cared about her didn't give you an excuse to check out! I couldn't hope to fix you; you never wanted help. Staying mired in your grief was far too attractive. I tried so hard to pull you out of it! Pushed you to strive for a higher promotion to take you away from it all. Wasn't that enough to keep you busy? I tried to give you a baby–something to care about. I… failed," said Red before puttering out as she realized the armrest would not answer her. Shaking her head in disbelief, she looked into her wet hands again, this time, finding her own reflection.

"You, of all people, should know I tried–more than anyone else would've. When he started drinking every night, I tried to claw my way back into his heart. Even if he didn't give it to me, I would take it. But even picking at his inadequacies didn't cut it. He was still gone, sunken neck deep in pain. I hate him, but he has every right to hate me too!" cried Red, sobbing in torrents as her accusers remained solemnly silent. She had to be honest with herself. The truth had to find its way to the surface. Absolution was the first step to freedom.

"I *really* needed him to be someone different! It wasn't just for him. I was never *satisfied*, ever. Deep down, some part of me enjoyed letting him know just how unsatisfied I was. He needed someone strong, but I'm too weak–even now! Oh, this very night, *they* are after you! He's alone as I am!" screamed Red, stumbling downwards. She had to see him again. Lumbering over to the kitchen, she felt her bare feet grow cold from the floor tiles. The messy drawer always had something useful in it. Unfortunately, she would have to settle for something less than her husband–a map would have to do. Uncapping the pen, she began to furiously mark it up. Since the armrest had neglected her company, the man on the drained bottle would have to do.

"Surely, Carrion would not let the case die: he's here for a reason. By now, they must have visited that doctor again. They won't come back here, either. Perhaps… the station. They must have the Deputy on the case now. He must know where they've gone," whispered Red, dropping the pen to rattle against the table. There must have been some way she could make it there.

The pen rolled a tad further before falling off the table entirely. Her eyes followed it, catching on something: her drink from her meeting with the thing.

Something about it was not right–the taste had been off. The liquid writhed and squirmed as if it wanted to consume the world itself, claiming everything. It demanded acknowledgment. Reluctantly, after prying her nails under the cap to unseal it, she stuck her finger in the liquid. Instantly, her finger burned from the inside, out, causing her to frantically dash to the water jug from the plant. Fearing the worse, she grabbed a cleaver and was about to become a small bit more like her husband when the pain stopped suddenly. She stumbled back to her chair gasping, still grasping the cleaver tightly.

"I drank this! That must be the *only* reason I considered betraying him! Right? There must be something in this... That masked man must've snuck in and poisoned it. Surely if he could sneak into my attic, he could have done something fouler. What sort of thing could do that to someone?" questioned Red aloud, continuing to study the dancing liquid constrained to its glassy prison.

Her husband had to know about the masked man and this foul substance. If it made its way into the Strayer plant, it could be the end for all of them. With the drought, they were barely churning out enough clean water as it was. Price-gouging had already set in. Surely the man with the empty eyes would be aware of that fact, lying in wait to strike. Eventually, she caught her eyes once more lingering on the bottle-man.

"I care about you. I'm so sorry I hurt you. I couldn't patch that big heart of yours in time. You would never have started drinking if I looked past myself a..." she said before stopping herself; he had made those choices himself. They were a pair of forlorn sinners, but what was gone was done. All she could do now was fight for a present that seemed out of reach–that baby needed them both to care for it. Even picking up groceries had been harder... As grim as that was, it was reality.

Her child would not be born to an empty plate.

Readying her boots, she went back to the floorboard. The knife gleamed silver-orange back into her eyes. It found its way into her pocket, along with a dozen other useful things, including a compass, a dropper with a sample of the liquid, and a crumpled map. Digging through their mounds of dirty clothes, she grabbed the Constable's heavily tinted glasses. He had always worn them at important meetings with the force to hide the white thing away. Foxtrot nuzzled at her foot as she bent down to pet him. He had been saner of late but seemed to be losing energy at a concerning rate. Ironically, it missed a master that despised it.

"I am going to find him, I promise," declared Red as a reassurance to Foxtrot and herself, studying the empty room around her. She found some of her sewing cloth, tying it around her head to cover her hair. It finally had a use, after all. A few scarves found their way around her face. Finally, layering some of her husband's coats, she looked considerably bigger. Red hoped such an intimidating façade would get her far. Marching towards the door, the only object of any true color in the room caught her eye: a ruby-red rose. It was the last thing he had bought for her. Some part of her hoped that would change. Her fingers swept over the wilting petals, causing her to smile profusely.

"Just like that one from so long ago. Back when... we loved each other. He had so much heart and such big dreams to follow suit. What a gift he had for picking the reddest rose of them all. Always said my hair made it look pale in comparison... I was his crimson rose. Maybe I still am," said Red silently a she tucked the flower in her pocket, carefully closing it shut with a pat of her hand before making a declaration—one she was sure of.

"To every rose a thorn. I will never hurt him again."

CHAPTER FIFTEEN: SOME FISH AND A BODY

"**W**e're here! At the outskirts of the Cistern, just like you asked!" shouted Winston while preparing to open the cabin door for the Professor. If he could do nothing else for him at this point, kindness would have to suffice. As a reward for his good deed, the door slammed open, just nearly clipping him. The slippery sand below, however, brought the boy to his knees.

Emerging, the Professor stepped over him, scratching the growing, inflamed red-green rash on his left hand–so bothersome. The Constable followed, feeling his coat pocket to make sure his nightstick had not been nabbed again: it was still there. Winston scurried back up to his feet as Carrion commanded him.

"Winston. Stay with the carriage. We should be back soon enough. Keep vigilant watch over these vicious, alligator-infested waters..." finished saying the Professor dramatically, clearly enjoying the horrified, pale face before his. He could not imagine what the boy's face would contort into upon meeting a real alligator.

"Don't mind him. He's just messing with you," reassured the Constable to Winston before pretending to wrestle some phantom alligator. Shaking his head, the Professor grabbed the big man's hand, brandishing it like a war trophy.

"Yeah. Says the man who lost his finger to one of those blasted things. You're fortunate it never finished you off, one course at a time until there was nothing left but a carcass," said Carrion extra venomously, leaving Winston, skittish, inside the cabin. Snickering to himself, he remembered how fun it was to play along with the rail-man's antics sometimes.

Brushing the rail-man hand's off, the Constable began to make his way through the murky mud encroaching on the sands. Hearing the shrill cry of a gull, the Professor took a moment to stare into the drained depths of the Cistern before commenting on it.

"Shallow... This body, did they reclaim it yet?"

"No. The force isn't equipped to deal with things like this. We don't even have a proper morgue. The ground usually just swallows them up, and rain puts them to rest. Suppose that's one way of going back to dust,"

"What a lovely anecdote–your point?"

"Whatever's left will be here. I don't like how quiet everything is... Not that it's ever terribly loud. Everyone is going to stay holed up inside until the rain returns. Which, honestly, sets the perfect conditions for someone to come in and tamper with things. Is there any chance *they* could have known to strike now?" asked the Constable before yawning. Such things barely made their way from his brain to his mouth.

Sleep had been an elusive mistress, almost like her. Soon, he would be able to make the world right again. By then, the patter of drops would restore the natural order of things, easing his mind to rest–even if he had to rip them down from the sky himself. The Professor smirked, spotting something in the distance; he was almost to his great prize. He spoke, barely masking his excitement.

"Such superstition for such a big man! Maybe *their* shaman made enough sacrifices to send it away... Tell me now, though, what seems so terribly wrong with the world? Anything real bothering you–beyond hocus-pocus, nonsense?"

"All of it just seems wrong: the blank book, Herbert's untimely death. He knew me, I swear. Now, this Guess character is embroiled in this growing mess–throwing lies about without any care in the world. They must be related somehow... Is there any chance he helped to develop whatever was smeared on Herbert, an unwitting test subject? Surely, you catch my meaning?" asked the Constable, trying desperately to lose the chains of doubt that weighed heavy on his feet.

Carrion had to know more than what he told him–beyond his confession. How preposterous could his stories grow? It was simply baffling that he could not remember where his tattoo came from but cared enough about it to seek answers, just like how Herbert had been about the book. Was he the only one out of the loop?

The Professor itched his hand roughly against his coat, noting how puffy it was beginning to grow. Perhaps Herbert had the last laugh after all.

"If you keep throwing about such wild speculation, you might manage to hit something, after all. Guess is certainly worth investigating a bit more–his ties to *them*, at the very least, are evident. If it comes to it, you will gladly wring his neck for me, will you not? Our dearly departed friend showed us how effective that little tactic can be," replied the Professor sarcastically, running his hand along his throat; it felt like the old man's iron grip still held it for dear life. The smell of something awful, however, was far more potent than any mortal coil.

Strewn about haphazardly in red strands, butchered parts of a corpse littered the surface of the mud, lacking even a semblance of humanity. Stooping over for a closer look, Carrion pulled two long black gloves free from his coat pocket, stretching them tightly over each bony ridge with a shrill squeak. He picked at the pieces, searching for something of value in what seemed valueless. Wincing, he growled at the remains before him as the large man questioned him.

"What are you searching for?"

"Time to do your police work for you... If you must know, any form of identification. If removing a mere digit from a literal corpse is already too morally dubious for you, I am left to pick through this... mess. Whatever came upon him was clearly well-prepared, yet there appears to be no presence of everyone's favorite 'murder-liquid,' eh?" sneered the Professor, beaming proudly from his exceptionally clever naming. The Constable sighed, waiting for him to continue onwards, wholly oblivious to how pathetic his quip sounded. Snarling, he decided to offer another piece of sage wisdom.

"One day, precious Constable, we will end up like him. Whether it be as a whole in a nice tomb or a thousand pieces in an unmarked ditch, our fleeting spark will burn out all the same. Life is our struggle to keep that little thing going a little bit longer. Do not bother wasting your time worrying about whatever comes after. We cannot afford to leave something behind, wasting what little strength we have. Surely, you agree?"

"I do not," sternly disagreed the Constable, thoughts clearly drifting elsewhere. How could he come back? It was far too soon to try; she could never accept his apology–not after what he had done. The thread was stretched too thin to be reeled back in. One bad brush of a finger, and it would snap forever. Now that the case and her well-being were intertwined, things were even more complicated... He would find a way. The Professor caught a speckle of blue grow on the rim of his island, and that was far too good to leave unpicked at.

"It comes with age, I suppose. One day it will smack that head of yours hard enough for it to click. But, you are not even present right now, are you? Thinking about everyone's favorite wretch again, are we?" asked the Professor spitefully, rubbing the spittle on his glove. He was quite pleased with the perpetual state of limbo the Constable had placed himself in. Endless yearning could not be as destructive as having to face something broken every day. Although if his assumptions were correct, Red was likely long gone, perhaps sharing a tent with Herbert's last wife and a considerable population of rats. Surely, she was nested comfortably on whatever measly fortune they had!

Clenching his fists, the Constable briskly trotted to gaze into what little blue the Cistern offered his thirsty eyes. Tiny grey-black fish drunkenly swam about, nipping at each other's tails. Something was simply wrong with their movement–like invisible hooks pulled them to patterns. Sticking his hand into the murky water, he felt it immediately jerk backward, burning softly.

To confirm his suspicions, the big man pulled the vial free from his coat cautiously. Comparing it to the waters, surely enough, he found that they had the same underlying gleam. Collecting a sample with another vial, the large man almost felt like a proper officer before shouting with horror as further realization struck him.

"Professor!"

"One moment, can you not see I am busy picking at a corpse? Yes?"

"Obviously. Did you take a look at the fish?"

"Why yes, Constable. Making use of your trained eye from the force, no doubt. Look at them swim around. You ought to go make friends with them–whisper your sweet nothings. Might make for poor conversationalists..."

"Their motion in the water is all off if you catch my meaning. It looks too similar to the sample from Herbert to be a mere coincidence. What if Guess somehow contaminated this place? Causing these fish to swim around, burning them from the inside out. It's no wonder they are so... damaged. Perhaps Herbert..." said the Constable before being silenced by the wave of Carrion's glove, covered in drying red blood.

"Supposing you are right, which requires an immense suspension of reason, why are the fish still flopping with life?

That little dosage was enough to kill Herbert. Furthermore, why would he put it in the Cistern?"

"I don't know... Perhaps he wanted to see if it could be filtered through the Strayer or not. I think it's time to test it with her,"

"Being?"

"Ms. Flores, or Karina as she prefers to be called. She said that she was a chemist–something we are sorely lacking in this case. With some luck, she might be able to identify what's in these vials... She really seemed eager to help you, especially," said the Constable emphatically, appealing to the rail-man with what little energy he had left. Something clicked inside the Professor's head as a cool bead of sweat danced down his neck. For a moment, he thought he saw a ghost of the boy dancing in the glint of the vial. Regaining his composure, Carrion shook off the shivers before speaking.

"You said the town waits for it to be filtered by the Strayer? No one is drinking this?"

"No, not as it is. Between the shallowness and poor quality, it's simply unfit to drink. The Strayer plant typically processes it for treatment and distribution, the closest thing to a monopoly here. With the rain gone, our 'relatives' around our borders have raised their prices. Without that plant and its reserves, we would be done for..."

"Best to keep it operational then, eh? We might consider telling your boss to put some of your fellow goons around it,"

"We need more evidence first. He is a rather hard man to convince of anything, and my recent behavior may have... not helped any. If we can identify it, maybe he will listen. Would you like to see Karina?" asked the Constable, catching a small pink blush poke through the Professor's skin. He was beginning to suspect that he had a heart, after all. Furiously indignant, Carrion pointed accusingly at him before replying.

"Of course not! She has her uses, though. I would, however, like to make use of her expertise. Besides, my kidneys are far too comfortable right now. Yes, yes. We can bring her those samples, and she can cast her enchantments to divine an answer,"

"Ah, so it's magic because you're poor at it? Kind old nuns must be sorcerers to you. The orphans must be their familiars,"

"Silence. Shall we see if Winston has successfully guarded off the carriage from those monstrous alligators, or whatever the hell I made up this time?" asked the Professor, sneering, as he threw his bloodied gloves into the ocean. It was already contaminated, anyways. Stepping over the remains, the rail-man cocked his head–something struck him as odd. Like the vial, there seemed to be an ethereal quality to it all although he could not place the feeling. He spoke up again, willing to risk sounding like a fool for once.

"These remains are familiar,"

"What makes you say that? It is far too grisly for me to make anything of it. I can't even stomach looking at it anymore,"

"For once, dear Constable, I am unsure. I just have some... intuition,"

"We'll see, but probably not. I pray that we reach the source of this mess soon," declared the Constable. His island rejected the red sunlight that threatened to devour it. With a solemn nod, the pair made their way back to the carriage, feet pattering through the mush. Winston had taken up a piece of driftwood, threateningly waving it about to ward off anything hungrier than himself–quite an impossible feat by this point. Smiling weakly, he almost gagged, catching a glance of the small red droplets that clutched to the Professor's soles for dear life.

"You have returned! Were you able to find out anything from the body?" curiously asked Winston, nearly impatiently. The sooner this affair ended, the better. Keeping the pair from doing anything foolish was far more difficult than leading Honeysuckle.

"A few things. Not the least of which, our dear Constable sees things in the water–perhaps a wiggling, bodacious mermaid, waiting for an *excellent meal*!" shouted the Professor, roaring with laughter at his overwhelming wit and intelligence. His companions were less impressed.

For once, Carrion was right: they had seen the body before.

CHAPTER SIXTEEN: ELEMENTARY

P acing frantically, Karina bit her lip in anticipation of the knock that would echo through the heavy wooden door any moment. Earlier, a man from the plant, swishing documents around with ease, had promised her that shipments would not be delayed again. It had been a day since he had been by, and her less-than-loyal patrons continued to seek drinks elsewhere. She was beginning not to blame them.

Stanton's was on the decline. Its customers had dried up with the rain, perhaps hidden away in the same secret place. No angry-red papers had arrived, but she knew they would eventually. Some of her equipment could fetch a pretty penny, but... such decisions were too dreadful to linger on. For the time being, she was not `in danger of being foreclosed upon. One good visit from the Constable and the others would help her more than they could know. Yet, the idea of giving that man more to drink made her skin crawl; it could only do worse things to him. Papers could not actually be angry anyways, right? Even if they were, they could not yell, after all.

She had to speak with them all again, even if it meant staying up to an absurdly late hour. They all had a charm to them, and more than anything, they actually talked with her. Some patrons mumbled to her, but such things were rather one-sided. The one, fiery green eyes and all, seemed to be hurting, scarred somewhere deep. Beneath all those rancorous layers and jagged spikes had to be a good heart. If he would just tell her about it, she could help him to mend it. Ultimately, he would have to want help on his own accord–prying never worked with his sort. The best she could do is knock at the door.

On cue, the actual, literal door creaked open, causing Karina to jump from a mixture of excitement and fear. Her bun threatened to leave the top of her head as her glasses clung to the notch in her nose. Marching in, the Professor led the trailing Constable and Winston inside with a particularly dramatic flourish. Masking her excitement behind an awkward half-grin, she motioned them closer.

"Mr. Constable! Professor! And Winston, of course. So glad to see you all again! How may I be of service at this fine hour?" asked Karina, bowing playfully.

"Ms. Flores, I recall that you mentioned having adequate to exemplary skills in chemistry. What made you say that?" replied the Professor, blunt as a hammer.

"Right to the chase, aren't we? While I wouldn't say exemplary, I certainly wouldn't say 'adequate' either. It's been a passion of mine for some time now, growing check to check. I had gone to school for a while, but this place can't just be abandoned. Although, I am beginning to suspect it will leave me... In any case, while the door's still open, the laboratory I cobbled together is yours to use–with my help, of course. With what little free time I have, I tend to work in there," declared Karina flatly, clearly offended by the Professor's poor choice of words. Straightening her glasses, she scowled, scrunching her nose in such a way as to keep them from shattering against the ground. Winston, leaning against the newspaper-littered wall, spoke up.

"Mate! Of course... or, would prefer madam? Anyhow, you have a lab? Is it a proper one with all the gizmos and such?

I've always wanted to see one of those!" said Winston with childlike glee, imagining glowing glass vials connected by tubes, surrounded by ice and flame alike. Amelia had been quite taken with a simple color-changing ring, hopping from one shade to the next with ease. Science could certainly construct bridges and medicines, but it could also make people smile.

"Winston, Karina is just fine. Yes! It has all the 'gizmos' you would expect. I have a feeling it might even have more!" she replied, grimace melting into a warm grin. Despite everything that happened to him, Winston continued to shine brightly against the surrounding darkness. Yet, small wrinkles crept onto his face, betraying his storied past. While it seemed strange that he would associate with someone like Carrion, she suspected he saw something more in him too. He had to.

"Although, I would be remiss not to ask: where did this sudden interest in my laboratory come from? Does it have something to do with Mr. Guess?" asked Karina forcefully yet gently. Sighing, the Professor replied curtly.

"You see, we *need* your lab. There is not any time to debate the finer..."

"Professor!" scolded Winston loudly.

"What? I am merely stating the obvious. Time is of the essence; remember the investigation? Of course not: you were too busy looking for phantom crocodiles. Perhaps a brief review is in order? We need the lab to test poison vials to expose Mr. Guess, destroy his livelihood, and most importantly, find the truth of where this accursed mark came from!"

"Goodness, I don't think my lab could be used for that..."

"Karina, please disregard him for a moment. Allow me to explain everything with a tad less vitriol and spite, so you can have a sense of what we're talking about, if you catch my meaning," calmly stated the Constable, using his hand to brace a rather indignant Professor. He proceeded to explain every point of their case, from the missing book to the untimely death of the Doctor, only leaving out any details he deemed too personal or embarrassing–anything about Red.

As he carried on, Carrion slowly retreated to the corner of the bar, sulking like a disappointed child. Every person that became entwined in his Fate only made things more complicated. Winston sat, listening intently to the Constable as if he had not lived out the events himself. Karina, unusually rattled yet fully engrossed, expressed rather colorful emotions–facially. Patrons were usually far less interesting, failing to send her hands rattling dangerously around glassware. Taking a swig of a drink she never planned to make, her thoughts spun widely as he finished speaking. She stammered before finding her words.

"Oh dear... wow. I expected all of *this* might surface with the investigation, but how did you get caught up in all of this, Constable? I thought the force was only really equipped to deal with burglaries and petty theft. If this vial is what you think it is... poor Dr. Herbert! If he's as poor as we think–how could he have known your name, Constable? And Guess! A simple brick-layer or a servant of some sinister organization? Lying about plotting bricks to me? I have so many questions. They will have to wait, though, as I suspect the Professor is growing rather impatient with me," finished saying Karina loudly, hoping her words would reach the deepest crevice in the room. Hopping off the bar stool, she strode over to Carrion, who jumped when she tapped him on the shoulder. Red-faced, he replied weakly.

"Impatient? Perhaps. Yet, I think I have the answers you are grasping for," said the Professor indignantly, standing up as he brushed off his shoulder. He continued his monologue perfectly, reciting the script perfectly he had so perfectly constructed in his head while waiting. Their yammering needed to come to an end.

"You see, I merely need to confirm the suspicions I have had from the..." said the Professor before puttering out as the Constable shouted angrily at him.

"Professor–get real! You and I have been *guessing* and *formulating* all this from the start! In fact, sometimes it feels like you're a good deal more lost than I am. So, sit tight, and we'll test this vial. Then, we'll know what's been going on 'from the beginning,'" mimicked the Constable in a shrill voice. The Professor stood up and walked directly to, or more accurately, into the chest of the big man. A hearty laugh emanated deep within him, leading the tinier man to sigh as he sat back down, utterly defeated.

"You two done yet?" asked Karina, clearly amused. The Constable shrugged and reached into his pockets, retrieving the two vials. Her eyes lit up, coloring her thick lenses, the moment they found the glow of the vials. They were remarkably unstable and volatile, screaming to be set free from their glassy confines. Taking them into her hands, she suspected it would react to nearly anything.

"You'll have to excuse my language, but what the hell is this? It seems hungry," observed the bun-headed-woman as she led them to a door located behind the bar. After unlocking a hefty steel lock, she motioned them to follow her inside, assuring them it could open again. Huge hanging wooden tables and suspended equipment were scattered throughout the room, all under a strange iridescent green light that seemed to penetrate everything. In the center of the chaotic arrangement, a prominent table featured dozens of pages strewn about it, covered in painstaking notes and sketches of yet unnamed things.

The Professor was in the process of pulling a vial loose from a rack labeled "Potassium Cyanide–X" when Karina swiftly doubled around to glare at him. He slowly put the vial back on the shelf, causing her to shake her head slowly before carrying on. Bumbling forwards, the rail-man smirked at the eclectic equipment around him. Clearly, every piece of equipment was so horribly mismatched and jerry-rigged haphazardly. Yet, he could appreciate how much ambition it took to throw it all together. Despite this, however, he was beginning to lose his patience.

"Ms. Flores, how long do you suspect this will take? I am sure the Constable's poor little ankles are beginning to give way under all that weight," said the Professor jokingly, clearly not as intrigued by endless flasks and droppers as Winston. Muttering a prayer under her breath, Karina frankly replied with a huff.

"As a man of science, you, of all people, should know that this sort of thing can't be rushed. If this stuff has any of the properties you suspect, possibly killing a man, we must take the utmost precaution when handling it. You all should make use of those goggles from that hanger," she said while pointing to a well-polished hanger containing a full set of goggles labeled as sterile. The Constable took a glance at the glasses before chuckling under his breath. There were no such things as half-goggles, after all.

"Karina, is this stuff really new to you? Never seen anything like it? If so, this matter is far more concerning, if you catch my meaning," said the Constable as his island chased all the green-lime lights in the room that seemed to blend. Her place was truly special, in no small part to its deviance from the usual greys and blues that dominated every other surface in town.

Nodding her head in response, Karina carefully poured both vials into separate beakers. Holding the pen in her mouth, she stuck labels on each vial, "One–X" and "Two–X?" respectively. Pulling a small dusty lamp from the ceiling, she was disappointed that its light failed to overpower the glow within the glasses. It even reflected off her glasses, which frustrated her all the more. Mind racing, she began to ask herself, as well as her company, questions.

"Do you all see how the sample from the Cistern seems to be less pure than that one? Clearly, this chemical can be diluted… Which means that it must have some sort of interaction disrupted by the addition of water. In all honesty, if someone had drunk this already instead of waiting for the Strayer plant to process it, we would likely have heard of several deaths by now. Since the Strayer is running late on shipments, people could already be turning to this stuff. Constable, when you stuck your hand in the waters, how unpleasant was it?" asked Karina slowly, poring over her chemical racks.

It seemed resoundingly acidic–perhaps it would react strongly with tissue? One section label particularly caught her eye: neurotoxins. There were so many candidates to consider, ranging from lead to glutamate. Of course, there could be another drug component... psychoactive ones like ethanol, scopolamine, and a good number of other things. This would lead to several tests and, more importantly, a much-needed distraction from the empty bar. She had hoped that particular shelf would remain empty. Scratching his finger, the big man replied after a pained sigh.

"Burned like hell. Took a few moments to feel any relief whatsoever," recounted the Constable, leading Karina to mutter all the more. She strode, nearly floating, back to the second vial, to cross off the "X." There was nothing better than a field test. So, spinning around briskly, she grabbed a shovel and marched out the back door without a word.

Winston stared at the Professor, who stared at the Constable, who stared at the door, which was left gaping open with mystery. Thumps of dirt, followed by a squeal of excitement, only fanned the flames of their growing intrigue. Returning to the doorframe, Karina held a bloodied brain high toward the sky like a war trophy. They all gasped, even Carrion. She sighed humorously.

"It's a pig brain! That was the only proper way to store it, cold storage and all. And yes, I didn't kill the pig for it! I had the butcher do that for me. He said it wouldn't be proper for me to have done it although I don't think he had the faintest idea of what I would do with it. Remember how we're trying to find how *they* poisoned him and what they did it with?" said Karina, grinning ear-to-ear with glee. Everyone in the room, including her, breathed a shared sigh of relief until she withdrew a rather wicked serrated blade.

"If you are squeamish, I would look away now," added Karina, dissecting a large part of the frontal lobe from the brain, gently moving it to a plate. Picking up a pipette, she dipped it gently in the first vial before holding it above the lobe in sheer anticipation. Everyone watched intently, all for different reasons.

"At last... my moment of clarity! You must love a good show," said Carrion anxiously while picking at the charred remains of his hand. The glove had somehow irritated it worse, helping it to turn a bit bluer. Of course, that would not matter soon enough. A hand was a small sacrifice for answers. Breathing in, Karina squeezed the pipette. A tiny drop fell on the lobe. Nothing came of it.

A second drop. Still nothing.

The third drop resulted in a similar fashion.

In focused increments, Karina dropped the remaining solution on the lobe until it began to sizzle. Collapsing on itself violently, the surface molted upon itself, decaying as large bubbles burst on the brain. Soon enough, there were gaping holes in the surface, seared around the edges, leaving strings of flesh.

"Oh, dear. That's... that's... We must stop this, and whoever is behind this," murmured Winston anxiously, as his hands clenched the cool pendant he had grown increasingly fond of as of late. Somewhat dumbstruck, the Professor gawked at his shaking frame. Rarely did he express himself in such a way of weakness. Yet, the underlying graveness frightened him... It did not suit the boy.

Chucking the pipette in the garbage, Karina swore that, at the soonest convenience, the rest of the vile liquid would join it. Clenching his fists into formidable boulders, the Constable thought of a grey-white body in a wheelbarrow, carted away to be dumped into dirt and filth. They could not let that happen again. Carrion glanced at the hateful marking on his hand, hovering the burned one underneath it before speaking up. For once, though, their interests aligned.

"Winston, I must agree. Every path we have charted has led me here to this place. I am so very close... so very close now. Soon, I'll have my truth, even if it kills me," declared the Professor, choking on the words as they left his mouth. A bit peaked, Karina interrupted his ultimatum as fast as possible to clear the curses from the air. Such hateful things did not deserve a home.

"I... We would be remiss not to try the weaker solution on the other lobe," suggested Karina quickly, emptying the pipette on what remained of the lobe. Breaking out in small spasms, the meat pulsed in parts. Yet, none of the tissue decayed, leaving her with an answer.

"It seems my assumption was correct: this version is far from lethal. It must impair brain signaling somehow, possibly contaminating it with lead. Dear goodness! It's so acidic!" exclaimed Karina sorrowfully as she dumped the remaining pig gore into the trash. Seizing his chance to speak, the Professor made his grand proposition.

"It must be Dr. Guess that made it. When I spoke to him, he claimed to be a neurologist, someone with the expertise to help create this. Perhaps *they* contracted him to help produce it. Herbert was just an unwitting test subject, and naturally, another loose end to be cut off. However, it does not quite explain why Herbert knew you... Well, it doesn't matter. Guess is still breathing for the time being, and we have plenty to take him down,"

"We should report him to the force immediately," declared the Constable with extra vigor, sensing his chance to have his heroic moment realized. Red, and everyone else for that matter, would be safe from whatever threat Guess had cooked up, and the Professor would discover his so-called truth. Everything would be better. Cocking his head, Carrion smirked with indignation.

"Those bumbling idiots? I think not. No one can stop me from reaching my truth, save the Fates. I've got the strength to keep them back, too. The force would never believe a lackey like you anyways. Mystery liquid that burns bloody brain tissue? How farfetched is that?" asked the Professor rhetorically, glowing against the Constable's reddening face. Hoarse, he spoke.

"Carrion…"

"Please… call me 'professor.' Then, we will talk,"

"Professor, we need a warrant to arrest him–not the simple whims of a pack of vigilantes! That is the only way he can find real justice for his crimes. With him in chains, we can get him to tell you everything you've ever needed to know. We can't let Guess produce any more of this stuff; it'll contaminate what little water we have left. Do things right, just this one time," pleaded the Constable as his island bore straight into the Professor's soul, without fear of sinking in its murky depths. Bending to Carrion's side, he cupped his hands around his ear.

"I can't afford to lose her too," slowly mumbled the Constable in pure anguish, lips trembling as the words bounced in-kind. Fingers twitching, the Professor backed away hastily, nearly tripping. He whipped around, let out a muffled curse into his coat, and then went back to face them. The rash on his hand had metamorphosed into something new altogether: a hungry green blob that wanted to devour any fleshy bits that remained. He bit his tongue, spitting the words out to ease the pain.

"With accordance to your primitive principles, I will indulge the stupidity of reporting this to the force alongside you. Make it quick. I personally want to oversee whatever lovely fire that consumes his property in its entirety, burning his empty dreams to the ground. Who is it that I have the pleasure of speaking to for us?" asked the Professor sarcastically, pleased to have forgotten the searing pain for a moment. Something was stirring, though, deeper within that could not so easily be scratched.

"My boss, Deputy Reiner. I don't think he's taken a good liking to you, in all honesty. He's a traditional sort and very stuck in his ways at that: it will take concrete evidence to make him believe any of this," explained the Constable dourly. Their last meeting had certainly not been ideal, but the Deputy was a reasonable man. With enough evidence, he would have to believe them. Besides, he was like a son to him…

"Old fuddy-duddy, then? Can't wait to meet him. His head

is going to spin when he finds out all of this has happened right under his nose–how very oblivious," said the Professor sourly, already considering the numerous ways he could persuade the obstinate old mule to move, prodding and all. Preparing a vial with the deadly solution, Karina offered it to the Constable.

"Show this to them. If they need a live demonstration, bring them here. That vial *cannot* be opened under any circumstances. Don't shake it, and don't even dream of putting it next to an open flame," said Karina before slowly pausing, catching a glance of the Professor's mutating hand. Brushing aside the big man gently, she took his bloated hand and held it against the light. He tried to shake it away, but her steely grip was not going to budge.

"That's gnarly, Professor. I need to treat this with something,"

"No. That will not be necessary. I have seen..." said the Professor before being cut off by a less-than-subtle push by Karina into a nearby chair, causing his eyes to widen in sheer horror. Winston chuckled, playfully patting the Professor's shoulder, causing him to hiss violently.

"Constable, would you make sure that the Professor doesn't worm around too much, so we can try to salvage what's left of his hand?" asked Karina, trotting out of the door to the outside. He would not allow her to see it, but Carrion smiled somewhat genuinely–something quite foreign for him. The Constable clamped his hands over the Professor's shoulders with a gleeful smile of his own. Naturally, the rail-man's scowl returned when she walked back with a bowl brimming with ice.

Laying the bowl down on the armrest, she placed his talons deep into it, causing him to sigh in relief. The coolness flooded him, climbing from his fingertips to his wrist. Perhaps this little exercise was worth it after all. Watching the color slowly drain, Karina drenched a towel in stored rainwater she had left from the plant before wrapping his hand in it tightly. He tried to dash away, and this time, his jailor merely pointed back at the chair, causing him to sit down with another sigh, far less motivated by relief.

"You know, this lab is sort of a marvel in a place like this," sheepishly offered the Professor, struggling to articulate thanks. Karina knew it was sort of a backhanded compliment, but any attempt at decency from him would not be treated with too much contempt.

"Thank you! That's thoughtful of you to say although I don't know how much longer all of this is going to go on. Competition has been bleeding this bar dry; I'm beginning to suspect that may be the least of my problems soon. They'll have to kill me before they take this lab, though," declared Karina with a hint of humor. Taking the damp cloth off his hand, she returned with a bandage, stealthily wrapping it to keep his eyes away from it.

"Business will likely improve–once the rain is back again, of course. Don't waste your time worrying about things like that. Everyone here is so fixated on the weather! Though, I must ask: where do you get all of this? You have quite the haul... is it stolen?" asked the Professor in a particularly serious tone. It was a sad attempt at humor, but Karina giggled a little bit as her eyes narrowed dramatically.

"Wouldn't be any other reason to keep all this stuff bolted down, now would there be?" asked Karina, faint dimples almost visible. The last of the bandages covered his hand. More importantly, the swelling had improved vastly. The Constable heaved the rail-man to his feet as his hands flailed wildly to stop him. Once the Professor was up, he dusted off his coat in protest and offered proper thanks.

"As a gentleman, I feel as though I should repay you,"

"No! Putting aside a bit of your stubbornness, even owing to a considerable nudge from the Constable, is enough for me. Take care of yourself, Professor. Don't do anything *too* daring. If you need a live demonstration for the force, you know where to come. Constable, good luck with the force and their antics. Lastly, Winston, always a pleasure seeing you!" cheered Karina as she led them back to the bar. Double-checking they had cleared the door, she shut it firmly. Such precautions were fully warranted. She had nearly lost a finger to that vile thing once.

The Constable's eyes, murky and not, drifted to a rack of bottles along the wall. He was parched beyond all measure. Yet, he knew it would just burn away at his insides, stealing the color from his world sip by sip. It had already grown so pale; it had no more colors to spare. No matter how awful things there were to see, bloody red patches of a corpse and all, he wanted to see things for what they were. So, he turned away. Karina's brow furrowed in disbelief: he had seemingly changed more in a day or two than he had a whole decade... She could now do her part in ensuring that his choice would stick for good–she owed him that much, certainly.

A customer sitting at the bar shook his head in disbelief– not at their emergence or eccentricities, but shock at the prospect of finally getting his favorite drink. Karina could not afford to lose any more customers, so she shouted out a few more words of encouragement as they fumbled out.

"Constable, I have to say... Even though it is bad for my business, I applaud your strides in sobering up a tad. I'm here for you... whether you have a drink in your hand or not. My door's always open... Keep coming back, all of you! Things get lonely sometimes," shouted Karina, unsure how her time with them had already ended. They would have to be back. This patron, though, in the meantime, would have to do. In the process of shuffling out, they all said their goodbyes in their own unique ways.

"Thanks for the hospitality, Ms. Flores. I mean, Karina!"

"Karina, you're a lifesaver in more ways than one. We have a fighting chance to stop *them* now. I'll be sure to come back for a drink or two, don't you worry!"

"Farewell, Karina. Thank you for saving a few of my digits," said the Professor flatly yet with an underlying sense of sincerity. Opening the cabin door for the pair, Winston situated himself on the box, suffering the discontented neighs once again. It was certainly better than what was to come.

The Constable was puzzled: Carrion was peering out in the dark, solemn and silent, save for his bandaged hand, which twitched violently. Surely the water did not do that to him–was he feeling something beyond pain or annoyance? A feeling that might outlast stepping on a tack or pulling a muscle?

It was not his place to decide, but if he had to wager on it, he would have supposed so. Finding himself sinking into the backrest, he figured that question could wait until another day. Yet, a small glint of gold grabbed his eye. It was still there. He could not bring himself to put it on, but it could not be left to rust away in such a lowly place.

He pocketed it.

CHAPTER SEVENTEEN: FLUX

The Professor knew what would follow: another memory, this time, sparked by mere children. How they danced around like lunatics, playing as if the rain still splatted against their coats. Yet, they were so much more than that–pale echoes from far-flung faces that remained out of reach. The phantoms would hold court soon, and the little brat with braids, such a hateful little judge, just missing a gavel, would arrive. Feeling his brain twist in on itself, Carrion slumped forwards, fearing he had somehow managed to ingest something in the laboratory. If he had, the pain would have been so much more tolerable and merciful than what he felt.

"Not much farther, Thad! Come save me from the monster!" screamed a voice, so close and yet so far away. It was drowned out quickly, though, by one that sounded remarkably like his own, asking the only question that seemed to matter anymore.

Who had he become?

It sharpened itself on his insides, goring him to the core. Naturally, the stabbing pain came too–they were not lovers to be separated. He felt the brushes batter against his bare feet. That damned coin still weighed down his steps although he swore it had been flung out of a window–it remained an anchor, still.

Soon enough, the light began to fade. The sky looked down in dark disappointment as the sun retreated to the horizon in defeat and expectation alike. Mother and Father would expect them back soon. Thad panted heavily as the Professor clutched his stomach tightly, leaving a five-pronged pit.

His legs sunk deeper into the carriage as mud caked the boy's legs. Letting go was no longer an option. Arms were of no use–not anymore. He continued past withered trees and thickets. Cuts soon joined the mud in tandem, but they made for little opposition against his will. Soon a voice rang out in the encroaching darkness. Here came the freefall.
Sinking...

    Sinking...

        Sinking...

            Sinking...

"I'm right here! Can't you find me, little Thad? Always the dumb one. Well, how long will you take?" cried a voice in the trees. The Professor was there now. He had failed at stopping himself from slipping; the only option was to finish the memory or be consumed by it. The pain had to stop, somehow.

"Get down here right now! I'm gonna tell Mother and Father about this!" shouted the boy, accompanied by more cries from the trees.

His gut ached as the Professor felt himself climbing up the branches of a colossal oak tree. Thad's anxiety died somewhere during his ascent. The girl chucked things at his head as if to knock him off–unusually weighty apples, primed for punishment. What a foolish girl... Apples could seldom compare to the warping of the mind. At the summit, Thad saw his sister's emerald green eyes, nearly identical to his own.

It was about to happen. Or, more precisely, it already had.

"Don't do that again. I wouldn't have anyone to pick on without you," said Thad flatly while pouting profusely. His arms crossed over one another, and her tiny mouth managed to make a remarkably deep scowl.

"Just shut up. See the moon? Isn't it beautiful?" asked the star-eyed girl as she pointed to a place beyond. Carrion screamed until his voice gave out, but it was cut off as the shards of thought-glass, wrapped around his throat, tightened. She could not hear his cries, only Thad's useless yelps.

The Professor wanted to tell her everything about what would happen in a few moments, but he could not. Struggling only caused more pain... All was set. In vain, he clung to a false hope that, since premonitions were not subject to laws or reason, his screams might reach her. Suddenly, something pulled Carrion back by the neck. The other stayed, naturally, bound by unshakeable chains.

Hurtling back...
Hurtling back...
Hurtling back...

Hurtling back...

The Professor was back in the carriage again. Empty, but in one piece next to a sleeping Constable, with a ring wedged halfway up his finger. Oh, how easily he had fallen! Even now, control seemed to slip from his fingers like coins.

He feverishly muttered to himself about strength, about fear. It was always hard to remember what he was really fighting for; reminders were certainly in order. All he had to do was vomit a few more lies, and then the daggers would leave his stomach. A little more bravado, dashed with a genuine sense of bravery, would be enough to find his most wonderful, golden truth, that would send the ghastly apparitions away forever.

He had to be enough for all of them–it was the only way. Nothing smiled upon the weak, save for the weak. The old vows said themselves before he passed out.

For the Constable. For Winston. For Thad.

Thud!

CHAPTER EIGHTEEN: THE LONG TALK

"It happened again, didn't it? Don't know what brought it on this time," said Winston gravely after he had wedged the carriage door open with great effort. Honeysuckle neighed its tremendous disapproval, but the poor thing could wait a while longer. The Professor was slumped rather unresponsively on the seat with his hands clenched tightly around his stomach. Putting his hand on his forehead, Winston was met with the familiar sensation of burning-wet flesh. Amelia had endured that pain for too long, and yet, some part of him selfishly longed for her to last longer, no matter her condition.

Carrion's episodes were beginning to emerge again... The "case" had taken its toll on him. At least the Constable maintained some semblance of peaceful sleep, however long it would last. Straining his arms, Winston managed to lift the Professor out of the carriage that he had crudely parked on the edge of a ditch, laying him on the dry earth.

Bending down next to him, he studied the sky. It used to amaze him: the splendor, the grandiosity of creation. Only one thing mattered now. As the starlight danced across his eyes, he thought he heard her cool voice from someplace distant yet nearing–she had always loved the night, darkness and all, for giving little lights a place to rest. Gasping for breath, the Professor forced his body upwards, straining his eyes to adjust to his rather unexpected surroundings before Winston spoke.

"You were... out again. I had to stop the carriage because I heard you hit something in the cabin. Is your head quite all right? The memories are coming back again, aren't they, mate?" asked Winston carefully as Carrion just continued to stare into the deep blackness of an empty sky. He saw the emeralds flick around the little lights that threatened to color them. Eventually, his lips pursed as he found his words.

"Yes. I suppose I should thank you for carrying me. Guess you are proud of yourself for finding me in this state again?"

"I'm a good deal more observant than you might think, mate. I've just been thinking of a way I could really help. There's never really a wrong time to have this conversation. Do you reckon we can sort through all of this now?"

"Since you insist, I will indulge your curiosity but do not burden me with your concern. This time... the memory was familiar yet unfamiliar. The boy was back, running about a forest to find some wayward girl, presumably his sister. I do not know what to make of these visions... I have no power over him. Then, the pain came along, and that miserable little bastard took me again! Maybe I cried out from the sheer sight of the runt," sourly spat the Professor, swatting at the growing number of mosquitos buzzing about his bandaged hand. They were thirsty for blood.

Winston sighed again, trying to pick locks that threatened to keep Carrion in chains forever. She would have had the right words to console him–like a proper locksmith. His fingers tightened around the pendant, allowing its coolness to enter his weary body. Lips poised to speak, he was interrupted by the Professor speaking.

"This cannot keep happening... Not now–I am so close to

the end. Winston, I will finally know what I am, who I am. Everything is falling into place except for me. If only, no… Damn it! I must be more. Think of it! I will never have to wonder again, toiling away at drawing breath. It is so *very* close now; I can almost strain my arm to reach it. Ah, what am I doing? Relishing in my own weakness? None of this should bother you, anyways. It's not your business and nothing for you to fix," declared the Professor weakly. Beads of sweat trickled down his neck, moistening the grass below, drip by drip–if only they could carry pain like tears did…

"Stop! Listen to what you're saying! So rarely do I speak my mind to you, but I have let this fester for far too long. I worried I would hurt you more than I could help, but I was wrong– we should have had this conversation ages ago. I should have intervened sooner. Carrion… I know who you are. You're a good man!"

"Now, Winston, this is hardly a time for empty humor,"

"I have never been more serious in my life since… Ah, my words fail me. If you cannot believe me, believe in yourself. Believe that whatever comes of this mark, or anything else for that matter, there's a good heart in ya…" said Winston earnestly before being cut off by the Professor, who swung his hands frantically, as if to bring the sky down to the earth. Veins bulged on his forehead like little blue worms, threatening to poke through his skin. Winston's weak smile slowly melted away altogether as Carrion cried out in sheer disbelief.

"After all these years, you still do not know me at all! I'm not good, Winston; I've never been good. Your youth has clouded your judgment with this silly, fallacious thinking… So, that is why you have stayed around, eh? Putting up with everything I have put you through to save me? I run you through hell and back, and you still think there's something 'good' in me left to pick at? After it all, you still don't know what I am? The things I've done… I'll spell it out for you, then: I'm no saint…"

"Carrion,"

"Tell me, how many innocents are arsonists–with a fire

burning in their heart that desperately wants to free itself, lungs thirsty for the ashes? None. Even if I could, why would I choose goodness? When has it been anything more than an inherent, crippling weakness? A gushing wound? I say, away with all of it! I've never been good, but I've always been *strong*, which is the only thing that matters. Show life you are its master while you still can," swore the Professor with swollen spite. Winston shivered, realizing that he had to break through his horrid carapace with force. Removing the thorn would require more than a gentle tug... Mustering his confidence, he channeled every insult, every lashing thrown his way, into a fiery, poetic, and ultimately liberating declaration.

"Pitying yourself some sort of villain? You remember all the things you regret, but not an ounce of what's good stays in that head of yours! You only see what you want to see, eyes fixed on chains, instead of the locks! Don't you see it? You have... No, you are the key to your problems! Underneath all those layers lies something worth fighting for. Why do you think I have followed you around, no matter where your crazed schemes lead you, mate? I know there's still hope for you. I need you to believe in that hope even if you don't believe me. So help me if you don't face those memories down! They have power over you, Professor, and you continue to remain a *prisoner* of your own making."

"I am no prisoner!"

"Yes, you are! This case will never fix your life–it doesn't matter what we find or who we stop. It will only leave you grasping for more! You must want more for yourself; dream of a future worth changing for! Make peace with your past that brings ya to your knees! Choose a brighter future just as you've chosen this life for yourself!" pleaded Winston as the Professor's head drifted towards the earth as his hands trembled. He was almost too silent as the mosquitos claimed their great prize. Surely, he would curse, shout at the sky, or cry some great injustice, but instead, Carrion simply replied sorrowfully.

"I never chose this, Winston," finished murmuring

Carrion, tearing off his bandage in airy-strips. They fluttered away to where he knew not. Winston had never been so adamant about anything. His bitterness and sorrow managed to make themselves manifest in such sultry words. He must fancy them as one of a kind–what a fool! Even if Amelia's death meant something, how dare he compare his pain to his! Who was he to preach to him? Carrion looked upwards, trying to see the child beneath the white-grey streaks of hair. Winston peered back, finding what light he could before continuing to speak. He had to be at his best–he demanded it.

"I know. Believe me, mate, no one chooses everything about their lot, for better or for worse. I hadn't the foggiest idea I could even drive a stagecoach, but things got clearer! Sure, there were more than a few detours along the way, but that's where I ended up settling. There's something freeing about always being in motion–reliable, as fluid as it may be. You got to keep moving forward!"

"Why?"

"To find love, and a true one at that. You cannot hinge your life upon one answer, some all-enveloping mystery that casts a shadow over everything else. Even banking on people is a risky venture because... well, everything has its time here. Yet, while you're still going, you can always choose to make of life what you can. Goodness, I know that I didn't choose..." said Winston weakly, struggling to force the words out. His lips stung more each time they creaked open.

Taking off his glasses, he wiped his waning eyes against a simple yellow handkerchief. She was there at that moment, making it all bearable. Even though she was so far up, he could tell that she was proud of him, with lovely, golden honeysuckles in her flowing locks. Shutting his eyes, he prayed softly, eventually continuing.

"I needed her to make it–more than anything else in the world. If it was my choice, she would be sitting here, not me. But you see, I had no say in the matter. *His* plan was bigger than that. Of course, I couldn't see that then, rendering me an angry little man with no one to take it out on. I... couldn't stand seeing her that way. Every part of me wanted to run away, sparing myself the pain. We were still so young. The color draining from her face... her back slowly slumping against the bed–it was all too much. At that moment, I had a choice: stay or run away to spare myself. Ultimately, I made the right one; she made it easy on me, though. Said I was more scared than she was as she withered away... When she passed, I felt the warmth of her hand fade away, but the coldness that grew never left this," cried Winston painfully before letting the pendant dangle from his neck freely.

It weighed so much... Yet, it was all he had left of her– one part comfort, one part sorrow. It was all or nothing. Neck slickening, the Professor bit deep into the pinky depths of his tongue. He wanted to tell him his weakness and split the gash in his heart wide open, but what good would it do? Winston already knew better than anyone else. Yet, he held onto the damned thing. His head drooped downwards, color draining as the words sucked the remaining life out with them.

"Of course, I had a few weeks to talk to her before her passing. Even when it strained her, she greeted me with a smile, even when it hurt her to... One day, I'll see it again, and besides, there's plenty to still do here. Where does that leave me, mate? To cry or shout? Give up? No... It leaves me with my life to live. Every day, I choose to try to live rightly, even though I keep on failing. I'm not perfect–not even close. But no matter what comes to me, I will continue to live with purpose... meaning. In this place, goodness can seem like weakness, but true strength is choosing a different way–a narrow one at that. These memories have their clutches on you... you must beat them, or they will continue to best you. Please, fight back! Confront them or continue to pay the price. I didn't want this conversation to happen this way. You know I..."

"Do not apologize. Never apologize to anyone for anything, ever. Spare me your sympathy! All your incessant bemoaning... What do you want me to say? I could tell you of every time I have slipped... No, sunk deeper into these places–that dreadful boy wanting to seize my mind, ever closer to taking control. I never know if I'll come back. You cannot understand such a burden, what it feels like... Losing yourself. I just know can't," declared the Professor, wheezing as his hands clawed at the dirt, its grainy surfaces clinging to the folds of his fingers.

Crickets chirped as the pair sat in silence for some time. Gasping for air, Winston sat dumbfounded, nearly defeated. Everything he said fell on empty ears. Unsure of what else to say, he decided to try and break the tension.

"Do you reckon the crickets will have a chance now? Seeing as we haven't heard them gurgle since we got here, they must have finally found a way to sing their songs," said Winston, laughing weakly, leaving the Professor to break out into dark laughter before he replied sourly.

"Does it matter? You know their life is so short anyways,"

"That's one way of looking at it; there was a time I believed that too. Over time, I've come to a simple conclusion–the only one that I can. Without death, life would be meaningless. Try to imagine what a boundless existence would truly feel like, Carrion. If we were all here for, well, forever, there would have to be a lot of coachmen. There would be too many people to drive about, even for them, with few places to go. Mate, what could be scarier than that? Knowing that your actions were but a drop in such an indifferent pond? Death weighs heavy on your shoulders–what scares you about it? Maybe that's the root of your problems," suggested Winston, gently pushing his drooping glasses back upwards, failing to make anything clearer. Clearing his throat, the Professor spat on the ground before begrudgingly answering him.

"I am not scared; there are so many more... fruitful places for fear. Yet, of course, I'm not ready! I will hang on for as long as people like Guess continue to scamper about without a care in the world, stealing away *my* truth. They will face justice,"

"Who says your justice is absolute? Carrion, your own future is what matters. Not vengeance, not answers. Surely, you, of all people, can have a heart for others! For having so little control over yourself, you sure want to tighten the noose around others, playing executioner,"

"You know *nothing*! Good people lack the spine, no... the resolve to truly punish the guilty. As the bodies continue to pile and the pyres burn, where is goodness? Can you find it in their dead eyes?"

"Compassion is stronger and sharper than any blade. It has the power to change hearts, reaching places nothing else can touch. Showing mercy, kindness even, takes far more power than cutting someone down..." said Winston before being silenced by a short swing of the Professor's hand. Carrion roared indignantly.

"How dare you presume to lecture *me* of all people? Who do you think you are?"

"Your friend! Listen to yourself... Tell me this, Professor: if compassion is so weak a force, then why have I traveled with you for so long? If mercy is so weak a force, then when I found you, why didn't I leave you to the ditch? If my hope for you is so weak, then why did I have this conversation with ya at all?"

"Naivety–you have yet to shed your sweet little innocence. Still having hope! You are ever the ignorant young buck, prancing about without a care in the world,"

"And you're a stubborn mule of a man. You haven't listened to a single thing I've said, have you? Too ensnared in your own pity to see straight. I've been through lifetimes in my short time here! I know you've suffered hardship, but it's no excuse to fall deeper into misery. If you continue fixating on this case, the answers you so desperately crave will destroy you! Mate, if for nothing else, hear me now: *I* will not leave you to your destruction. This 'case' will not triumph over you. I swear I will not allow this obsession to take you!" triumphantly declared Winston, wrinkles folding defiantly in exultation. The inviting stars could gleam a while longer in their solitude. The Professor, red-faced and horrified, screamed.

"You don't have a choice! No claim over me! Go back to the carriage now!" screamed the Professor, words slurring into the contractions he so despised. Feeling his tattooed hand twitch, he saw little blue blots pulse on it as it rose. Angling back with a mind of its own, his hand drew Winston's eyes upward, carrying a sort of curiosity before realization struck him across the face.

"Don't *even* dream of it,"

"Leave me,"

"As you wish, master," snapped Winston, slowly backing away toward the box. His glasses gloomily glided to the tip of his nose; he did not bother to push them up. It was far easier to tame a horse than a mule. He knew that Carrion only had so much control over himself. If only she had been there... Surely, she would not have failed.

Although he was beginning to suspect that words, altogether, were not enough–he would have to choose his own path. Which, quite frankly, was the most frightening bit of it all. Winston heard the cabin door slam shut as what remained of his thoughts faded into the cool night air. The Professor's hand, or more accurately, the mark that tore into his skin, looked deep back at him. It called him weak, weak, weak.

He knew what he had to do. The other voice, the one that never stopped echoing inside his empty heart, had to be silenced. Fear had been so easily traded for a fleeting delerium that threatened to upend everything that had been built. Winston had truly blossomed into a liability. And such things were meant to be discarded.

"For Winston."

Carrion did not pay it too much attention; the best vows were meant to be broken, anyway.

CHAPTER NINETEEN: DEBATES AND DISPUTES

E yes creaking open, the Constable found himself awake, with a ring kissing his knuckle. It balanced his hand, missing finger and all, making it feel lighter. He studied the heavy hue of the metal against the red-orange morning ligh: it glinted beautifully. For the first time in ages, the big man had been able to sleep without booze, which felt like Paradise.

Glancing at the Professor, he saw a restlessness, which permeated from every pore. His hand twitched as his teeth clanked against one another, causing his wrinkles to stretch across his ever-narrowing face. It was an all-too-familiar sight– an induced hangover in its own right. Whatever Carrion was experiencing was not sleep. A voice emanated from the box, slowly beginning to sound like Winston's: indeed, it was.

"Good to see you sleep so well... Not to say I was watching you sleep, considering how creepy that might come off. You might be the only one that managed to eke out any sleep. Just a heads-up, but we've almost made it to the force building. Although the word 'building' is beginning to seem a bit generous... At least it has four standing walls. Of course, no offense to you, mate," added Winston quickly, unwilling to alienate himself any further from his passengers. The Constable smiled before tapping against the glass gently.

"You're not wrong. The town's been fighting for ages to secure funding for a proper hall. Much less chance for the force to get anything out of it if the damn thing is never built. Some of the officials are... I'd rather not hurt your ears too much. They're just a pretentious lot," delicately said the Constable, realizing how little he cared to impress those people anymore. The tinted glasses would be the first thing to go when he returned.

The Deputy had always urged him to keep them on, sealing his sandy island away from the world. According to him, the pale thing was just too unsightly. What more he could have seen without them! For such small things, they kept him from her. The badge did too... Shifting uncomfortably, he wondered how much longer he would be content with being a nameless constable.

"I bet! With all their powdered wigs and fancy chairs, they must have little time to think about anything else. Of course, their delicate bodies probably sink into those really good, comfy chairs. Velvet paddings, cushions. Buttons. Surely, some of them must fly!" exclaimed Winston, allowing his words to uplift his spirits. A long night of contemplation only served to echo the truth he did not want to believe: he could not save Carrion from what was to come. The pendant felt so cool, so inviting; Amelia, her beating heart against his own, called him. Her stringy-gold streams of hair, so full of life, brimmed with promise. In a place where there was no more death or mourning, she sat on an oak tree, looking at the stars.

So, at that moment, doom and dread were utterly destroyed, demolished with finality. And that was enough. He gritted his teeth before mouthing one resoundingly simple word.

"Soon,"

It was not time yet. He would wait just a while longer; the

work was not finished yet. Hearing a small tap in response from the box, the Constable could almost picture Winston grinning like an idiot from the other side–he was not. Eyes flicking open, the Professor straightened his back, creak by creak, against the seat. Cursing, he poised his tongue to make words, which was becoming increasingly difficult.

"Are we almost there? No rest for the weary, eh?" asked the rail-man as silence answered him. Turning towards the Constable, he was greeted by a shrug. Shaking his head, the Carrion prepared to yell louder, but the big man's lingering gaze caused him to reconsider. He must not have overheard his most spirited debate with Winston... No wonder he looked like such a lost puppy. Smirking, the Professor chuckled lightly before the Constable decided to speak up.

"Is there something I should know about?"

"Nothing of *your* concern, Constable,"

"I would beg to differ. Winston's usually not the silent type. Considering our lives are literally in his hands, perhaps we should sort this out? Otherwise, we might be discussing this in a ditch. So, if you'd mind indulging me here, what happened?" firmly asked the Constable as the carriage ground to a halt. Capitalizing on this interruption, the Professor flicked his head away, pretending he had heard nothing.

"We're here," shouted Winston from the box as he studied what was sparingly referred to as headquarters by the force. It was just as poor as the first time he had the misfortune of passing by. Solemn bricks, plastered in a dull grey paint, were sealed with dark mortar. Occasional garish spots of color from the convenience store poked through the rest of the dismal display. Two dimming lampposts shined emptily against the hazy, dusty windows, which seemed to trap a century's worth of dust and crumbs.

Whoever renovated the place must have figured that a lack of any distinct color would make the place timeless, but they had unwittingly created a headstone. The silly grocers, who had previously occupied the building, had already sealed its fate, though, by choosing such an awful location. All the runoff from the rest of the town drained there. The force's last effort to make the place hospitable came in the form of a crooked wooden sign, which welcomed visitors to a truly unwelcoming place.

It was a sorry sight. Wedging the cabin door open, the Professor and the Constable marched ahead while Winston dragged behind, trying to ward off the smell of decaying food. The force must not have managed to get rid of all of it. Knocking gently, the Constable was ushered in by a rather timid man. The foyer was simultaneously confining and empty, littered with empty chairs and dusty photographs. The air was thick and stuffy, nearly suffocating. For all they knew, they were breathing the same stuff folks decades ago did.

A large file cabinet, gleaming, sat behind a decrepit desk. It looked as though it was the only thing that received care. After hacking up a lung, Carrion swore the walls were closing in around them–in the most literal sense. After leading them to the front desk, the man nervously smiled and greeted them once he had sat down.

"Hello, officer. What brings you to our department?" asked the man urgently with little patience, causing the big man to stiffen nervously. It was the first time he had not worn tinted glasses in the office in a long time–his first act of rebellion of many to come. The Constable spoke up, somewhat timidly.

"Mr. Beckett, we've met before. Normally, I'd be wearing something a bit different. I'm Constable Brauer... my badge is here,"

"Of course. I recognized you, glasses or not. But, our policy states that I must not discriminate between the force and the citizens of this fine town. You should already know that yourself, Constable,"

"Yes, Mr. Beckett. We have arrived with pressing business, and we must speak to the Deputy at the soonest convenience. There is a man in this town who intends to release chemicals into the Cistern, potentially poisoning anything that did come from the Strayer. The deaths are likely..." said the Constable before stopping himself as he realized that Beckett was tapping his pen with every word. Beneath it, was a yellow ticket that had a seemingly infinite number of zig-zagging rows and columns, demanding attention. The secretary tilted his head mockingly before continuing.

"I'm sure the Deputy would love to hear all about it! Despite all the nonconformities with the weather, he continues to report in every day. In fact, at the moment, he is not busy. Before that, though, I'm afraid you're going to need to fill out this ticket–in its entirety. This is for filing purposes,"

"Beckett, please. I don't think that will be necessary today,"

"I'm sorry. I didn't create the rules, I just enforce them. If you don't believe me, I would be happy to procure the handbook from that drawer over there. Would you like to look at it?"

"You're failing to understand the urgency of this situation: this is a matter of life and death for the people of this town. Someone may be unknowingly pouring this for their daughter without any shipments from the Strayer! This is above your rigid commitment to protocol!" roared the Constable, drawing himself to full height. Glancing upwards at the tremendous, though rather formless, mass before him, Beckett replied smugly.

"I don't think arguing will have that ticket written any faster. How about you and your friends go sit down and fill this out for me? It's hardly an inconvenience like you make it out to be,"

"Oh, I'll fill it out all right–every horseshit-coated line. Then I'll shove it straight up your..." said the poor Constable before once again being cut short. Placing his burnt hand on the big man's shoulder, the Professor bared his grisly yellow fangs in an apparently friendly manner, begging Beckett to try him.

"Drinking can do wonders to a man, Mr. Beckett. We would be happy to fill out this ticket for you–with the utmost haste, no less. Please excuse us for a moment," finished saying the Professor facetiously, attempting in vain to drag the Constable along with him.

With such a powerful declaration, they quickly realized that between all of them, no pen was to be found. Picking at the fraying edge of the chair, Carrion sighed at their sudden epiphany. Double-checking all his coat pouches and pockets, he sheepishly looked towards the Constable to do something. Searing with anger, he grunted at Winston. Sighing loudly, the boy slowly made his way back to Beckett, for, with good fortune, the penultimate time.

"You'll have to sign that pen out before you use it," said Mr. Beckett, sensing the question that hid behind Winston's lips before it managed to squeak out. A special, delightful giddiness glowed through his otherwise colorless face. The boy cocked his head, then replied.

"Fair enough. May I use this one, then?"

"I think you just misunderstood what I just said. Allow me to repeat myself: sign for it first,"

"Okay, mate... Listen to yourself for a moment. The reason I need a pen, to begin with, is to write your ticket. Ya see, we don't have a pen yet. So, I sought to settle that little mishap by borrowing a pen. Yet, you expect me to request a pen with a pen I don't have... Sir, I think you're the problem," explained Winston calmly, one word at a time, to restore some semblance of logic.

"Like I have repeatedly said, I don't make the rules. I merely enforce them. You seem resourceful; why don't you figure something out?" asked Beckett, sneering as he dramatically pointed back to the simply wretched chairs.

Defeated, Winston went back to mire in his shame. The Constable buried his reddening face into his hands, muffling a roar. Yet, the Professor had caught a scent–perhaps that of the kin of the famed Mr. Cheese. Surely enough, a little thing scurried about with a pen clamped in its jaw. Although they were not on speaking terms, Winston and the Professor locked eyes, communicating an unspoken truth. Perhaps all their rat-catching had not been for naught.

They both quietly got up, sneaking to opposite sides of the room to assume their positions. As the Professor screeched, the rat ran into Winston's hands, which quickly wrestled the pen away. Applauding the boy, he felt a faint smile fight to creep through his smirk–which he begrudgingly flashed for a moment. As the rat scampered back into the hole, he wished he could offer a more permanent solution to such disgusting vermin. It would have to pay another day. Yet, a dead rat could not fill out a ticket, so the pen would have to suffice.

After an inordinate amount of time, the ticket was finished, and they all stood solemnly in unison. For the first time, they were truly united. Emboldened with an air of absolute confidence, they marched to the front desk like a triumphant host riding on the eve of battle.

"My dear Mr. Beckett, here is your ticket," said the Professor delicately, dancing the ticket across the table. Holding their breaths, the men felt their confidence slowly sink into doubt as Beckett's eyes pored over it. Evidently dissatisfied, his spindly fingers withdrew a pair of reading glasses to hasten the procedure. Measuring the ticket for dimensions with the nearby ruler to ensure its authenticity, he slowly read each line quietly as to not violate client privacy–there were always prying ears, after all. Eventually, after some time, he spoke.

"For our purposes, this ticket is adequate. I would be remiss not to mention how the handwriting borders on downright sloppiness. However, that is your irregularity, not an insult to this system as a whole. As such, this is acceptable. I will put you in the queue, Constable. As for your friends…"

"Excuse me?"

"Professor, is it? And, the other one? Did you really think that one ticket would cover you all collectively? Did you actually take the time to read the ticket? Each one of you must provide a ticket for me. This is the reason why we have rules in life– for disorderly people like *you*," cried Mr. Beckett as something finally snapped inside the Professor. With a swift swipe, he snatched the ticket, dangling it rhythmically before the irate man's face. In his other hand, as if it materialized from nothing, came a lit match. He basked in the growing horror on Mr.

Beckett's face as the orange flames danced over the paper. A tiny pile of ash soon grew on the desk.

"Now, now. Playtime is over! We are doing this *my* way. You–yes, you. Those legs of yours are going to carry the news of our arrival to the Deputy with appropriate expediency. If you become too distracted along the way, and my poor colleagues have to wait much longer, I will begin burning whatever *precious* things I find in your desk. I will personally oversee that every rulebook finds a final departure to the abyss–a one-way trip, I must assure you. Do we have an understanding, Beckett?" declared the Professor forcefully as he rubbed the charred end of the extinguished match against Mr. Beckett's whitening knuckles. Recoiling sharply, he fell backward out of his chair, quickly scurrying to the back, not unlike Mr. Cheese's doppelganger. Winston, unmoved by the whole ordeal, simply asked.

"Was that really, really necessary?"

"Winston, for once, you were right about something. It really would have lost its charm if I had done it at Guess' place. You know, this serves as a nice lesson for all of us: sometimes the mere threat of something carries the same weight as doing it. Mr. Beckett is a logical man; I threaten his petty rules, and he crumbles into dust. Anything directed at those musty books makes him feel threatened, by extension. Ah, the wonders of man!" sarcastically spewed the Professor spitefully as the Deputy emerged from his office at last. Mr. Beckett trailed behind, head low. After straightening his silvery-white beard, the Deputy crossed his arms, which almost did all the talking before he did.

"If it isn't Constable Brauer. You look well–took my advice to heart, didn't ya?"

"Yes, sir, of course,"

"I like that. Men like us are above such things. So, could I have a moment alone with you? There's a lot to discuss,"

"Sir... yes, sir. Professor, Winston–I'll be back with you soon,"

"Sure. Take all the time you need. Winston and I will have some fun with Mr. Beckett in the meantime. He might get lonely without our company," cheered the Professor, splitting his mouth with a toothy grin. With a hearty pat on the Constable's back, Deputy Reiner led him inside. The door slammed shut, leaving the Constable with a moment to study the terribly familiar, yet unfamiliar, room. At one point, it felt like home. What could have changed? The room itself was hardly any different, save for stacked bills that threatened to break the table beneath them. Like the rain-starved earth, donations had dried up at the wrong time.

Inside a tight glass cabinet, a pristine uniform remained locked away, one of the few formal ones ever produced for the force. It shined, especially in the surrounding filth. There was a time he had yearned for his own–something with his name on it. Now, just hearing it spoken would suffice. Dinners, ceremonies, and the like paled in comparison to the thought of eating with her one last time. Perhaps Red still had her ring too, not sealed away in a cabinet...

"Now, I'm going to cut straight to the point: that Carrion fellow. Tell me what he's doing in my lobby. What do ya think of him?" interrogated the Deputy sternly, breaking the Constable out of his thoughts. Truth leaking from his lips, the big man felt like a schoolboy again, confessing to his mischievous deeds.

"He clearly has alternative motives for pursuing the death of Herbert. It's personal for him. He's reckless and impulsive, prone to action instead of thought. But, without him, we wouldn't have discovered everything going on. Despite everything he says, he's on our side for the time being,"

"Ah, but you'll never be like him, Constable. A cheat, a scumbag. Typical outsider! He's truly one selfish son of a bitch. You can just tell he has no regard for that Winston chap–emotionless and cold. Freaks like him have no place in this town, or any at all, for that matter. Too many of that sort in the world, though, so few people like us: we got to stick together. Some good folks must keep order among the monsters," lectured the Deputy fervently as the Constable felt his island spiral dangerously. As much as he tried to agree with him, he simply could not. The Professor was all these things, maybe even more, but generalizations did not fully capture him.

When his knuckles were busted, bleeding, and bruised beyond recognition, Carrion had given him his coat. When he had fled home, he took him to the one place that he thought would help. Above all else, he had never made fun of his eye or made him wear the shades... Despite every other insult he had flung at him, he offered him that rare mercy, which meant far more than he could ever know. As the Constable poised his lips to speak, the Deputy continued his interrogation.

"This discovery, what is it? Does it relate to Dr. Herbert?"

"Yes, sir. We believe that Dr. Guess, some sort of neurologist, created some sort of chemical weapon and used it to kill Herbert. I found a puddle of it around his body. Miss Flores, the bartender at Stanton's, gave it a look–the stuff is lethal. Even a little of it damages the mind if someone ingests it. Water changes it, so the bit in the Cistern should not be a concern. If it somehow got past the Strayer, though, we'd be in trouble. Sir, we need to move to arrest him. Guess must be behind all of this,"

"And why would Guess, a common bricklayer, make a 'chemical weapon?' He lives in a shack on the edge of town. Newer to town but he's never bothered anyone,"

"He's lied to everyone... for some time. In a drunken stupor, he confessed to the Professor about everything–he's been turning in reports about the brain to a mysterious organization. Herbert told me his father worked for a similar group before he turned up dead. *They* are probably bankrolling Guess' research. If this stuff, his creation, gets into someone's home, it could kill them, too. Sir, intervening could be the first *great* thing the force does for this town!" finished saying the Constable triumphantly, taking a deep breath. She would have been proud of him; he had a way with words, after all. Yawning, the Deputy offered only an upturned smirk for his speech, watching the big man's face sink in slowly. Taking one last moment to bask in the shock of the milky eye before him, he chuckled before continuing speaking.

"First, huh? That's precious. So, some shadowy organization has its clutches on our town? Going to poison everyone until their eyes crisscross? Son, are you finished yet with this preposterous charade? Guess you never dropped drinking, did you? Though with all this crazy talk, maybe you're dabbling in substances, too. I thought I raised you better than this…"

"You raised me to tell things as I see it; here I am, doing just that. I have no reason to lie to you, of all people! When my father left, you let me polish that cabinet over there–gave me something to do. You said one day it'd be mine. I'd never turn my back on that… My loyalty's been here for almost three decades,"

"You're still not fit for it. Did the promotion mean nothing to you? *So* swept away with the ramblings of a madman you'd present this garbage to me? It'd be better if the alcohol was talking–you'd probably be making more sense. Red's got to be ashamed of you… And your dear mother? If she was still here, she would be…" said the Deputy, puttering out as the Constable rose, locking eyes with him–pale and not. His neck craned up, shoulders straightening back. The words said themselves as his clarity grew.

"Don't ever speak of them like that,"

"You forget your place! When I took you under my wing, you were a bloody runt–a nobody! That father of yours left you with nothing. I pulled you out of the wreckage and tried to make you into a man. You were supposed to be better than the rest of the witless goons here. Was I wrong about you, huh?"

"Yes! You raised me in your shadow, holding your own petty dreams and ambitions over me–always out of reach. I never wanted a life of luxury, fancy rubbish, until you filled my head with lies! I had so little, yet you picked me clean… to the *bone*! When my mother died, I needed a dad, not a bloody buzzard, coming to finish me off,"

"Clearly not, you fatass buffoon. I…"

"Was I supposed to 'save' the force? Was the promotion

your blessing, your approval, to do so? I don't need it any longer! You hear? Find someone else to take from. I don't drink until I pass out now, pissing myself, not because of your scoldings but my own damn choice. So long as the precious uniform was fine, you could sleep easy. Look me in my eyes, both of them! I have outgrown you, old man!" shouted the Constable, skin flush with renewed life. His face burned brightly with restoration. Slinking forwards, the Deputy struck the table, before putting his fatty finger deep into the Constable's chest.

"You ungrateful little *shit*! I gave you your world– everything you have that's good is thanks to me. You're fired; you've gone rogue. Whether you like it or not, Brauer, you and I are two of a kind. You can pride yourself on changing, but you will never escape who you truly are–someone like me! You may never see me again, but you'll always carry me with you, deep down. Nothing you can ever do get rid of me. And, after life's set you on your ass, you'll come crawling back. When you're groveling before me like a wounded pup, I'll tell you what I always have: that it's men like us against the world!" screamed the Deputy as he ripped the door open, letting it hollowly thud against the wall.

"You're no man," replied the Constable simply, throwing his badge and nightstick on the ground. It was a small price to pay for freedom. Such burdensome things were better left behind. Hearing the door slam shut with finality, he breathed heavily before finding his breath. Winston came to comfort him as Carrion shook his head in disappointment before muttering.

"I take it he didn't believe us?"

"No. We don't need him or the force. We have everything we need to take Guess down," replied the former constable, leaky tears dripping from his island. As the splotchy white land continued to emerge from the waves, years of stress slowly melted away from his face–tears of joy and expectancy were much stronger than those of fear or sorrow. It was more than restoration; he felt better than before. One bold declaration managed to make it through his lips.

"It's time to finish this, once and for all."

CHAPTER TWENTY: THE INTREPID FORCE

Mr. Beckett sat panting at his desk. The Carrion fellow had given him quite a scare. Overwhelmed with nervousness, he felt his fingers feverishly pore over the rulebooks, carefully checking each page for creases. Although if he were being fair to that threatening rule-breaker, the Deputy had been the one that truly set his crumbling hands into motion. He had been given strict orders to turn away any visitors for the remainder of the day. Strict, being held at gunpoint.

Not in a literal sense, of course. Something in the Deputy's icy glare conveyed far more than a cold revolver to his head. It typically was not policy to deny guests, of course. However, he had no drive to debate the finer details. Not when there was so much counting to be done–his personal set of pencils would have to do. The ones for visitors were unusually chaotic. There were six of them; one had a horrid, chewed eraser. Should he count it as being a pencil, imperfections and all?

His palms continued to sweat and glisten as thoughts scattered. An eraser alone was not a pencil. Surely, plenty of people had bumbled about with their chewed pencils, and no one would question if they had a pencil. It was about the lead–the sharpness, the precision of it all. The first pencil felt sharp against the tip of his finger: it was sufficient. Yet, the second from the pile created a far more acute sensation. The first no longer seemed sharp by comparison, threatening the order of things.

He could sharpen the one, but what if it became too sharp? Another imbalance would be even more unacceptable. Mr. Beckett intended to fix problems, not create more of them, after all. He felt his concentration slip from his fingers as a dreadful noise threatened to penetrate the door. It almost sounded like human breathing. Seeing as how the door was locked, per the Deputy's policy-breaking instruction, whatever was out there could wait. There was no need to compound such brutish behavior. The thuds devolved into a senseless harmony, culminating in a few names.

"Arthur! Reiner!" sounded an awfully irritating, muffled female voice. It was another problem, just like that blasted eraser or dulled end. Disobeying the Deputy by opening the door would be against policy, but so was his instruction to keep it shut in the first place. Ultimately, policy was divine–the Deputy was just a lowly servant of it, as he was. Letting a woman in was simply the lesser of two evils. With a key in hand, he slowly stood up from his desk and strode through the empty lobby. As the lock clicked open, a towering figure emerged in a particularly heavy coat and tinted glasses that suggested little humanity was beneath them. Tightly wrapped fabric obscured the rest of its face like the bandages of some great mummy.

He had been duped, played for a fool. This was no woman crying for help; rather, a reaper coming for him far too early–such a disorderly demise! The figure cast its shadow over him as he made his peace. Truly, all the fear of the Deputy had been for naught. Slowly backing away, he stumbled on his feet, falling to the ground. As an invisible scythe raised above him, something most wondrous caught his attention: a red strand of hair poked free from the reaper's cowl. Swallowing, he asked cautiously.

"Ms. Loxley? Is that you?"

"It's Mrs. Brauer. Are you all right?" asked the figure, who was probably not Death, who offered her pale hand to him. Unwrapping the many scarves coiled around her face, she pocketed the glasses. It was indeed the so-called Mrs. Brauer. He was always so skittish–time had changed nothing. She chuckled lightly before continuing speaking quietly, as to not disturb him any further.

"I've got to speak to Mr. Reiner immediately. My husband is in grave danger,"

"I'm afraid that won't be possible, Mrs. Brauer. I have been given strict orders to ensure no guests are seen at this time,"

"From whom, exactly?"

"The Deputy himself, of course. He was quite adamant with his instruction,"

"I see. I'm sure he'll make an exception in this case. Let me speak to him, and I'll work this out for you. What do you say?" asked Red rhetorically, already determined to see him, even if that meant kicking down the door. He raised his hand in a vain attempt to stop her, but she quickly brushed him aside as she marched to the office.

With one last ditch attempt, he tried to grab the edge of her coat, but, instead, fell on his face once more. He stayed down. As the office door creaked open, his ears perked up. A few words and phrases managed to creep through the door as much as he fought hearing them. It was simply against policy to eavesdrop on his superior. Yet, he was only human, after all.

"My husband... grave danger... some sort... must... something... Herbert... he's... gone... a few... please help... find..."

"Calm your... he was... while ago... husband... rogue... fired him... Carrion... bad taste..."

"He... no... couldn't have... you... know... where... has... gone?"

"Not... concern..."

"Excuse me?" asked the voice with stinging indignation. The words tore through air and door alike. They would be heard.

"All he told... lies... Herbert was no..."

"Explain... this... violent liquid... burns like... seems to control... wine..."

"Lies... more lies... not truth... why he... fired..."

"Still... he is... like your... start... case... find him, now!" screamed the voice angrily, demanding something far greater than acknowledgment: action.

"Too much imagination... for... woman..." said the other voice before being cut off by a sharp slapping noise. If the words passed through the crusty old building, then that dosage of pain reached the Cistern.

"You... the force... will find him... I know... being hunted..."

"Out... with you... no business with us... or *them*..."

"I... find him myself... when this... you'll... be fired..." finished saying the voice as the door sprung open, hinges crying for mercy. Mrs. Loxley, fuming with searing anger, stormed violently through the lobby like a raging tsunami. Hopefully, the Deputy would have a far more pleasant reaction to his choice of letting her in.

"Good luck, darling. You're hysterical!" shouted the Deputy, spittle dripping from his lip. Removing a handkerchief from his pocket, he dabbed at the growing sore on his face, spitting a glob on the ground before slamming the door shut. The woman frantically rewrapped her face, swearing all the while. Yet, her eyes lingered on a match left on the table–Carrion had been there, which meant that her husband would be around, too. Beckett would know something...

"You–tell me where they went," demanded Red, snatching the match to wave it at the weasel before her. He shook his head a tad bit too vigorously, so she grabbed him by his collar, holding him up to see his reflection in the shades.

"You're really putting me out here, mister. I'm not feeling terribly kind today, either. Where is my husband heading?

Answer me!"

"Something to do with Guess! I swear he didn't say anything else," cried Mr. Beckett as she released him. Satisfied, Red kicked the door open, darting back into the street. The trip had not been a waste after all. Palms weighty, Mr. Beckett took a careful recount of his pens–he could never be too sure they were not disturbed by the chaos around him. He heard the door creak back open, and he knew what followed the clunking footsteps behind him.

"Now... Look me in the eyes," demanded the Deputy sternly as his gaze once again aimed through Mr. Beckett's head. Sheepishly, he lifted his head to look back into the barrel. Expecting bullets, he was instead serenaded with barbed words from his superior.

"Don't ever do that again–you hear me? The force doesn't need anyone who can't follow orders, yellow-bellied and all. Just because all the real men are dead and gone is no excuse for a sorry thing like you to sully this post. To think some of them died for an embarrassment like you... A lowly son of a bitch, a motherless wretch... a bloody coward. But, you know all that already, don't ya? Say that for me; *say* it!"

"I'm a lowly..."

"I'm not going to wait much longer, Beckett,"

"Coward,"

"That will suffice. Know your place. You are less than the dirt on my boot, utter scum! Don't you ever disobey me again. As for those rulebooks... The time for such things has passed. My boys never used to need those silly things. I'm really doing you a favor, you hear? I'm setting you free. Thank me!"

"Sir, please! Have mercy!" wailed Mr. Beckett in pain as tears began to stream down his face without any care for the papers below. Those books were his only guidance in such a disorderly and cluttered life. They were all he had. His withering hands twitched violently, threatening to rattle off altogether. They cried injustice.

"Burn them all! Don't bother sparing one of them. I never

want to see those bloody things ever again. Oh, and while you're at it, those history books over there can join them," declared the Deputy, sadistically grinning with infectious glee. Knees buckling, Mr. Beckett continued to sob, eventually falling to the ground for the last time. There was nothing to count on the ground, nothing to quantify, nothing for guidance. Too many cluttered papers, too many messy books, too much excess, excess!

There was no hope.

"Cheer up, son," sarcastically said the Deputy, clapping Mr. Beckett's decaying back with a hefty pat. Bending down quietly, he cupped his grizzled hand around Mr. Beckett's ear, injecting one last bout of poison.

"If there's anything left when you're done, it'll give you something to wipe away all those tears. Besides, everything's gonna be all right soon again. Just like the good old days. I promise."

CHAPTER TWENTY-ONE: A GUESS AND A THEORY

"**N**o jurisdiction, no nightstick. You are not even a bloody constable anymore. What am I to call you, Brauer-boy?"

"Mr. Brauer is just fine. Just as your first name isn't... Well, what is your first name? For all your titles, I've yet to hear your most basic one," said Mr. Brauer jokingly, shifting his tone as the Professor's bloodshot eyes narrowed. As dusk had set in, Carrion remained unnervingly still against the lost light. Yet, no stillness could mask how low his shoulders hung, drooping from the arms that weighed them down. His sideburns flared unusually violently, hair flying from his cheeks. He was resoundingly crumpled yet unmistakably defiant.

The former constable swore to himself that he would remain vigilant. This wayward kite would not be lost; he would not be swept away in the night. They would take in Guess, settling the matter for good. Everyone would be safe again... Perhaps, even, the rain would finally return. Although if he were being honest with himself, his bare skin no longer recoiled at sunlight's heated touch–it welcomed it. Things had changed, or more simply, he had.

"As for bringing Guess in, the formalities will be worked out later. Vigilante justice is usually frowned upon, but he has likely committed crimes elsewhere–surely someone wants him. Besides, the nightstick was a bit of a toy. Look at my hands, Professor. These clumsy things were crafted for one reason: breaking stuff with brutish force. That nightstick would have only gotten in my way," said the big man jokingly yet truthfully as he released the pressure between his knuckles. A cacophony of cracks hissed free from his hands, save for the one place where he was missing finger. The Professor, with great effort, stretched his frail arm around the big man in an apparently friendly manner.

"Finally! There may be some use in you yet, Brauer," exclaimed the Professor, with a hint of sincerity. In-kind, Mr. Brauer playfully clapped the rail-man on the back, nearly knocking him to the floor of the cabin. Regaining his composure, Carrion basked in the glory of his renewed tool.

"Such strength, vitality! You've taken your knocks much better than I thought possible. When I first met you, I saw you as Red's witless, senile footstool–a shell of a man! Yet, that is exactly why there is something wholly remarkable about you. For all your excessive mediocrity, you knew you wanted more. Wading through her lies, you have reached the precipice of freedom! Throw away any pretense of love with that wretch. Stop treading that thin, thin line, Brauer. Let go of any notion of honor, of goodness. Keep a decent fear about you, relying on yourself. That is all you need to make it in life," finished lecturing the Professor, emeralds engulfed in red cracks.

Swallowing deeply, Mr. Brauer found himself unable to mask his disappointment at his words. It was a jarring reminder that, despite all of Carrion's projections of courage and stability, underneath was a scared little man afraid of being hurt again. Yet, he was terribly hell-bent on his path toward destruction. Such bestial values were bound to fail him eventually–sooner rather than later. Sighing, Mr. Brauer realized the Carrion he had met days ago was the same person before him now. He needed hope, however small.

"Professor... I *am* a shell of a man, missing more parts of myself than I can count. Red wasn't there for me when I needed her to be, but neither was I. Every choice I made was my own. When my mother passed, I tried to drink it all away, leaving Red without her husband. Things only got worse as we grew apart... Sure, her 'comments' were never meant in kind, but I pushed her to that place. Honor is the one thing separating us from *them*... Being decent in a world like this, Professor, is choosing to be more..." said the former constable before being cut off by the Professor, who cursed bitterly.

"Oh, how it pains me, so! I was wrong about you! You're still drowning in her lies while keeping your terribly *high-minded* thoughts in the clouds–like Winston and all the rest. Ignorance is the world's plurality," finished saying the Professor, seething hatefully before coughing violently. He pulled out his now nearly ruined handkerchief, spitting into it as Mr. Brauer shook his head in disappointment.

"Carrion, no one ever loved you, did they?" asked the big man earnestly, trying to pierce through a fading façade. His emeralds betrayed him as something that may have been a tear streaked down his face. Searing against his reddening skin, the little droplet was soon lost to the cool air.

"Doesn't matter. Besides, what would you know about it? Always blathering on about your lost love... pathetic. Cry me a river! The love others have given you isn't worth spit: she's not coming back–you will only be reunited in dust. Accept it! Become something new, rejecting such wasteful things,"

"It's not meaningless, just because it doesn't last! Professor, you need to listen to yourself. Every time we've confronted death, bodies, and all, you've stressed the importance of living life to the fullest. I hated hearing it, but you're right; one day, we will join all those bodies we've seen–in the ground. I'm not getting any younger... But, that doesn't make every day we live valueless; it makes them even more special. Goodness knows time's changed me, but I accept it now,"

"Don't use my words against me! We are nothing more than walking bombs, waiting to go off. Our fuses are lit, and our time is set. There's only one thing keeping me from a premature dirt nap myself... truth. Love, goodness even, is such a meaningless pastime, leading only to heaps of weakness and misery. Overcome life by thumbing your nose at it for as long as you can. Seek your own ends, above all else,"

"A long life doesn't make a good one, Professor. Fear might keep you breathing, but is that really life? You're scared of what real life might feel like–all the mistakes that are bound to come with it. What are you living for?" asked Mr. Brauer carefully, causing the Professor to recoil sharply. His eyes threatened to pop free from their sockets as he spat the word out.

"Answers!"

"To what question? If it's bringing Guess in, soon you will have your answers. But, if it's about who you *are* today, you'll only be sorely disappointed. We don't even know what this symbol means yet! For all we know, it could be just that: an hourglass–nothing, more or less. If that's what you're living for, whatever the answer, it won't be enough. You're troubled, but you can change. Think of Karina or Winston! They care deeply for you. Is that a weakness?"

"Shut it! I will not suffer your miserable mockery any longer. You, and all the rest, are insufferable! When I've taken out Guess, everything he stood for will burn into cinders and ashes. Leaving me with my answers... and all of you, in ignorant squalor!" declared the Professor, words dripping with spite. He turned back to the window and was silent. Grunting, Mr. Brauer fiddled with his fingers, failing to surprise himself any longer with the tiny gap; he was beginning to not miss it at all.

The carriage stopped suddenly.

They had arrived. His island swam in shallow waters, widening as it was pushed to and fro. Guess' manor had seen better times, particularly since their last visit. His sculpted face, now broken many times over, was strewn about in fragmented shards across the lawn, denying them their chance at eternity. The formerly lovely gate, torn ajar, issued an echoing creak against the wind. Strangely corrupted, the marble was tainted to ruin; pale white arches had devolved into a sickly yellowish shade of their former glory.

As Winston opened the door for the Professor to step out, he heard a sharp breaking noise beneath his foot. Broken glass was strewn about the whole walkway–quite the warm welcome, indeed. The windows were shattered, toothy grins beckoning them forward. If the wind had been any worse, the former constable suspected the whole place would come crashing down. How could Guess be the culprit if this happened to his home? Were *they* displeased?

"Here we are… I didn't think it would be this bad," said Winston slowly, clutching his pendant for all the coolness it had left. Spitting on the ground, Mr. Brauer struggled to ease his nerves. A small part of him still hoped the rain could just fall, washing all his troubles away. But, he knew it was not so simple. The trouble they were about to face could not be run from any longer–and it was part of them, too.

Winston's eyes flickered with fear. Yet, after whatever happened between him and Carrion, he was still here. Perhaps bravery was his greatest gift. The big man could do for some of that himself. Taking a deep breath, he spoke up, earnestly.

"As bad as it is, we wouldn't have made it here, or frankly anywhere, without your help, Winston. You're going to be a damn hero, sticking out your neck for people who aren't even yours, if you catch my meaning,"

"You are my people. I wouldn't have it any other way, mate. Don't let her go, you hear? I never want to see that ring on the ground again…"

"Enough sappy nonsense. You all should be clapping about this wreck! Someone's already started our work for us. Let's find where he's weaseled himself into," said Carrion, interjecting rudely.

"Professor, I'm not finished with what I'm saying," declared Winston as Carrion creaked his head, studying the hourglass on his hand one last time. Swallowing deeply, he replied sourly with a smirk.

"Can't it wait? I'm so close to *my* truth, Winston. Are you going to get in my way again? Dissuade me from my path?"

"No, not this time. Wherever you go, I go. There's nothing I can do to stop ya from choosing this, but I'll be with you no matter what happens. Whatever we find in there will not make me abandon you. I hope you can see what I see, in time. There's a good heart pumping in there, and above all else, you're my friend,"

"Enough of this charade. Guess awaits," muttered the Professor, sweating mercilessly as he slipped through the gate. Did he really think such a parlor trick would work on him? Even if he meant it, it did not matter. Unless... something was growing within–nerves? Feeling in his numb body? It would go away soon. The fruit of his doctrine would soon bloom. Wheezing painfully, he felt his breath threaten to flee his body altogether as he defiantly twisted the door open.

A figure, leaning over the railing of the mezzanine, drew their expectant eyes. Crushed flowers, perhaps the very same nightshades, littered the floor in disorderly patches of yellow petals. As they slowly made their way inside, the thing tapped his cane with pressing urgency. There they were, as expected: Carrion, Loxley's human baggage, and a witless ferryman of the damned. He would show them the truth as he had been shown–the world awaited, after all.

"*My sweet children, have you come for Dr. Guess?*" rasped the thing that may have once resembled a man. Ignoring the rest of the ghoul's features, the Professor's emeralds were transfixed on the hourglass engraved into his lovely mask. Clenching his hands tightly, the Constable put himself in front of Winston, gently brushing him behind. Something inside clicked... this could be Mr. Guess, now with a mask affixed to his face–how grotesque! The windowed faces sang their pain with the roaring wind in chorus with the Professor's echoing cackle.

"Yes, we have certain business with him. You would not happen to know anything about that, would you, dearie?" asked the Professor sarcastically, sneering all the while. His hand danced over his favorite coat pocket, barely restraining itself for the fun ahead. Pointing his wrapped, bony finger at him, the Councilman continued issuing his proclamation of judgment.

"We would indeed! We are the Councilman, speaking and acting for them. Dr. Guess is long since gone, but fear not... We are here now, despite the apprehensions of Ms. Loxley," triumphantly declared the Councilman, stretching an open palm upwards toward his guests with sheer glee. Furious, Mr. Brauer sounded back in righteous protest.

"Keep her name out of your filthy mouth! Whether or not you're Mr. Guess, we're taking you in,"

"I regret to inform you that Dr. Guess is dead... But, not to worry, we are here. Your tender concern is noted; we will make no effort to escape. After all, we are exactly where we mean to be," exclaimed the thing joyously, straining what little his lungs had left to give. Winston grew ghastly pale as the pendant warmed in his shaking hands. It would be time to see her again, soon. He knew it.

"Liar! So caught up in your own delusion, you pitiful worm! I must say, you have gone above and beyond to conceal your identity... Cutting up some old body to fool us? All that lovely brick-laying nonsense? You even dressed the part with that precious antique on your face. All this fanfare and conspiracy just to poison some waters? You really are just a petty serial killer with some clever antics. If *they* are so real, surely, *they* must be too important to bother with you," accused the Professor as he pointed the match back at the talking-thing.

"We do not lie! There is no time for such games. The body at the Cistern is your proof. Is one body not enough? Such a shame that not too much of him is left: the leftovers rest in a watery embrace. Enough idle chat! Let us drink together. You have many questions; we have many answers," replied the Councilman before leisurely

strolling further up the stairway. He had a pronounced limp–
his left foot dragged behind the other. Grinning eagerly, the
Professor took Mr. Brauer by the ear and whispered silently.

"He's a *cripple*. Can't put up too much of a fight, eh?
Running isn't in the cards for him. We can continue to
entertain this, for the time being," said the Professor confidently,
scratching a match head against his coat nervously. They went
up the stairway, past the mezzanine, as the Councilman opened
two grand doors leading to a room that would never be dined in
again. Cautiously, they followed him in.

Taking his place at the head of the table, the Councilman
seemed unfazed by the doors slamming shut behind him. Mr.
Brauer supposed that Guess could have sat there once. Now, his
body would never find rest. Just like with Herbert, they had
failed again. Innocent or not, he had not deserved being diced
up to bits–no one did. The gentlemanly monster before them
was hideous. Who inflicted those burns? If enough of his face
remained beneath the mask, would they even recognize him?
Perhaps it did not matter, anyways; whoever he was would face
justice all the same and pay fully.

A match danced between the Professor's fingers, so easily
slipping into his clutches from his pocket. After so much time,
he could finally unmask the truth. With enough gusto, it could
probably be off in no time, sparing him from any miserable
discourse at all. Philosophy would give way in a single yank...
One good tug, and everything, at last, would be bare. Yet,
a seasoning of theatrics never killed anyone, so he grinned
smugly, waiting eagerly for what would surely come.

Overhead, a hanging purple-gold tapestry covered in little
hourglasses swooshed lazily from the creeping winds. What
little color they held was swallowed by the draining, empty
sockets behind the mask. Discontented, he reclined back like a
sullen disciplinarian, hand resting on his cane like a ruler. The
Councilman spoke.

"*This place–so much history! All so utterly worthless.
Mementos, memories, lives, hopes, dreams, and fears... all gone. Our*

dear Carrion, you are wayward like these things: dead and empty. A husk. You have no purpose..." finished saying the thing with absolute conviction.

"I didn't come here for rhyme or riddle, you freak! You'll breathe only as long as you remain useful. Start talking, or..." said Carrion spitefully before slowly puttering out. He could not manage to finish that thought, yet, that very fear would surely provide the strength he needed! Besides, there was a first time for everything. The big man cursed under his breath before interjecting.

"Enough! This madness has been entertained for long enough. You're overstepping. We're taking this man in, alive. He will face some sort of real justice, even if Reiner refuses to deliver it. This... obsession has consumed you for way too long: let go of it , Professor. I don't want to make this choice for you," swore the Constable, towering above the truly little man before him. After everyone had poured into him, how could he still even consider that as an answer?

"*We are flattered! He wants to slaughter us. Making such a bold change already, now that you have been set into motion. Your answers... Do you remember them, Carrion? All those years wash them away? Let them stay buried; they cannot save you now. That is where the healing starts...*" said the masked man before his words were overwhelmed by raucous laughter from the green-eyed man. Carrion, losing all control over himself, broke his glass on the table, cackling more. He spoke.

"A comedian! Three words! I'll spare you not one more. Who. Are. *They?*"

"*What an absurd question! You truly crave your past life. We are men of change, gifted with clarity in a world blinded by fog and smoke to forsake their past above all else. We wage war for the present while others still cling to lost things. We are The Society!*" declared the Councilman triumphantly with many voices, winds carrying them downwards to oblivion. Winston felt the very last bit of coolness dissipated from the pendant altogether.

It was almost time.

"*The Society...* A fitting name for a bunch of ruffians and thugs, leaving behind every bit of humanity for some unreachable thing? Time is a gift, spent or unspent. This empty hourglass is a lie," said Winston, a formidable lamb before lions.

"*Do not insult us with your petty thinking! Faith buys you nothing, only offering false promises and half-truths about a better world... Action is the only way to change. Let the Past and Future rot, the Present gleams in our palms!*" recited the Councilman feverishly, burning alight with words that were not his own. Pouring himself a glass of wine from a bottle hanging on the wall, he awaited their deluge of endless, meaningless questions to rebuke. He had been taught well.

"Enough of your insipid sayings! Taunt me no longer; I demand an answer! Why have I been marked? What is this poison?" screamed the Professor incoherently, waving a vial that had been in Mr. Brauer's pocket a moment ago. Taking a delicate sip of wine through the narrow slit, the Councilman dabbed the edge of his mask with a handkerchief. Enraged, Carrion marched toward the Councilman until he was restrained by two boulders coming down on his shoulders. How dare Brauer hold him back now!

"*The Serum–our greatest contribution. Power and dominion trapped in a bottle: control-incarnate. Do you not recognize it? Why do you desire to have such painful memories again? You are a free man begging for chains! That mark is liberty, just like ours!*" replied the Councilman, spilling the swishing contents of a vial over the tablecloth, reducing it to nothingness as it sizzled.

"There are some things that can't be controlled... People are one. I would know... Setting people in eternal motion, no breaks, doesn't give them any real choice. Especially by burning their brains half to death," declared Winston fervently.

"*Short-sighted imbecile! So easily it reduces the strongest to feeble children, inclining them to look to authority, to structure. The Society gives them their great purpose! More than endless parables and fairy tales. My body is living proof of the sheer power in the bottle. The strength to build up and burn down! A means to inflict real change!*" screamed the Councilman, voice wavering without any doubt–his path was absolute, after all. Tilting his head, he revealed a bloody seam that followed the edges of the mask, passing his ear. Putrid, burnt flesh poked through the seam of the mask, almost begging to be freed.

Carrion wiggled underneath his own fleshy prison, struggling to break free. His tool had decided to find its voice at the wrong time. A phantom pain scratched at the insides of his formerly burned hand–the audacity! It would not stop him now, no more than some big man's silly pair of hands. As Winston made his way beside them, Mr. Brauer decided that the Professor had folded enough. It was time for a confession.

"So… one Herbert wasn't enough for you, huh? You exploited his father for research and decided his son was too much of a loose end? Once Guess put out, you had no use for him, either?" asked Mr. Brauer, struggling to draw the right words through his holed mask.

"*Yes, of course! They are dead: a lineage best left in the dirt. One's toil resides in the bottle, and the other is filled with it… Meaningless, all of it! His extravagant abode is now a hearse–this one, too,*" rasped the Councilman before roaring with infectious laughter. Shaking his head slowly, Mr. Brauer remembered the old man's lifeless body. He had done him more good than he would ever know. So, while he was dead and gone, he had outlived far more than his home–a true legacy. It was time for his killer to face justice. Winston spoke up for the last time.

"All this bloodshed… for what? Something that takes away such a basic gift? You've lost it yourself, clearly. Do you know what it feels like anymore, mate–freedom? Was what you gave up worth it to birth this monstrosity?" asked Winston with conviction, drawing nearer still to the Professor. As Carrion squirmed, the thing's head shook violently, dangling loosely from its socket. Convulsions seized him; his arms frantically waved, spasms sending them flying in crazed swings–even dashing his glass to the floor. He cried.

"*You cannot fathom the forces at play! We are their chosen* instrument! Freedom is a fair price to pay for purpose in this empty life... What do you have, little man?" screeched the thing, struggling to make the mantras make sense again. Though he was restrained, Carrion's tongue remained loose as ever.

"The world is gnawing itself apart in entropy. What makes you think you can do a damn thing to stop it? There is no order–not here, no... Not anywhere. We have such a tenuous grasp over reality; only a few even have the strength to graze it. That bottle changes nothing! What truth do the *common* folk have? Would they know if it slapped them across the face? Some people are born to be nothing, mere meat-puppets prancing about as the Fates will it. Filling their empty little heads with nonsense doesn't change a damn thing," preached Carrion angrily, emeralds glinting defiantly. Composing himself, the Councilman gripped his cane tightly. His words gushed out, oblivious of themselves.

"*Coward! We are all empty vessels, waiting to be filled. We choose submission; others need a catalyst... a perfect power. A small price to pay for something far greater than preservation... transcendence! You are bound by humanistic fragility, believing your fetters are inescapable. Yet, it is overcome! The Serum, alone, has the power to build up and burn down–inflicting real change... Fate itself brought low by reverent servitude!*"

"Submission? My knee's not bending until it's lopped clean off. Not to you or the Fates themselves... My path is my own! So, spare me your lies, you freakish idealist! No one's redeemable–not worth saving. We're all animals, struggling to hide our shame away. Bunch of bloated pigs content in our troughs, oblivious to every string pull. You see, I know what I am! And, I don't give two shits about changing. Truth is the one thing worth clinging to in this living torment we call life. I'm about to have it. Take it off for me, will you? Drop the language antics... What say thee, o cruelest of bastards?" asked Carrion, worming out of the big man's arms. His tirade continued with each passing step he took toward the silent, hateful thing before him.

"You think, you, alone, know true pain? All of those nasty

burns make you something? Skin deep! Of the flesh! All of them. I've been pierced by different daggers, not of steel, but sterner stuff–leaving scars that will *never* heal... It doesn't matter! We're all fucking broken! But, I'm gonna make it just long enough to have my answers, then it'll be lights out for all I care. Give them to me... Give them to me! Now! Or, I will tear you apart with my bare hands... Answer me, you freak!" screamed Carrion deliriously as he flailed his body toward the masked figure, who fished in his pocket for judgement.

"*Enough of this charade, charlatan. Denial perpetuates every fiber of your being. You know your past, and yet, allow it to consume you wholly–there is nothing left to save. Take my mercy–prepare to be set free from it all!*" declared the Councilman as a revolver, loaded, materialized into his hand.

It fired.

Winston leapt in front of Carrion as the steely bullet tore through the air, thirsty for blood. It bore through the guardian angel, collapsing with him to the ground. Mr. Brauer, frozen in horror, watched the scene unfold before him. Scampering to his feet, the rail-man screeched before ramming the Councilman like an enraged bull, knocking the revolver from his hand. It slid across the floor as the masked thing fell backward while his cane slipped from his fingers. Mr. Brauer fought for control of his own body, struggling to limp toward them, step-by-step. Growling, the Professor bared his fangs, pouncing on top of the animal before him.

Carrion's reddening eyes were murder, and his talons, wet with hatred, pierced deep into the other monster's shoulders. A hideous laugh echoed from his jaws as spittle dripped down his lip. Soon enough, he sent the thing's precious spectacles flying against the wall before the glass exploded into brilliant shards. Struggling to draw breath, the Councilman strained to reach his cane–it was out of reach. He was running out of options.

The former constable limped drunkenly toward the revolver. Any second now, it would all be over. Winston would be fine; he had to be. One more bullet would make the world right again. His cracked hands, scabbed-over in black clumps, shook at the mere thought of using it. He had barely even held a gun... much less fired one.

Wedging his rough nails underneath the mask, the Professor viciously tore at the thing's mask. Unmasking the truth was much easier than he had anticipated! The wounds reopened, bubbles of blood crackling with nervous anticipation. The rail-man paid no heed to his crimson claws, feeling his own blood rush alongside an intoxicating feeling that permeated every fiber of his being.

He claimed his prize. Shredding flesh cried out in vain agony as the mask gave way to a horrific, gory, burned, inhuman face. It was not Guess; in fact, it was not anyone. Strings of dead vessels upheld their claim to the edges of the mask as a crimson pool began to seep from the Councilman's head.

Mr. Brauer was almost there... just a little further. All he had to do was shoot the bastard dead. Surely that would not be so hard? Winston would be good as new; they could patch him up in no time. Red would finally be safe, too. Everything would be okay.

Seizing the moment, the Professor tightened his hands around the Councilman's neck. Thin, blue lines of fat bulged between each finger. The thing continued to gasp and scream which only invigorated the monster to squeeze harder to make more wonderful music, more lyrical screams.

Snatching the revolver from the floor, the big man weakly held it up. It shook profusely in his hand as his trigger finger twitched violently–slippery with sweat. So easily it could have pulled it, should it had been there at all... But it was a stump. So, for the first time in ages, he was acutely aware that it was gone. As the pair struggled on, and the gun continued to bob in his hand, he realized it would not have mattered: he never had the strength to fire it, anyways.

Grunting, Carrion denied the thing each and every attempt at breath. Losing too much blood and air, the Councilman finally wedged his fingers around the cane–pulling a hidden blade free. He slashed the assailant across the face, summoning what little strength he had left to kick the clawed-thing off him. Scurrying to the window, he jumped straight through what glass remained–the rest was lost to the night. Breaking free from his trance, the big man gave chase to the phantom.

Leaving Carrion, a dying Winston, and a mask paid for in blood.

CHAPTER TWENTY-TWO: THE TANGIBLE LOGIC

"**W**inston!"

It was a bad gunshot wound. He was already coughing up blood–lots of it. Rushing to him, the Professor, with a reddening brow, knelt. With his coat, he dabbed at the boy's leaking stomach in vain, yet Winston just sheepishly smiled at him.

"What did I know, mate? That whole 'Bullet Logic' thing must have some merit to it," said Winston weakly, grimacing to form a half-smile. Carrion felt tear after tear slip down his cheeks; he could not hold them back any longer. He placed his hand on his neck to feel a faint pulse. It was not going to last; they both knew it.

"I'm so sorry... I never wanted this. You're not like me in any way. I was supposed to be the one to pay. My body, not yours! This is my fault! I... I..." said Carrion stammering, unable to form the words he needed to say. Winston placed his red hand on the Professor's shoulder, leaving a bloody mark while his other hand motioned him to take the pendant off his neck.

"I told you I would *never* leave you–no matter where you went. You're my best friend. But don't ya get it? I'm about to see her again: Amelia. I've kept her waiting... too long. Death isn't so scary when you're looking at it. Just a shroud, waiting to be peeled back. She's there," said Winston softly before hacking violently as he reclined against the wall. His glasses crept down his nose, eyes reddened by tears of sadness and joy. He struggled to continue.

"This pendant right here–remember how I didn't drink to honor her memory? Suppose it was the only thing that kept me from letting her go. But now, I'm ready. I don't have to carry this cold burden any longer; it's warm where I'm going. You can't live that sort of life, Carrion, a haunted one. Don't let grief *consume* you... Promise me you won't let it, will ya? Promise me..."

His body crumpled over the ground. The Professor smeared his tears on his coat, lamenting over Winston in the midst of his sobbing.

"I abused you for years! You don't deserve this... Every day, I treated you like scum when you were the only person in my life that ever cared–that gave a rat's ass about me! Please, don't go. I can't make it without you. I... I don't have anything, anymore. You can't die! You haven't *fixed* me yet. Please forgive me! Forgive me for what I have done to you! All the unforgivable things... free me from this pain... these shackles–free me!" he wailed as the light dimmed in Winston's eyes. His body began to go limp. With a last triumphant effort, he fought to see the underlying light in the Professor's emeralds one last time.

"I..." said Winston, puttering out as he drew his final breath. As his eyes shut, his body rose, eventually settling on the ground with a newfound calmness. Carrion clutched the pendant close to his heart before taking one last look at his one and only friend.

He fled the mansion as his vision failed, bloody blot by blot. One stubborn bit of gravel, though, had other plans, taking him to the coarse ground. Everything became redder before growing dark. His world continued to collapse around him, giving way to the next.

III

CHAPTER TWENTY-THREE: VERTIGO

Carrion buried his head in his hands. Blood continued to pour out of his forehead, sputtering like a fountain. Even if he had wanted to stop it, he knew it was far too late–which seemed like it was for the best. Hooves pounded in the distance, and he suspected the carriage followed them. Gone, like everything else.

All he could see, taste, and feel was an ashy red. Forcing his eyelids to break the cakey seal that shut them, he saw something in a puddle, the last remnant of the rain: the boy, Thad. He had only seen through him before, but now... He could see him. His eyes were striking, just like his own: green as emeralds but not dimmed. No... they gleamed with a resplendent brightness–hope. Soon enough, the puddle gave way to redness. And then, the boy was gone, leaving the pale face of a ghost: his own.

"Go away. Memories can't hurt me anymore... nothing can!" shouted the Professor spitefully as his consciousness continued to seep out of his head, drip by drip in little plops. Surely, his wounded pleadings fell on deaf ears, if anything listened at all. In any case, he would have to cry out louder to be heard!

"Please, I don't have enough of me anymore! He's dead, buried to waste away! Too little strength, too little fear... *Little* Thad couldn't save anyone, so how could he hope to save me?" asked the Professor bitterly, slipping to the other place without any battle–he had nothing left to fight. Besides, who could win a war against themself?

Sinking...

    Sinking...

        Sinking...

            Sinking...

"Brother-dear, you're zoning out again. Moon must have gotten to your head... Doesn't Mother have enough to worry about?" chastised the boy's sister, grinning ear-to-ear. The body had to speak his words! Such impudent stubbornness–every attempt at seizing him failed. How he longed to be more than an observer, bound to such an empty vessel, some silly meat puppet!

At least there was no pain to distract him this time. Daggers floated around him with edges free to soar. Droplets of blood hung in the balance, too. The aching had at last subsided. Perhaps this was what death felt like... entrapment in a singular moment, relived over and over again for an eternity–no feeling at all.

"Enough for now, I suppose. Mustn't keep them waiting," answered the girl rhetorically, beginning to find her way down the tree. He took one last look at her, invisible tears warming against his skin, to remember her face just before the memory of it would be ripped away forever.

Eventually, she found her way down, calling him some derogatory thing. The Professor felt Thad climb down as the harsh bark carved anchors, white streaks, into his hands far more tangible than mind-mist. Then came the question, right on time.

Who had he become?

Carrion laughed darkly, cursing all he knew. Those words always managed to worm their way back, wholly meaningless and absurd. His truth had escaped with such flighty carelessness... Without it, how could he hope to answer such a silly question? He barely knew who he was–much less who he had become. Oh, green eyes. The boy had them, and he did too. Thoughts weaving together to form a monstrous tapestry, his truth was made manifest.

He was Thad, and Thad was him. Inseparable, coexisting in the same blood and flesh. How could he forget–Thad was their given name. Or, more completely, was he not Thaddeus Carrion? No wonder the boy dragged him back to face the truth; he craved an acknowledgment of his existence from himself.

Now, even the forms were blurring together... What a cruel fate! To see something so pure, so innocent, reduced to a sullied shell, repressed beyond reach! Strength and fear were far too jealous for another voice; the boy was nullified. Thus, Thad had suffered all his miserable choices, without so much as a voice.

Impatient, men in black, greedily stealing the moonlight, emerged around the tree. One rushed for her, leaving Thad for another burly brute to hurl over his shoulder. His weak arms pounded against his muscular back to no avail. She screamed, naturally, but the forest ate her words.

Soon enough, she, too, was snatched as the man chuckled all the while. Thad forced his tear-stricken eyes open one last time to see an hourglass that burned on the man's hand, edges flaring like a red-orange wildfire. Eventually, darkness set in, which did not matter anyways–the duffel bag stuffed over his head denied any attempt to keep the light alive.

He wanted to tell him to hold on–that it would all be okay. But, he would not dare lie to himself. All his pain... just to die in a ditch. What a way to go out.

Then, came the needles... which were not pleasant, but little Thad could barely feel them, anyways. His body had slackened numb against the chair forever ago, bit by bit, as all feeling floated away. The bag was long gone, but it still hung over his face. Sometimes he could almost make out her face, light shining in her eyes but it was so blurry. Words hung in the air.

"These children are weak! Unfit to receive their purpose,"

"They are what we have. Time is of the essence... the others are gone now. Let us keep ourselves grounded on the present,"

"The past is dead,"

"Indeed. Let them stay buried! These children are flagbearers of a better world. This iteration is perfect... It gives them value,"

"A worthwhile risk,"

"For the Present," replied the other voice, which soon faded into Thad's gut-wrenching wailing. As it burned down his throat, stabbing at every hidden thing, he dared to hope the screaming would stop for a moment–a second, even! But, it did not; for not all the cries were his own. So, he gave in to the chorus.

The cold chair was a poor conductor. Not his sister. Mind warping on itself, memories became twisted and entangled into one another. Not his sister. His nails dug into the armrests of the chair as they all faded away. Father, followed by Mother and everyone else–all gone. Not his sister.

"You can't take her from me!"

She was gone, of course, in an instant like dust to the wind. The coin weighed like death in his pocket. Pain, an enveloping fog of honed things, pierced his brain in a suffocating embrace. Memories, poked to pieces, cried out too, but so quickly they were silenced.

Yet, one voice remained, telling him to go on. But, he was too weak. His iron will crumpled into resignation, fears giving way to acceptance. Saying his goodbyes to himself, he gave up. And a burning sensation claimed his hand, overcoming all else, willpower and thought alike.

The Professor woke up.

"He's gone... gone, for good! How much did *they* take from us? From me? Where is she? Where is my sister? My mother, my father? *They* took them from me! *They* took *everything* from me!" screamed Carrion, teeth clattering like little headstones.

He sat in a large green expanse of moss below soaring, four-winged, black birds chirping songs of woe. Two moons shimmered in the sky, reflecting what little light remained in the sky. A dark mountain range, rotten teeth, loomed in the distance, protected by an insurmountable divide.

Studying the hourglass in his hand, he laughed at how ignorant he had been. That fiery mark was the last gift from his most successful procedure, not a tattoo! A boy sat across from him: the usual suspect, Thad. Tilting his head curiously, the boy asked simply.

"Are you... me?"

"Yes, you stupid child. Some part of you must have survived the murder-liquid they shoved down my throat, or should I say ours? Clearly, logic is no factor here,"

"What on earth are you on about? My mother and father are well although I don't think we have the same ones. How did you get here? Was it... hard?"

"Harder than you could possibly imagine. I never wanted to end up here, wherever this place is. Some part of me wanted you to stay buried beneath all those chemicals. Ah, this past of ours is something, isn't it! Or, is it your present? Oh, I'm not brave enough for that conversation, yet. Hallucinations are a beautiful thing. You've been crying out to me for some time now... So, what do you have to say for yourself?"

"Like you said, I'm you: Thad Carrion. I'm seven years old, and I..."

"Spare me! Not a professor yet, eh? You must be some incomplete fragment that slipped through the cracks of annihilation—how remarkable! Have you heard of a man named Winston? Is he here too? Doubt we went to the same place, but who knows? Having to put up with you must be a special kind of punishment,"

"As if. You sound like her; you know that? Always bossing me around. How about this... I'll tell you about Winston if you tell me what's gonna happen to me,"

"What would you like to hear? That you'll end up just like I did: alone in a ditch, bleeding away. No one cares, and no one cries. If you're lucky, maybe they'll let you rest there. If not, the crows will have another rancid meal. That must satisfy you! Or, would you like to know more?" asked Carrion bitterly, seething with pure hatred at the little wretch before him. The little boy broke out into tears as his began hands wildly rubbing at his face. Whimpering, he recoiled away.

"You don't get to cry, weakling! You couldn't even save..." shouted Carrion before stopping himself. Slowly, he rose, walking to Thad. Bending over on his knee, he pulled a handkerchief free from his pocket. Dabbing at all of the teary-wet splotches, the larger Carrion whispered, nearly silent.

"I... *shouldn't* have said that. Winston cared about you more than you know. He was trying to pick through all of me to find you. Must mean something, I suppose. That's why I want to see him again—before whatever comes next," finished saying Carrion delicately, with all the sincerity his weak lungs could muster. Thad took his hand, eyes slowly meeting a pale reflection of his own. Then, the boy spoke, albeit in squeaks.

"He's past the big hole in the mountains. I've only heard echoes. Keeps to himself,"

"Thank you... That chasm isn't natural, is it? You ever crossed it?"

"No... It is quite deep,"

"Mind over matter, my dear boy. Thinking a bridge into existence will be the easiest thing I do today,"

"I've tried. Strength doesn't get you too far here,"

"Ah, that's a lesson for later, my boy. Watch and learn," said the Professor, raising his free hand to the divide. Within a mere moment, it spasmed violently, each finger twitching wildly with a mind of their own. He fell to his knees to hack violently.

As it turned out, sheer willpower would not be enough to materialize a bridge. Surely, this iniquitous hellscape was his punishment—and like life, there would be no silver lining, rendering him a Sisyphus. Yet, at least he had a boulder. The boy drew closer to comfort himself, but he simply brushed him away, growling.

The ground shook, laughing boisterously at such a feeble

display. Spiraling rocks tore through the ground like wriggling worms, to mock his hand. The boy shook his head before making it known he had been right.

"Told you so,"

"Silence..." murmured the larger Carrion, scratching madly at his sideburns. His words were not enough. Yet, the vow he thought he had discarded remained.

So, his shaking hands, soul-spindles, pulled the pendant's chain around his neck, clasping it together tightly. Breathing deeply, he peered downwards into the gap. The little rat was right–it was resoundingly treacherous. He had to find a way to handle it. The sky faded into deep indigo, moons drawing ever nearer to one another.

"There must be another way," declared Carrion, finding a way back to his feet. Straightening his coat, he began his pilgrimage, step by step. Moss made for a measly foe. Thad shouted to him.

"How do you know you'll reach him?"

"I do not; I must continue as though I do... Guess that's faith, huh?"

"It's not safe,"

"Really? How insightful... Stay here, and I will come back to you. This place hardly seems forgiving–what a lousy purgatory. Though I suppose one can't really get 'deader.' Guess that remains to be seen, eh?" said the Professor jokingly, turning to make one more glance at himself. The mirror had denied him that luxury for ages.

"I didn't mean the gap. There's a voice on the other side of the mountains. Talks for a lot of people. Be careful," warned the boy, causing Carrion to roar with dark laughter. Eyes bulging deliriously, he replied in a jubilant manner.

"Oh, how very delightful! That voice will be silenced soon. I'll start with his precious tongue. I'll take him apart, bit by bit. Already had a promising start in that regard. Disregard the yelps, will you? Be a good boy: I'll be back soon," replied the larger Carrion.

The moons continued to eclipse one another.

CHAPTER TWENTY-FOUR: CONVERGENCE

The lichens soon gave way to jagged, obsidian rocks. Past the pit, dark mountains loomed overhead, too timid to touch the moons.

Carrion was beginning to hear voices–ones he would much rather forget. Perhaps the winds were playing cruel tricks on him, conjuring dead voices to dissuade him from his path. He could not dwell on the spiritual for too long, however, because his shoes had become far too bothersome. The soles had melted away some time ago. Beneath his bare feet, stones hissed with heat, burning toes together. Just as quickly, though, they were snapped apart by the cold ones.

Annoying as they were, none of the sensations could match the burdensome weight cast upon him by the growing subterranean cries below. Such heaviness wanted him on his knees.

"Shut it! Your insufferable cries do little to dissuade me from this path. I am strong! Fear has gifted me much. So, don't bother wasting your breath!" declared Carrion defiantly, angrily trudging forwards. Somewhere along the way, his feet had become fleshy slush, which sunk into the thirsty rocks below. It became increasingly uncertain where his legs ended and the ground began.

The moons grew brighter, like two eyes lighting up with eager anticipation for his each and every stumble. What a lovely spectacle he was! At this rate, he would be slurped up whole, lost to obscurity. But, he did not relent. The show would go on.

So, like a natural performer, he carried on, arriving at the great divide after what felt like an eternity. Time had lost all meaning: hours, days, centuries were all the same. The serrated black pillars, looming in the background, seemed to desperate to chew him up–and spit him out. So, in sheer defiance, he screamed again.

"You think the deepest depths of this pit can stop me from seeing him? Or the highest heights of the mountains? Winston would have gladly done so much more to save me. He would have told me that I was worth it–that I was a good man and worth saving. The misgivings of a moron, no doubt, but coming from a much better man than I could ever hope to be..."

The voices, hecklers, drowned him out effortlessly.

"Is this what you want?" cried Carrion, throwing one of the stones into the abyss. It hung in midair, floating lightly. The smell of his own burning flesh, however repulsive, could not stop him now. Neither could the cool stones which provided little solace as they numbed what remained of his limbs still.

"I don't care if it takes a million of these bloody things and an eternity to place them. This place is scenic! Why be a complaining bastard when I can be a working one?" said Carrion as he began to carry more stones over. He would build a bridge! Perhaps his mind was unable to conjure a real challenge, after all. Satisfied, he continued talking to himself, to the amusement of all.

"How many would kill to see their mind–to see the horrific machinations that provide for the spinning of the wheels? Even their grinding is a perfect song. I truly am an ungrateful son of a bitch," said the toiling man, strained by stones that only seemed to grow in weight. It made for a shoddy distraction from the voices, particularly the loudest critics. Those wailing banshees could keep their silly rocks; surely, he did not need all of them.

How many eternities would go by before their voices gave out? His own was already puttering out. Bending down for breath, he heard crackles beneath the torn earth. Putting his dry lips against one of the cool stones, Carrion answered one of the most familiar echoes. If he were lucky, it would be enough to shut them all up for good.

"Mother, my time with you was cut short. Clearly, life had different intentions for me than you did. Don't worry anymore! That scared boy you knew is gone–long since dead. I'm far better off now. Perhaps some of your stories of great heroes of yore finally wormed their way into my head. Yet, I must confess that I don't know quite what to do with my birthright: this heart. It *begs* me to stop. Who am I kidding? You'd be disappointed that I tried to throw away the one part of you I still carry. Still, it clings to me. There might be time… Ah, don't worry about me anymore! My sister must need attending to. You will not be forgotten again. Goodbye, find peace," cried Carrion, feeling the words slip loosely through his crackled lips. One voice sizzled away into the wind. Yet, the screams did not falter. Eternity hurdled forwards with indifference–so too, did Carrion. The bridge grew stone by stone until one voice, particularly influential, got so loud that it earned a bit of the limelight.

"Father. I didn't become the man you wanted me to be. That probably won't change. 'Lies aren't becoming of a man like me,' eh? Oh, I was the runt of the litter, then. Now, I'm hardly better; the whole 'professor' thing is probably a sham in itself. Well, at least I'm still kicking–at least, I think I am. What else do you want to hear? Praise for you working yourself to damn-near-death? I never knew you, but you managed to feed me. For that alone, you're a much better man than I'll ever be. Guess you really knew more about sacrifice than anyone else. Go, then, and labor for them! Mother must be famished. I have no more need of you. Goodbye," cried Carrion, head hung in exhaustion. It was time to make use of that unfortunate streak.

The stones had grown so terribly cold, claiming his fingers

one snap at a time. He had to work faster: stumps would hardly do the trick. Surely, a few more centuries would yield a bridge–it had to. In vain, he tried to drown out the final voice with his own. It was not her show.

"Symbolism in my own mind? How wondrous! Are these stones my mistakes, my sins? Do my plights amuse you?" questioned the Professor sorrowfully, quickly throwing a particularly blistering stone back down after a particular voice, hers, eked through a fissure.

"No... not her! Plenty of these things are about for construction. That rock isn't special; it *can't* be," whispered Carrion, nearly pleading. His hands, formless and fingerless things giving way to structure, continued to pass from cinder to ice. Every remaining stump was as entangled and entwisted as the eternities that joined them. The voice grew louder, demanding acknowledgment. Something, likely blood, dripped from his ears.

"This is my mind! Not hers... One damned voice can't stop me. See, the bridge is nearly complete. You can't deny me this, dead-thing! You are nothing more than unspoken words. So, come then, phantom! Call me a failure!" screeched Carrion deliriously, lip quivering in sheer fear. The earth, clearly offended by his lousy display of bravado, booed before swallowing him up.

He fell beneath the sands. The voice... it was undeniably hers. His body fell limp, feeling fleeing from his weakening frame. The marked hand clutched above the searing stone, struggling to pull himself free. Strength spent, he relinquished himself to the mercy of the suffocating maw around him. Then, it spat him out. Gasping for breath, Carrion clambered upwards, choking on sand and words alike.

"Sister, oh, my dear sister! Here we are, reunited at last–in life, death, or some half-space in between. I could beg for your forgiveness, but I'll spare you my pathetic pleadings... Penance is action, after all! You weren't always nice, anyways. Ah, worry not! Your vicious wit lives on, for now, in me! You know, it baffles me how our folks saw your edge but not mine. I've honed it since, so it's rather unmistakable now. Not for my own good, but for the good of others! A burden I bear for everyone! I will never allow someone to be taken from me again. I can still save Winston… and avenge you. Those men, those roaches… I didn't have the strength to save you then, but now I do. They'll sleep with maggots… I sure wasn't a good brother for the little time I knew you, but it doesn't matter now. Arbiters of vengeance face their proper punishment too, after all. Well, your life will not have been taken in vain–you hear me? Rest well, wherever you drift," declared Carrion as his limbs found form. The last stone rested in his hand. So, for the last few years, he made his way across the seemingly infinite bridge. He gazed upwards; the two silvery moons fully eclipsed one another, becoming one. From the remains of his hand, the stone fell into the last place it could fall into. It was done.

The bridge chimed. Falling on his knees, Carrion sobbed uncontrollably. Each tear sizzled against the gleaming black stone. Strength nor fear had made the path before him. No… It had come at the cost of another empty vow that he thought would merely clog his throat and stay his feet. Yet, Winston… He might be saved, still. One final voice found his ears.

"You did it! The abyss, the chasm, has been bridged. We're connected now. You faced your past… our past… and survived," said Thad gleefully, laughing as his apparition faded away into a sudden gust of wind.

"Wait! Boy, come back!" screamed Carrion as Thad's voice echoed from inside, reverberating. Clutching his chest, he wiped his messy tears on his coat sleeve. Drawing himself to full height, he peered into the abyss.

Some things would remain lost forever, swallowed up by the dark. Yet, each and every stone he paved represented a small part of something that survived: whispers of a name, bitter regrets, faint traces of a mother's warmness, wayward dreams yet unrealized, and hope of a better future. Voices were free to soar, no longer bound by earth and stone. They had coalesced, becoming one thread, weaving rock and memory together into a bridge that dared to cross the chasm.

Whether he knew it or not, Thaddeus Carrion was whole again.

Yet, still so wonderfully broken.

CHAPTER TWENTY-FIVE: SMALL MIRACLES

F ailure.

When he was a member of the force, Mr. Brauer would have made a report, producing paragraphs of paperwork all dodging that simple word. Now, the word seemed to suffice, burdened by unimaginable horrors he could never forget.

Winston was gone... His murderer had slipped out of that window with such grace–ease, even. Blood caked over every part of his face, he had still managed to waltz away without a care in the world, from the second story, no less. Naturally, the rain still lingered in the wretched clouds.

Nothing had prepared him for this, nothing at all. When he had trudged his way back to the manor, everything was gone: Carrion, the carriage, and perhaps most surprisingly of all, the body–gone. He had failed every oath he had ever taken. The one time he was needed, he failed, seized by cowardice. Reiner was right: he did not deserve a uniform.

Yet, there was still one person he could save now: Red. Bounding down the sidewalk, he found plants shriveled beyond recognition, crumpling against the turbulent air of his steps. As orange light broke itself free from the horizon, continuing to bathe its lost children in light, they remained lifeless as ever–except for one, a blue-white beauty that threatened to hurl itself at the sun.

Home was so close now. His fists ached painfully; he had no idea what to say.

"Red... I..." practiced Mr. Brauer softly under his breath, words puttering out as they convicted him of their lateness. No, it was all wrong. Beginning with her name was rather presumptuous, considering how he had treated her. Surely, she would slam the door in his face, leaving him with nothing left to fight for. There had to be a way to soften the blow. The big man dangled the ring gently in his hand, slipping it from one finger to the next. So many broken secret things made for quite a weighty thing, indeed.

"I'm sorry for..." whispered Mr. Brauer carefully, choking on each simple syllable. What good could declarations be to nearly a decade of discord? How would sweet words do him any better than they had before? Nothing he could say would ever be good enough, but it would beat saying nothing at all like he had for years. He needed her more than ever...

Then, he saw a figure coming closer to him, covered in heavy coats, among other things, with his shades...

"Red?"

She quickly threw off the scarves and the heavy shades as she ran up to him. Wrapping her arms tightly around him, she laughed as her eyes grew wet.

"I found you! I found you..."

"Red, I don't..." said Mr. Brauer before she drew him closer in her arms. She could finally feel his warmth again. And, as her tears climbed down his neck, he could almost swear, for one beautiful moment of old comfort, that the rain had returned. The loss was permeable; it was more than real.

"No. Don't say that. I found you, and you're safe–that's all that matters. Let's get home now. We're no strangers," said Red slowly, cautiously releasing him so they could make it the rest of the way home.

She figured that healing words, like barbed ones, were best delivered at a steady pace. If she had spoken too fast, it would have been another meaningless, vain expression falling on expectant ears. Conversely, burdened words would have provided enough time for him to be lost again–perhaps out of reach, forever. So, silence suited the walk back just fine; there would be plenty to discuss soon, and they both knew it.

Hearing footsteps behind hers as their door creaked open, Red found her breath. As his body collapsed over the fraying sofa, which creaked under his weight, she knelt beside him as the big man spoke.

"Red, I don't where to start... No matter what she used to say, words never came to me naturally. So much has happened... But, I still have you. You're still here," said Mr. Brauer thankfully, clutching her hand tightly. He had never felt so much pain and joy together in his entire life. Such bittersweetness drained him like nothing else.

"I know. Words aren't enough sometimes," sorrowfully replied Red, placing her soft hand along his rugged face. Her nails, clipped cleanly, allowed her fingertips to finally meet the terribly unfamiliar, hairy surface that rested beneath. His face slowly crinkled into a weak smile as his eyes met hers. In-kind, his fingers ran up her neck to her porcelain face, amazed it was not iron-wrought after all. He grew flush before speaking.

"This is different. It's been so long,"

"Too long. You sound... different. I had almost forgotten what you felt like,"

"I had too," replied Mr. Brauer, shifting slightly. He would have to relearn his old tricks now. Suave charm had no place in a loveless marriage, but now... Perhaps it would have a chance at a new life once more. Red tilted her head, playfully feigning annoyance with a smirk. Leaning forwards, he twirled her hair, nearly snagging it in the process. She grinned before realizing that her husband had much more to say–something more pressing than the news of the distant yet ever-nearing birth of their child. Buried words dug themselves free from his mouth.

"It wasn't your fault that we drifted apart. When mother passed away, and we tried so hard to conceive... All I had left was whatever purpose Reiner saw me fit to perform. So, I tried to live up to everything he believed about me–and up to what I thought you saw, too. Somehow, I thought my whole world could be made right by company, promotions, or even drinking... How wrong I was. As you kept knocking at my big, stupid head, all that kept banging around in there were silly thoughts of being some great man–when I wasn't even the man you needed!" bitterly exclaimed Mr. Brauer, sinking deeper into the sofa. Red shook her head, breaking into fresh tears, not of sorrow but joy.

He sounded so much like his old self–his old mannerisms and expressions had come home, too. Beneath the pain in his words was feeling, and for that alone, she was thankful. Yet, his wounds were so raw; she had to help him heal. Swallowing, she tried to think of a few magical words that would wash them clean, but they did not come to her. So, a few more could not hurt.

"Honey, it wasn't just you. I couldn't find a way to help you out of it. All my prodding and pettiness only drove you deeper into sleep... I was so concerned with dragging 'you' back to me that I didn't think about where you were, to begin with. I should have looked past myself more..."

"No! You gave more than enough... years. I was so overwhelmed by it all, you barely reached me. I felt like I was being swallowed up; everyone needed a piece of me. There wasn't enough to go around, and that worthless promotion only managed to make things worse. Drinking made for a sorry solution... Though, even there, I couldn't escape anything. There's a silly little heart etched on the table at Stanton's. Could've been done with a fork, for all I know. It reminded me of us when we would have been the sort to make such a thing, if you catch my meaning. In all honesty, I wanted to forget you; I will never forgive myself for how hard I tried... But, I couldn't. I need you–now, more than ever... There's something I have to tell you,"

"I'm all ears. And, there's something I have to tell you, too. Tell me everything first, though. We've got all the time in the world," replied Red, realizing that her news was no longer a burden that she alone would bear. Perhaps it would be a blessing after all.

The pair embraced tightly. Mr. Brauer felt the hair rise on his hands, covered in dark red lines of blackened scabs. They had stopped hurting but had not fully healed. Red turned a burgundy shade as she caught a twinkle in his good eye. Her eyes drifted briefly to the other before she could catch herself. Immediately, his face, too, reddened a bit like a tomato as he turned away. She shook her head before leaning closer to stare directly into his island, without a hint of doubt or disgust. Breathing in, she made a declaration she should have made to her husband long ago so that he would never wilt under someone's gaze again.

"When I first met you, you had a silly pair of glasses on. I couldn't half-see your face... just that mane of yours. Sort of figured you were blind at one point. The day you asked me to walk the market with you, you had the bloody things on. Of course, in some sense, you were blind, so as you tripped, they came tumbling off. You look just as red now as you did then, but you have no reason to be ashamed. I married every part of you. I've done a poor job of showing that these past couple of years, though, haven't I? All my stupid insults and games have made you hate something that's beautiful–something that's uniquely yours. If that eye is so damn unflattering to the world, let them gawk at us! I don't care what they think. I only care what you think about it, now," comforted Red rather brashly yet gently. He blushed proudly, color rushing to his face. Overwhelmed with reinvigorated love, he felt his words gush out like blood from an open wound. All the newfound warmth was soon lost, replaced by numbness that threatened to overtake him. The ensuing words broke them.

"Winston's dead. Carrion is missing..." said Mr. Brauer

bluntly, struggling to keep his eyes off the ground. His chin quivered as he bit down deep into his tongue. Red drew close to his arm, cries barely becoming muffled. That could have been her husband... If she had handed him over to him, he would be gone. The child would have been fatherless–all thanks to her.

They sat there for some time. It got no easier; perhaps, it never would.

Eventually, growling in anguish, the former constable roared at the sky. He raised his hands, the useless things that had never been worth anything to anyone, that could not even pull a trigger, to pound them against the wall once more, finishing the job for good. His knuckles, still horrifically swollen into yellow-blue mounds, cried for mercy. In disobedience, his fingers contorted over one another, half-trying to form fists– meaty things that would do the trick, once and for all. They would be gone; no more empty lies of strength or power left to swindle him. Pulling it back, he sent it barreling forwards, yet, despite his intentions, his fist would not budge. He blinked in pure shock.

Red held it back, alone. He could hear her gasping for breath against the sheer force and iron willpower driving his hand. Every vein in her arms pulsed like little blue suns of sheer adrenaline. Her teeth sharpened against one another as she cried out in pain. Eyes widening, arm falling back, he stumbled backward, collapsing to the floor. She wept.

"Never again... Never hurt yourself again. I don't know anything, but I know you can't do this again–not again. You know, I heard all of it? I still did nothing. As you broke your hands on the bricks, I did *nothing*! I had the audacity to think you got what you deserved. If anyone deserves that sort of pain, it's me! You deserved someone whole–not a broken mess like me! So vain, so empty, craving some stupid dress shop... I couldn't give you *anything*. When your mother passed, I... wasn't even there. I wasn't even able to give you a child. What sort of woman am I? What kind of wife am I? How can you even bear to look at me? To think anything I'd say would be worth spit now... You don't need me at all–never did. At least, when you leave, you'll never have to see my horse teeth again. You'll never hear my poisonous words ever again. You'll never hurt yourself... for some *horrid bitch*. Never... never, never... again..." cried Red as she, too, hit the floor.

She shook violently, teeth gnashing as saliva dripped down her lip. Viciously tearing at her own hair, she began to line the floor with ginger tufts, eventually crumpling into a ball as her hands just kept swinging. His own hands shaking, he gently held her raging fists, full of red-orange streaks, still. Trembling all the while, he reached his arms around her, pulling her as close as she could be. From the ashes and embers, a small warmness grew. Stillness set in. It was enough.

Grunting, he lifted her up to the sofa. Her eyes stilled, followed by her flaring nostrils. They breathed in deeply, together, one by one, until breath felt like breath once more. Mr. Brauer spoke his peace as she clung to him closer.

"Don't ever destroy yourself for someone like me... I'm not worth it. Red, you spent so much time trying to reach me that you forgot to look after yourself, all these years. You could've started that shop already if it weren't for me... And now, for a moment, we tricked ourselves into thinking all the pain could just wash away, yet here we are–on the ground, hurting ourselves. I suppose both of us had hoped every little broken thing would be mended by touch, by words. Guess it's not so simple. We both have a way to go, don't we? It'll be one hell of a journey, but don't think for one moment that I would leave you to face it alone. We are far too messed up to heal each other... But, together, we can share our burdens–and for a while, that'll have to be enough. All we've got to do is stop hurting each other... and ourselves. Our mistakes don't have to decide where we end up. What I said to you that night was unforgivable... There won't be a day I forget it. And, frankly, I'm in nearly as many pieces as I was then. But, I *need* you, and I hope you still want me. Perhaps, together, we have a chance to make things right again. A chance is worth fighting for," said Mr. Brauer softly, stroking her hair gently. She clutched her belly before murmuring into his ear.

"Yes. I'd like that very much,"

Red straightened her back against the sofa, running her fingers through her hair to see how much she had lost. It could regrow. Given the right care, anything could have a chance at a second life. The plants, shriveled beyond recognition, still clung to life. So, surely they could too.

"I was so lonely while you were gone. Somehow, you felt further away than you ever had. I felt locked inside even though I had a key. Everything was barred, covered in locks of my creation. Guess that's what being a prisoner feels like–waiting, hoping, dreaming that one day, everything would go back to what it was, without the faintest idea of how to get there,"

"You are no prisoner. You'd waste your life waiting for me to come back while I drink my life away. I *don't* want to go back to that well anymore. I should never have left you in that place... I can't believe you waited,"

"I have waited years for you to come back–a day is nothing. Still, trying to make things better is not going to be easy. Improvement is going to have to start with both of us being decent. I haven't thought about stuff like that in a long time,"

"Yes... Hard as it is, we must have hope," replied Mr. Brauer, eyes wetting as he realized just how much he sounded like Winston. That starry-eyed man somehow had managed to stay bright in such pervading darkness. Now he had been snuffed out, yet his light continued to shine. Swallowing deeply, he knew what to say. If mother could hear him, she would have been proud.

"You know, Winston had a wife at one point... She had passed away, and he was there, no less. Never would have guessed that when I first met him, but he had been through things we have been fortunately spared from. Can you imagine that? Still managing to smile and laugh after all of that? He knew something was keeping him,"

"What do you mean?"

"When I lost the murderer in the market, I went back to Guess's place. Carrion was nowhere to be seen; blood was all over the floor. It was awful... I wanted to throw up. I made my way up to the second story, then–I don't know how to say this. Winston's body was gone, like it had never been there. I checked every room. Eventually, I made my way around the grounds. He simply vanished,"

"Vanished? Honey, he died. He couldn't have..."

"I know. Someone must have laid him to rest. I don't know who, and I don't know how, but Red... something about that gives me hope enough to believe we'll be all right," slowly said Mr. Brauer as fire erupted in his heart, invigorating his soul with searing sparks of love and passion. As his color was restored, his eyes began to see, causing the formerly dingy, grey room to erupt in newfound warmness. Red's hair grew into a familiar, lovely golden-orange. He leapt into his moment of clarity.

"There is some good in us, this town, this world, still. Something or someone good is looking out for us! Even drowning in crushing despair, good somehow persists. His body wasn't just left in filth. He was taken care of... Is it so crazy to think that we might be taken care of ourselves? I just can't believe that everything is just all rotten, all cruel. Everything may seem like a mess, but some things must happen for a reason. We were meant to meet, and everything that has happened since must have meaning to it. What we've gone through doesn't determine our future, but we can step from it to something better,"

"After everything... how can you believe that?"

"Red, how can I not?" asked Mr. Brauer as the pair held each other tightly. Foxtrot, still a lively sort, came in barking obliviously. They were both quite happy to see him, and he was particularly happy to see the big man again. As he swaddled the little thing with his delightfully oafish arms, Red fought the urge to laugh. It would come out pained, but she could not help herself. A squeaky little giggle found her way out from her lips. Soon enough, his rather boisterous laughter joined hers. At that moment, she knew it was time. She spoke up.

"Art. There's something I need to tell you," said Red cautiously, catching how his island jostled when he was greeted with something so terribly foreign yet familiar: his name. She would try to use it more.

"You haven't called me that in a long time, Ms. Loxley. Sometimes I forgot I was even called that, once,"

"Now, now... you were the one who insisted I call you 'constable.' Said it made you sound more important,"

"Ah, but I'm not trying to fool anyone now, am I?"

"I never knew why you were so concerned. It seems to me your hands could do all the talking,"

"They still can," replied Art as Red took his hands, scarred and all, and looked into his eyes. Whatever news his mind could have possibly dreamed of, it paled in comparison to the reality that his heart had craved for so long.

"I'm pregnant!" gleefully shouted Red as his eyes widened with amazement. Hoisting her up gently, he swung her around, thankful he still had some strength left in his hands to do so. He certainly was not ready, but at that moment, everything was just fine. They had each other, for now.

"I'm a father. Arthur Brauer, a father. Red Loxley, a mother,"

"Brauer... Red Brauer."

CHAPTER TWENTY-SIX: CRUX

The black columns solemnly cast their judgment on him. Their spikes cut deep into the sky, bleeding light between their peaks. Scampering off the bridge, Thaddeus Carrion gazed upwards. The twin moons were truly indistinguishable from one another, shining together as one with resounding finality. They could never be separated now. The horizon continued to roll backward, always managing to just be a bit further away. How it taunted him! Yet, his bare feet, charred beyond recognition, carried him forward–their numbness, nearly reassuring. He had felt pain over lifetimes, thousands of years, which he supposed nearly marked the first second of eternity.

"Life and death, good and evil, strength and weakness, bravery and fear, action and inaction. Tell me now, o cruelest of bastards, where are they now? In this hellscape, these 'virtues' are no more. What remains? A vengeful husk who carries a meaningless truth. My guilt is as eternal as this place–beyond time, beyond meaning, beyond death," whispered Carrion as his hand clutched onto a shelf on the mountainside. The hourglass burned brightly below his gnarled, twisted fingers charred beyond recognition. It condemned him. Each blackened chunk of rock, bathed in moonlight, bent around his fingertips, beckoning him upwards. Winston was there... Who else could deliver his passage? All he had to do was claim it.

"Oh, silly Councilman–hiding here, in this desolate place. You cannot escape me. I will tear this world apart, piece by piece, until I find you, rending it all to nothingness. My family, my sister... They will be avenged. Winston, I'm coming for you!" shouted Carrion, hearing his weakening voice echo ever upwards. Surely, he was able to hear him now.

The summit was in sight now. As frost and ash alike choked his throat, he climbed on. As his bloodied eyes winced open and shut, fluttering as if they may never open again, he climbed on. As phantoms, the dead and living alike, taunted him, he climbed on. He had nothing more to lose. What could hope to harm him now?

Wedging himself over the ledge, he rolled over to fight for breath–something he might have taken for granted once. Gasping, he smirked weakly at such lovely irony: he was fighting to be alive in a place where he was almost certainly dead. As he scrambled to his feet, he was greeted by a familiar, clamorous noise.

"*Coward! All this talk from a dying man, living for nothing. You are a shadow, a speck of emptiness, drifting from vacancy to vacancy. What can you ever give meaning to? You could never save him; what hope do you have for yourself?*" wailed a particularly raspy phantom in the wind. Carrion swore he would make him regret every twisted word that came out of his filthy mouth. Seized with anger, he marched onwards with new determination. Wrath was beginning to become an old friend. Perhaps it would be possible to rip the mask off a second time. If not, he would have to settle for his face.

Eventually, he approached a clearing. It warped itself violently as rocks tore into shapes. They folded into one another, creating an hourglass. Slipping apart, the stones beneath

Carrion's feet oscillated, bucking him downwards. Rearranging one last time, the fragments interlocked to form a black gate. Fog seeped out, creating a misty-haze that sought to envelope him. On the top lay a single word, carved in thousands of chippings and cuts: *ruin*.

"Come now–face me. There are no more bodies to take your bullets,"

Without hesitation, Carrion journeyed inside. Things became even stranger. Plains of jade flowers dotted the ground, swinging rhythmically but emptily. The moon, hidden high above grey clouds, remained barely visible. Dark blots in the clouds promised rain but seemed hesitant to let it go, perhaps frightened that the flowers would merely drink it up. A few stones raised from the ground, floating in wonky circles, to form a pedestal for its object of reverence: a revolver.

"A gift? How thoughtful. It can deliver my gift to him!" said Carrion crazily, slowly brandishing his newfound weapon. Spinning the cylinder open, he emptied all the rounds, save one. They clinked gently, one by one, slipping down the petals before sinking into the ground. Carefully putting the cylinder back into place, he spun it gently one last time. Pocketing the revolver in his coat, he continued onwards, chuckling to himself all the while. Perhaps he cared for himself, after all.

"I suppose I should have kept a spare. What am I to do with myself after this? I am certainly worthiest of the next one. First, I must play savior... or rather, executioner? I suppose there's no difference!" said Carrion darkly as laughing soon devolved into wheezing–his lungs had long since been spent.

He skipped blindly through the greyness until a throne emerged. Before it, the masked thing and a stumbling man with glasses beside him. It was Winston... At long last, things could be made right. Every eternity had converged to this singular moment. The thing offered its last few caws.

"The broken man presents himself at last,"

Without hesitation, Carrion withdrew his revolver from his coat and prepared to fire it, but Winston leaped in front of him, stretching his arms out wide. Whatever he screamed, he could not hear it... Not that it would have mattered, anyway.

"Get out of my way! Not again!" screamed Carrion as he threw Winston aside without a care in the world for where he would land. Squeezing the trigger, he painted the throne red. The mask exploded into green-crimson shards as the body crumpled on the ground. A pool of blood issued around what little remained of his head, soaking into the crevices.

The flowers gulped it down before the petals burst in sick explosions of crimson color. Clenching the revolver, he bent down to Winston, offering his good hand–the one not marked.

"Winston, I am here for you. Please, come to me," pleaded Carrion, frantically trying to part the greyness with his flailing arm in vain. It continued to slosh all around him as Winston continued to sink farther into it. Hacking violently, he felt his lungs burning, filled with sulfur and soot.

"Please. Forgive me, now!"

"I can't believe I ever had hope for you. You're just like him; you know that, mate? The line's been crossed... There's no fixing you now. You were right about one thing: the lot of you all are animals! Except only one of you is breathing, and the other one isn't–you've seen to that, haven't you?"

"I had to! You could never hope to understand. He had to take the bullet–he earned it, even more than I did... Stop hiding from me! I saved you; *save* me!"

"Away from me! I wasted my life for yours... You're a wasteful thing, aren't you? So many excuses–you bloated bag of lies! Perhaps you fooled me too, feeding me bits of hope, but deep down, you always knew what you were: broken. I've got nothing for ya. Begone from this place!" screeched the figure as it evaporated into the mist. The grounds trembled, oscillating like the palpitations of a heart. As laughs echoed all around, the clouds released their icy tears violently, pelting the flowers to death. Climbing from foot to knee, the water began to engulf his entire body.

Perhaps Thad, or rather himself, was right: this was a

suicide mission. Clutching awkwardly at the revolver, he raised it to his temple. In vain, his glistening fingers pulled the trigger over and over–each time, he winced with disappointment. Laughing at the Fates one last time, he closed his eyes. Yet, as he began to feel the water inflate his lungs, he was glad. His limbs began to float upwards, growing stiff. Darkness setting in, his mind came to a simple conclusion: he would never find peace, in this life, or the next.

Hurtling back…
Hurtling back…
Hurtling back…

Hurtling back…

CHAPTER TWENTY-SEVEN: THE REVEREND

L ights danced, sloshing from greens to blues to yellows and back again. A thin white veil enveloped it all, letting the chromatic blobs bounce about it even more. Planes and frames intersected and crossed like ripples of waves, disorderly yet determined.

This must be death in proper–far more peaceful than he had imagined. No more searing stones or endless bridges of matter-thought left to torment him... Yet, even this could not be death as he supposed it should be because pain remained. This could not be the end. There had to be something more.

A bell chimed: it was holy. He felt his eyes strain to open against the darkness as something started to take form. Spots of light crossed a thin barrier, though not weightless... no, it stretched, as if it wrapped tightly around his head? It must have been fabric... specifically, bandages. His fingers tingled, nails catching against one another, as his chest began to bob up and down like an engine given new life.

The sound of steps grew closer. Shaking vaguely upwards,

his arms managed to rip the cloth off his face, granting him sight. His eyes adjusted slowly, painfully. A sloping wood ceiling lay above, making him feel quite small. Stained glass, in quite an assortment of colors, painted his face many hues. Taking a deep breath, he strained to pull himself up. A booming voice overtook the other noise.

"Oh goodness, you're awake. You had me quite concerned, in all honesty. That cut runs deep, and worse yet, Dr. Herbert isn't here to lend a hand anymore… Rest his soul. You owe your life to a miracle and… his teaching. I stitched up your forehead the best I could. Everything I know came from him,"

"Who is there? What do you want from me? Apologies, dissertations, poetics? Do I have to deal with that little shit again?" shouted Carrion deliriously, trying in vain to escape his cushy prison. The blanket was as heavy as it was comfortable, making for a formidable opponent, indeed. The man eased him back downwards, placing the bandage back on his forehead, not over his eyes. His prayers had been answered; the cut looked better.

"You're not dead although I imagine you're in shock right now. My name is Reverend Sharp. I'm the minister of this here town," slowly explained the burly, yet kindly, man as he took one last nervous glance under the bandage. It would make for a gnarly scar.

"You're not real. This must be the waiting room–for judgment, I assume! Are you here to make me look presentable? Don't waste your time. I was on the wrong side of the wager, I suppose," sluggishly said the Professor as he felt his words continue to slur.

"You're not dead! I'm not God either, just a helping hand for Him here on earth. Take a deep breath. There is nothing to fear now. You just need some rest," reassured the Reverend, seeing Carrion squirm under the blanket as if it burned him. Eyes continuing to dart around frantically, he replied callously.

"I guess I'll have to take your word for it. Assuming I'm not dead, you have my undivided attention… Ah, what has happened to me? It takes so little these days to take my ear. Say, Mr. Reverend, have you ever talked to yourself? Like, in your mind? I..." said Carrion, as his voice cracked before giving out entirely. The kindly man asked him to open his mouth before pouring warm liquid down his throat. His stomach rumbled a little less as he felt his back start to relax.

"In due time, I will tell you everything I know. For now, the only thing that matters is getting that cut to look better. I'll be back to check on you in a couple of hours. Sleep well," said the Reverend, drawing the bandage back over Carrion's emeralds.

"Wait!" shouted a voice that Carrion figured only he could hear. Sleep overtook him, but rest remained out of reach. Silence drowned his thoughts, save for the abhorred echoes, gurgles, of things lost.

"*You're scared of living... For Winston... No one ever loved you, did they... As you wish, master... I don't drink to honor her,*" screamed the voices, all fighting for control. Yet, above all, one remained. It did not cease nor yield. As his teeth gnashed away, he tried in vain to put his hands over his ears. Sadly, the whirring in his ears did not stop nor the voice... It was all the more dreadful, carving into his soul without remorse.

"*Believe that whatever comes of this mark, or anything else for that matter, there's a good heart in ya,*"

"No! I couldn't save you then... I couldn't save you now. There was never any hope of 'fixing' me... You spent your life on such a *wasteful* thing. Nobody cared for me except him!" shouted a crazed Carrion. He flailed like a fish upon the mat, throwing himself off the side of the bed. Curling into a ball on the ground, he continued to bawl uncontrollably. The yells soon devolved into shrieks. He was pain made tangible.

"*Somebody* save me from this!"

Dashing footsteps clacked against the ground creating a distant tempo. Hairy hands gently pulled him by his shoulders, setting him upright. Behind circular spectacles, his speckled blue eyes peered into Carrion. Disgusted by his concern, he tried to voice protest, but his words slurred into nonsense. Sharp spoke for him.

"I'm here. Do not be afraid. You've had enough rest, now, I suppose. Whatever has happened to you–I am so sorry," delicately said the Reverend as Carrion slowly regained his faculties enough to sneer indignantly before setting the old fool straight.

"Don't pity me! Everything that happened was a long time coming. Retribution for my past. I don't deserve to be breathing. I... should be dead although I'm not sure I'm alive. I certainly do not wish to be. Where are my manners? Oh, dear. You saved me, telling me you're not some sort of angel. I don't know if I quite believe you. So, unequivocally, is this judgment?"

"No. I'm just a man–a reverend but a man, nonetheless. You're alive–nothing short of a miracle. What is your name, if I may ask?"

"Carrion. Or was it the Professor? It was Thad in another life,"

"Carrion, try to take a deep breath. Your body is still in shock,"

"Nonsense! I've never been more sober in my life. Humbled, no... hewn upon my own logic. Bullets be damned. I've bridged the gap. There is no going back," cried Carrion vehemently as his eyes grew increasingly bloodshot. His yellow teeth crisscrossed, causing a terrible clattering to echo through the hall. Back arching all around, he began to sob, face down on rather rough tiles.

"Calm yourself!" shouted the Reverend, bellowing so loud that Carrion jerked to attention. Sighing, he muttered a quick prayer softly before placing his hand on Carrion, who recoiled sharply.

"Now, Mr. Carrion. I'm sorry for raising my voice. I just need you to remain as calm as you can. We need to make sure your recovery..."

"Calm? How, my friend, do you recommend I stay calm when he took a bullet for me? A wretch, a fleabag, a liar, and a cheat. An arsonist, would-be murderer, used-up test subject, abusive, good-for-nothing, better-off dead, sack of shit. He should be here. I'm not worth spit! I deserved, no... I earned that bullet. I *wish* I was dead," rambled Carrion as he began to vomit uncontrollably.

The Reverend rushed for a small bucket and eased Carrion's head over it. All the declarations of deprecation fell in, along with the other filth of the body. Every time he tried to speak, nausea overcame his will. Fearing his patient would lose consciousness again, he placed a pillow next to the bucket before pacing the sanctuary, nervously praying.

After a long while, Carrion finally forced his gaping mouth to shut. Pulling a small handkerchief free from his coat, the Reverend dabbed at his mouth. The rail-man's body had caught up with his whole mind. Covering his own mouth with his purple handkerchief, he quickly but carefully carried the bucket away. Eventually, he returned, asking one simple question.

"You feel any better? I thought you were about to lose all your fluids in one go,"

"I suppose I do. That was a first for me–crazy thing. I've never vomited before. Guess all that waste stored up in me, eh?" weakly exclaimed Carrion, sneering, as he seized the armrest of the nearest bench. His body felt weak, but his mind felt sharper after the ordeal. A cool sense of calm had replaced the delirious, all-consuming sense of sorrow. He was certainly not lost to himself.

"Suppose some things are better left unexperienced, but your recovery is what I prayed for..."

"See, I'm going to have to cut you off, right there. I'm not some religious nut. Save your prayers for someone who actually believes in them,"

"Really? You seemed particularly worried about your ever-after,"

"Ah, semantics! I was merely testing..."

"Mr. Carrion. I have one simple request for you: try to be honest. Lies will not serve you in this house,"

"If you want an apology, you will have to try harder than

that. Saving me for some sort of heavenly reward? Do you think I owe you anything? I was ready to pass into nothingness. You denied me my *perfect* death," lied Carrion as he hacked violently. Clutching his stomach, he slumped downwards, closer to the increasingly familiar ground.

"You don't mean that, Mr. Carrion. In truth, I helped you because you needed it. When I saw you bleeding out on my pavement, I saw someone who could not save himself–not a crown. I did not save you for any kind of blessing, and I certainly cannot save you from anything that goes deeper than skin,"

"What is that supposed to mean? Are you a seer, a prophet? Going to spin another yarn for me? Some more fairy tales?"

"No. Carrion, I can bandage you, but I cannot mend your heart. That is what is truly broken. Something is missing,"

"Lies… Lies, most dreadful! I fixed myself. I never needed a good book. I have thwarted the Fates at every turn; my destiny is my own,"

"From what I presume, you have lived your entire life by that accord. Where has that led you? A sidewalk, wasting away,"

"Don't you dare judge me! My entire life has been nothing but suffering. Everyone around me, torn asunder, ripped from my fingers! I felt my sister waste away… pumped full of living death. You know *nothing*. Here, you sit a comfortable distance from reality until it comes to your doorstep–you repugnant hypocrite!" cried Carrion, hissing, as the Reverend sighed gently. If it were only so simple to escape sorrow… No wooden sanctuary could keep him from that.

He had time to reflect on such matters. Apparently, the entire faith had been upended because the Almighty had decided to spare them a few days of rain. His last sermon had been given to an empty room where he was almost certain none of his congregation could hear him. Even the choir refused to come back. Night after night, he pleaded with God to bring them back, rain or not. There was no answer, then.

There was no answer now although it seemed that God had other plans for him. The previous night, he spent in prayer, begging to help someone, when he had heard a stirring outside. As it turned out, the Lord had delivered exactly what he had asked for–at His doorstep, no less. This Carrion fellow was clearly hurt. He knew all too well what that felt like. So, as it turned out, he was exactly where he was meant to be. The Reverend replied softly.

"It would not be the first time I've been called that. You're right, to some extent. I've made a lot of mistakes in this life while telling others to do otherwise. I pray for the conviction to do what's right, and I still slip up. But, every morning when I wake up, I pray to follow through–even knowing that I can't. I'll never be perfect, but He is,"

"Sounds like a loser's proposition,"

"No, it allows His perfect mercy to manifest. This place may seem separate from the outside world... I believe, if anything, that's what draws feelings to the surface. So many people have come through here–some once and others never again. I have learned to live with that. When someone you know for over a decade turns up dead..."

"You don't just find another charity case?"

"No... It's never been easy, never will. Just because I know there's a good shepherd waiting for them doesn't make it any easier. Now, with the rain gone, all I can do is pray they are safe. So, while this suffering is not my own, I bear it anyways as a sheep without the rest of his flock. My shepherd makes it bearable. Darkness will not overtake the light; God is not through with you," said the Reverend warmly as he offered something more tangible than promises.

Leaning down, he wrapped his arms around Carrion's squirming body. Embracing him tightly, the rail-man felt his frame stiffen. He had not been hugged in so long. Instead of fighting, his chest loosened, and the pendant called to him. Pulling back, the Professor straightened his back against the bed. It was not the time to bear that sorrow. He spoke.

"You know, Winston would have really liked you–all that preaching... Such a shame he isn't here to chat. Always sputtering off nonsense about hope. I cannot believe in it myself, but the more I see others… It has some merit–words I thought I was incapable of speaking. You know, I will never believe something good awaits me. But him, wherever he drifts, perhaps it is in peace,"

"There is no greater love than to lay down one's life for a friend,"

"Picked up poetry in your spare time?"

"No, not at all. That's just a verse,"

"Perhaps there is some truth in that book after all, eh? Though I could never have faith in some grand architect beyond my sight watching over our universe with cold indifference, I'm happy you can… and that Winston did," said Carrion, head drooping downwards as a sigh crept through his lips.

The checkered floor beneath him told a different story. Cracked tiles in their blacks and whites cried out. Not in pain but exaltation. Their smudged surfaces told stories, kissed by the trotting heels of the lost. They had sacrificed themselves to deliver their steps. Every crevice, a carving of momentous weight. Burdens were bare on their dingy faces. Bending downwards, he traced his finger along the seam. His nail cut deep into the slit. Pulling his hand back, a small cut had traced the edge of his finger.

"This place certainly tells a story,"

"Indeed. What is your story, Mr. Carrion? Who do you choose to be?"

Who had he become?

Golden silence. The shrieks, the anguish, receded back into nothingness. His present life, consumed with suffering, was decided by his past. How could raw willpower hope to change it now? Truth hidden behind the memories of a child changed nothing. He needed to be whole again, but he would have to settle a while longer for brokenness.

Hatred, as warm as sunlight. How could it not permeate to the deepest depths of his soul? Arbiters of vengeance had to be strong. Yet, he felt weak. Agents of retribution were fearful. Yet, he did not fear. Vows–what were they, anyway? They were bound to fall adrift, dead in the waters, empty and hollow. How could he even honor promises made to the figments of his own mind, much less himself...

An open palm. It beckoned him away, away, away. No, not yet. The burnished figure would have to wait a while longer. Peace and reconciliation were prizes for a clean man, not a dirty one. White silk was for saints. He could never be pure again, not after a thousand embraces by the waters. The red ran too deep, and it was not going to get any cleaner.

The past was dead, yet alive in him. He could never let go of it, but he could still shape it. When he was born, he was formless. Then, the hiss of a branding iron cast him into something. But, the embrace of something just short of an angel shaped him into someone... a person. Perhaps some choice remained yet as the Fates tightened the noose around his neck.

"Mr. Reverend, could you spare your ear for a moment? There are a few things I would like to relieve myself from... some even I may yet do."

CHAPTER TWENTY-EIGHT: ON EDGE

The Councilman gasped for breath, collapsing against the harsh edge of a wooden booth. His chest heaved violently, struggling to compensate for lungs that had long since given out. Steadying his hands, having done so more times than he could possibly remember, he pulled a lighter free from his coat. Unwrapping a bandage, he bit down hard into it while he pulled the blade free over the leaping flame. Satisfied with its roaring reflection, he took the blade and seared his own wounds shut. Without the mask, he was free to scream, but the thing did not–flame brought healing. Or, perhaps some primal instinct, profoundly promethean, had at last seized him. He sighed at the mere thought.

The air tasted wet. The burdensome mask had made such a sensation impossible for so long. His skin had numbed long ago, but unseen droplets made their way through the cracks that cut through his flattened lips to his tongue, where sensation had somehow survived. Little blackened nubs, once called teeth, had served their purpose to protect it, providing one last paltry comfort.

If the rain returned, it could trickle throughout his whole body with reckless abandon. And he would taste it... It could not undo his rotten face, but perhaps it could give new life to something within, deeper still.

He sheathed the blade before running his twitching fingers over the deep blood-red marks buried in his neck. When he was but a boy, his father had told him that a warrior without breath was no warrior at all. If someone managed to take it away, by crude force or love, they rendered their opponent nothing more than defenseless prey, and such things had no power.

If he continued to struggle to breathe, a tracheostomy would be the only way to continue *their* work for a little while longer. When it was finished, he would be free to die. The church loomed over him. Smirking, he wondered how many prayed for a future they could not see, wasting their lives for a thankless purpose, dying without meaning. Yet, he was thirsty–parched, even. So much so that if someone appeared with water, churchman or not, he would have gladly traded his breath for it.

Had *they* not given him his share? Was speaking for *them* not enough? *Their* words seeped into pores and thought alike, burned scorch by scorch into his stubborn skin. *They* had given him a glorious purpose, making him beautiful. Every slice, through the guilty and innocent alike, had provided the means for a better present. *They* had broken the cycle of human fragility! And yet, his thoughts remained dangerously far away from reality, drifting to faraway springs.

"Forgive me for my weakness!" he cried, biting into his tongue. How could he possibly uphold the Code in such a sorry state? He did not dare to speak on *their* behalf–all words would be poisoned by his debility. If only he had the mask! It had chiseled his face into eternal perfection, giving way to *their* words with ease. Now, his own voice threatened to creep through... The sayings would save him!

"*For the Present... For the Present...* For... The Present... For..." he cried out in utter anguish, trying to make the words sound real. Every breath felt shallow, scraping against his insides like a foul razor blade. Cool water, even a drop, mercy-incarnate, would give him a moment of respite... no, relief. If he could stretch his arm far enough, he could pull down the clouds and heavens, dripping with life. Squinting, he tried to make out where the gray line of the earth met the endless emptiness above.

Freedom, autonomy, control–all forsaken for a sliver of purpose. What could the sky offer *them*? Or him, for that matter? Would throwing down the stars to suck their light dry satisfy his unquenchable thirst? No! Ungratefulness had consumed him after everything *they* had done for him. The mask was far too precious a gift to receive another... Yet, if he still had it, he would have been glad to give it up for a drop, too, just moistening the very tip of his tongue.

Behold! As if his secret desire was made manifest, there was a well, a red-brown brick holy site, waiting for its patron. No doubt, it sloshed with watery freedoms and salvation, overflowing with eternal purpose not bound by time or death. Surely, *they* would not see his hands touch it... They worked to free themselves from the terribly dry earth as his back arched upwards. As he slowly arose, his knees buckled, forcing him to clutch his cane. Then, he was certain *they* could see him.

The blade had been given to him at the beginning, reminding him of what supported his each-and-every step. *They* would always be able to speak through sound or steel. Those too stubborn to find true meaning, Carrion and the rest, would all receive the message one day. He was simply a pale reflection of himself, a pity.

Was he himself not just another blade in need of mending? A dull edge hardly created sharp noise; how else could *they* speak and be heard? Surely one sip would not make him a sinner! Trudging his way closer, step by step, he looked longingly at the well, brimming with liberty. Coughing sickly, he felt his knuckles crack as lost souls fought to hiss free.

All the killings had been necessary, each scream merely a chorus to *their* purpose. He had to be certain of that. Mutilations, although grisly, were simply another facet of an unpleasant act done for a righteous cause larger than himself. Even if *they* were wrong... He was just an instrument, after all. Though what remained of his soul, caught in an eternal drought, cried otherwise.

The Society had almost broken him–*their* finest tool and most treasured speaker. Not through use or wear but punishment. When the flames had surrounded him, fingers charring together as the mask was given to him, he wanted to die. It was supposed to make him stronger, yet he had never felt weaker. What a violent crucible! Was he really any better than before? When he was reborn, did he rise as a phoenix or remain smothered in the ashes? Was he any more worthy to speak for *them*? Or did *they* leave him a broken tool with delusions of importance, of power?

Grimacing darkly at his cane, he pulled the blade free, falling back to his knees. Such heretical thoughts: he had been fooled by a mirage! How could he possibly know what was best for himself? He had so easily forgotten what a purposeless thing he had been before *their* intervention. This thirstful lust had consumed him; the fountain was a pile of deceits that threatened to undo everything he believed in.

Studying his reflection in the silver-red blade, he looked into his own eyes and found nothingness. The well had something... There must have been something more than half-truths inside it. Oh, it was within reach now! All he had to do was claim it. The blade, fully aware of his thoughts, answered with steely voices that clattered around his head. He could not silence *their* voices. If only he had more power...

"You cannot leave me–not now. You are far too weak to draw breath without me. Who else would carry your steps? Who else can make you beautiful again? You deserve these things... and so much more. Would you sacrifice your purpose for a drip of life from the well? They have already chosen you, most honored tool, for work. What more could you possibly desire?"

His hands shook violently, trying to sheath the hateful

thing. Soon, it was in the cane, but it kept speaking–even more loudly. If he could release the bitter thing to the barren earth below, his hands could cup together, bringing one last sip of peace. He would not have to be a thing any longer, being called a son one last time.

"Do not relinquish what little power you have left–it is your birthright! Do not dare to hold that gift with such contempt. Cast your shadow over the weak! Rob them, viciously, of what was taken from you. Let not your blade or senses be dulled now. Take me one last time, and finish your task. Overcome the cycle one for something larger than yourself. What is one second in a lifetime? The waters hold no power now. Not for you."

Hobbling to the well weakly, he chuckled to himself deliriously. He had already sacrificed everything for his purpose–what more could he offer to the well? A demand for sacrifice was simply unreasonable! What power did he have left? Without the blade, he was nothing. Surely, he deserved to keep it! After everything that had been taken from him, he was owed such a lovely crown-splitting steel. After all, his greatest power was stealing it from others. How dare the well ask for it? What god could be greater than *them*? With stubborn defiance, he cried out in exaltation.

"We reserve our right to take! For the present," cried the thing before spitting on the ground. With renewed vigor, it marched forward with hardened conviction, face contorting into an all-too-familiar shape. The well's soft voice fell on empty ears. He would kill them all–and relish in it.

So, *their* arbiter of justice passed through the final trial, and a lost man died his final death.

CHAPTER TWENTY-NINE: A LESS-THAN-HAPPY REUNION

Arthur Brauer awoke from hibernation. As his eye adjusted to the beaming orange light, just narrowly creeping through the windowsill, the rest of his body slowly stirred to life. He had hoped it would be match-light, but it was not. Red, still asleep, clung to his arm, so he gently slipped away. Pulling the cover back over her body, he took one last moment to hold her hand. She would have a while longer to rest.

Their discussion had gone long into the night. Reiner had been no more apt to help her than he had him. The Councilman had broken into their home with ease. She had to be taken somewhere safe; Stanton's seemed like the only natural choice unless something else came to mind. Karina's lab was remarkably sealed off... She had been gracious enough to help them so far; she would not abandon them now.

Today, Carrion would be found; he hoped, alive. He had been in such bad shape when he left him... But, for looking so frail, he was a tough old bird. Perhaps someone had stepped in–

the very same someone that put Winston to rest. Mr. Brauer slowly began to dress, hesitantly leaving the raincoat on its hanger. Should it begin pouring outside, feeling like a drenched moron would be better than carting that heavy thing around anymore. It could be company for the shades, now buried deep in the dresser.

A knock, unmistakably, came from the front door.

Taking a deep breath, he withdrew the Councilman's revolver from the nightstand. He hated keeping such an awful thing, but his intuition that *they* would rear their ugly heads again had proved true. No one would touch her. Whoever was out there would have to go through him—every part.

More knocks, one right after the other, sounded.

Clamping one meaty paw over the doorknob, he pressed the gun against the door. Biting deeply into his tongue, he waited for the next knock. In a second, he could throw the door open and squeeze the trigger before the miserable bastard would ever get a chance to lock eyes with him. It cocked, and he was ready.

The last knock dully echoed. He slammed the door open, nearly causing it to fly free from its hinges, as the figure before him fell backward. Readying the revolver, Mr. Brauer pointed it straight at his head, preparing to end whoever it was. Finger or not, he had the nerve, now.

"Brauer! It's me!" screamed Carrion, who was evidently still alive, although that condition seemed to teeter dangerously closer to the contrary. Putting the revolver down, the big man felt his jaw fall limp in disbelief before he spoke.

"You're alive... How?"

"Good question, astute today, aren't we? Thanks for deciding to extend my lease on life... You're certainly not the first one this week to try and shoot me,"

"After everything we've been through, you're still a smartass?"

"No... I suppose my roguish charm got the best of me. After you followed the masked thing, I stayed with Winston. He was...

lost. My body was giving out. I crawled until everything became red. I 'dreamt' of many things, fire and water alike. When I woke up, I was in church, of all places. Apparently, the Reverend had found me in a puddle and carried me there–out of the 'goodness' of his own heart. Claimed something Dr. Herbert taught him saved my life. Man, the Fates have a sick sense of humor. He insisted I take the good book although I talked him down to a hymnal. Must have done his old Christian heart well,"

"He's a good man. Told me that, should Red ever get pregnant, he'd helped me deliver the baby. Funny thing is, he might have to make good on that promise now,"

"Oh? Guess you're staying with her, then?"

"I suppose so. She's asleep still. I was about to send her to Stanton's, so I could look for you," said Mr. Brauer honestly, deciding their usual game of vagaries was no longer worth playing. Carrion shrugged before asking something simple.

"Why?"

"Look, I don't know half the hell life has put you through. Whatever 'truth' you were after has bought you nothing more than new pain. We're both cruising towards destruction, and Winston can't set us otherwise anymore. It's our nature, but we don't have to act that way. Life can be a bitch… I won't leave you to face it alone. Not when there's got to be a silver lining to it all–something worth fighting for. We can both choose to be something better, together,"

"Savor what I'm about to say and don't expect to hear it again: thank you,"

"Ah, shut up and come inside. If our ruckus hasn't already woken her up, I don't know what will,"

"As you wish. I'll do you a solid–I'm making myself at home. Prepare accordingly," replied Carrion as the big man led him inside. They sat down where once they had, the first time around. The cut on the rail-man's forehead looked remarkably well off, despite the dried blood that caked it. Mr. Brauer figured it would make for one hell of a scar. It was a shame that it had to come at the cost of someone else's blood…

Smirking weakly, the big man looked down at his favorite stump. He had never quite worked up the courage to tell anyone the truth about it. As it turned out, badgers could be quite hormonal little beasties... Unfortunately, he had found out the hard way–the rest of the finger had to be taken off. Mother had a way with a cleaver. If anyone had asked, he would have indulged them, now... even Red. There was nothing left to hide.

"You're alive!" exclaimed Red, not only thankful that he was alive but also her husband would not put himself in danger looking for him. There was a reason why their conversation had gone on so long; she could not bear the thought of losing him again so soon. She began to pour what was left of their water into cups. The shipments were terribly late, which had managed to get past all of them; there were plenty of fires about, in fairness. Carrion's face contorted into a half-grin.

"Indeed, in the flesh. I suppose congratulations are in order? Taking the scenic route deserves a bit more praise than the first-time floundering of virgins," said Carrion sincerely, bordering dangerously close on being kind–in his sense of the word, exclusively.

"Certainly. That was almost a compliment. I'm sorry... I shouldn't have..."

"Don't worry about it. I'm taking my licks like a champ. Do not bother trying to *tiptoe* around me. Be your snide self, with full confidence!"

"Touché," replied Red, snickering. He had managed to hold onto his particular sense of humor–good for him and bad for everyone else. Even if it was at her expense, he seemed like he needed a laugh desperately. Loss took without remorse.

"So... What now, my intrepid guppies?" asked Carrion simply, not knowing if there was an answer. Mr. Brauer scratched his mane, mulling over the many paths before them. The Councilman had to be stopped. The Cistern had already been poisoned, but the Strayer still processed clean water–unless it was somehow shut down. He spoke up.

"Honey, when did our last package from the Strayer

arrive?"

"Several days ago. The drought must be affecting their ability to churn out clean water. All I've heard from them is excuses,"

"I thought the Strayer processed the Cistern, not rainwater?" asked Carrion, starting to arrive at the realization as Mr. Brauer grasped at it.

"Perhaps if the Strayer realized there was a new contaminant in the water, they would halt production! They may have discovered the Serum was present and had problems trying to treat it... If the Councilman found a way to start production again, he could send out poisoned shipments to the entire community," reasoned Mr. Brauer, beginning to formulate a plan as the puzzle pieces interlocked in his mind.

If *they* introduced Serum to the water, it would make the second thing Karina mentioned–the controlling, brain-altering mixture. Once the town had consumed it, *they* could simply talk them into submission. After depriving them of water for several days, they would take water... from any source without any questions. The Councilman would bend their knees with thirst.

When they had seen her last, she had suspected it was some combination of a drug and a toxicant like lead. Perhaps she came up with a discovery that could reduce the effect? If she had found the composition, it would surely have been a start in treatment. Though, once consumed... They had all seen what it had done to the pig's brain.

Guess and Herbert's father had both contributed to the creation of the Serum. Perhaps some documentation had survived that could help Karina? Herbert had claimed they had taken every book from him related to his father's work save for the one he asked for... Yet, he had known his name before ever meeting him. If he had been untruthful, then he may have lied again.

Goodness knows the Deputy and the rest of the force were useless. Beckett would stall them until everyone was poisoned beyond help. Yet, if he could convince the other men to help him, they could provide the muscle to storm the Strayer. While they had only ever seen the Councilman, he could have other cronies under his wing. Promising a new order would certainly be appealing to those at the bottom.

Above all else, Red and their child had to be safe–though it was becoming increasingly difficult to pinpoint where that would be. The church... Reverend Sharp might receive her. He would not let them come to any harm there. It was plenty far away from the plant, too. Stanton's would be further though... He swallowed deeply. It was time to do mother justice.

"He's going to target the Strayer... Once he poisons the reserve, if he hasn't already, the people, dried half to death, will gulp it down with indifference. At that point, all is lost. We cannot allow that to happen. Karina was studying the Serum when we left–we can't do anything for someone that's ingested it. However, she might be able to make something to cut it off at the source. We have to find her and ensure the Strayer doesn't fold. We don't have time to pick apart Herbert's truths and lies anymore if you..." declared the Constable, beginning to like the way his words carried a bit of weight. Decisiveness suited him nicely; they would already be the Councilman's puppets had he not acted on a burning curiosity to crack a book open. Grimacing, Carrion shook his head slowly before making a painful observation.

"It's already *much* too late. Chances are high that the water has already been ruined. Even if Karina could whip up some magical 'cure,' everyone would already be far too gone to enjoy it,"

"Our shipment hasn't come in yet, remember? Karina sounds like a smart lass–she could figure out something," chimed in Red, handing their cups to them.

"Then we still have time, borrowed but valuable, nonetheless. I'll go to the Strayer and stop him. Carrion, can you make it to Stanton's? Karina will know what to do," said the Constable as Carrion continued to stare blankly. His emeralds bore through the cup into the water. He licked his lips before wiping his coat sleeve against his mouth, causing his nostrils to flare.

It reeked of blood–Winston's and his own. When he got up to leave the church, he stretched his numb arms through the old familiar sleeves. Sharp pleaded with him to leave the old thing behind to be burned. Such a hideous thing it was, torn and painted in red splotches that would never fade. Still, he could not leave it.

No more than he could abandon the pendant that weighed it down. His trembling hands reached down into the pocket, pulling it free. Teeth clattering, he raised the little python, wrapping it around his neck. He gasped and wheezed. One cup of life would have to count as a start for a thousand sips. The coat would continue to match its suitor, perhaps even more so if he continued to stain it as he feared he would.

Downing the cup, he solemnly shook his head before speaking his peace.

"No. You won't get all the fun and glory for yourself. We can find Karina and take whatever she dreams up to the Strayer. There, we'll end this–one way or another. You don't have to woo the missus anymore with a thirteenth feat, do you, Hercules? You've seen to that with the little bundle in her stomach. You can't let me off the hook now. Goodness, you needed me so damn bad that you were about to leave your own family just to find me! How could I hope to deny such an earnest request, partner?"

He paused briefly, nearly choking on the slew of his salty words. After everything they had been through, he deserved better than half-sarcastic filth. Speaking truly kindly had proved remarkably difficult thus far, so he decided to gift him with an equally rare gift: a genuine smile. It may have given way to what could have been considered kind words by a select few.

"After all, what good is hope when there's only one fool following in its stead? A pair's worth more, any day. If you give me a moment to get used to this strange terrain, then I might just go all in it. Once we lose big, debtors, Fates' cronies, tumbling in from all sides, we'll stand together. If that isn't a lovely, poetic sentiment, I don't know what is."

CHAPTER THIRTY: OLD DOG, NEW TRICKS

Karina felt lost. Early last morning, when usually even the most hardcore drinkers had found their way home, she was greeted by a raucous commotion. Mustering the courage to open the door of her lab, she made her way to the bar. Her developments on the chemical would have to wait for a while longer.

The room was bustling with people. At first, she thought she had finally inhaled some toxic fume that made her eyes go funny as her brain slowly died. However, they were very much real–and quite thirsty, at that. Loyal patrons, former patrons, distant ones too, and even people she had not seen once in the town were all there... all strangers.

They must have decided their collective aversion to stepping outside of their homes was less important than dying of dehydration. She could not disagree with their thought pattern–where better to get a drink than a bar?

Some were old, and some were young. One little girl had lovely hair that poked out every which way, no longer bound by a rain cap. Her hair had been like that once, but a bun proved to be remarkably less work to tend to, leaving her far more time to work. There were not many opportunities for such "girlie" things, growing up in a bar. Yet, she would not have traded her experiences for anything. Some of the patrons had pointed out how having a pint with her was just like having one with the boys. That did not bother her most of the time.

One time, some old woman, clearly set in her ways, came storming in. Leathery skin folding in her face, she asked why any decent woman would serve drinks to a bunch of drunkards and dregs. How could she hope to find a suitor in any of the hoodlums she served on the daily? Were her standards really that low?

She shook her head, trying to explain how her father left her the place to uphold–there was nothing else for her to do. The woman would not accept that. A lady like her ought to act like one–and dress like one too. Besides, she had to compensate for the rest of her. No proper gentleman would find some sloppily dressed stick intriguing. Not even the patrons would be that desperate, buzzed off their asses.

Karina asked her to leave, politely but firmly. Once she was sure the door had shut fully, she made her way back behind the bar. She pulled the lab door open, making sure her fingers were clear of the door before slamming it shut, before darting inside.

She cried. The green light barely touched her skin in the corner of the room. Not because of the hurtful things she said about the way she acted or looked–she had accepted those things a long time ago. There was little she could do to change them. Rather, the hateful woman had just reminded her how supposedly undesirable she was.

She did not see how being willing to get her hands dirty made her any less of a woman... any less loveable. Or, how that old coot would think taking care of Stanton's made her an embarrassment to her father–the very one who had given it to her. Her glasses helped her to see... Was she supposed to throw those away, too? Apparently, they dimmed her eyes, her one "redeeming quality," whatever that meant. She had certainly come prepared with plenty of creative insults.

It was not like she had not tried to look. In a town of its size, finding anyone, friend or otherwise, was a challenge— one she had not surmounted. Talking with patrons, while nice, was a sorry substitute for real relationships although she was increasingly unsure if she could discount such things. Perhaps the woman had been right, after all, although she had to believe that was not true.

Staring blankly at the little girl and the horde of familiar foreigners that surrounded her, Karina pushed up her glasses and smiled before greeting them.

"Hello everyone! How can I serve you all today, one at a time, please?"

"My family's running out of water... Daughter has had nothing to drink for days... The Strayer hasn't put out a damn thing in weeks! We won't make it much longer... I ain't sure what we're gonna drink this week... The Reverend's out of charity," sounded all the voices chaotically, like the scattered thoughts of a living organism made of many more. She had not known there were so many people in the town to begin with, so her own thoughts shattered with all the buzzing. How could she help all these people? Her last shipment from the Strayer was nearly depleted, and most resources from the lab were simply unfit for drinking.

She climbed to the top of the bar to try and count the squirming masses before her. Coughing into her elbow, she got ready to raise her voice. It had become far easier with time.

"Everyone! Please listen carefully. I have a little water left here... The rest isn't even close to being fit for drinking. Ingesting contaminants like that could have long-term repercussions..."

"How would you know somethin' like that?" said a voice in the mob, interrupting her. The heckler must have enjoyed the anonymity granted by the surrounding bodies. Another person shouted out.

"Put a sock in it! I've been to this place for a long time. Karina's worked with drinks for years, too. Surely you don't believe she didn't figure out anything this whole time?"

"Still doesn't have the sense to keep water for a bar!" cried yet another voice from the increasingly amorphous blob of people before her. She had her fill of it.

"*Quiet*! This place is mine, so you all will do the courtesy of listening to me. We all know that Stanton's is not turning anything out. I depend on that plant just as much as you all do. The truth of the matter is that bickering amongst us does nothing to make this problem any better,"

"So, what are we supposed to do? Lie still and die? I say we take this up with the sons of bitches that think we can afford to wait this long,"

"Yeah, they're asking for it. I bet they'll find something for us to drink when we're knocking at their doorstep!" said another, perhaps someone that had spoken before although it just as easily could have been some other person altogether. Karina's brow furrowed in confusion. How could she hope to speak calm into a roaring wave? Reason might not suffice, but it was her only weapon, so it would have to do.

"We can ask the force to make sure production can get running again. I already sent some colleagues for another matter–I'm sure, then, that the force is ready and able to assist,"

"That's the dumbest thing you've said yet. I went by yesterday: every window was barred straight up. Looked just like it used to: an old convenience store run straight out of business. Must be a real goose chase you sent them on, huh, sweetheart?" asked the person that was most certainly the heckler who instigated the trainwreck of what could only loosely be called a conversation they were having. Karina's fingers ran through her bun. This was not good... The Constable and the rest had not been back for days. Something must have happened to them, too.

"I say we tear open that door, there, and find out just how 'contaminated' all this water supposedly is. I don't even know her," said a new voice with utter conviction.

"She has no reason to lie to us! Right, Karina? You've poured us drinks for over a decade... Just tell us the truth," cried someone that previously defended her.

"It's not like she's got a man to take care of... All she's ever had to do is look after herself. Think she would change now, folks?" said a voice that may have or may not have been inside her head. Whatever the case, the mob slowly moved closer to the bar. The little girl's golden locks were lost in the encroaching darkness, which increasingly set in with every step. Karina curled her hands into fists and shouted furiously.

"What have we become in our hour of need? Thieves, barbarians, and ruffians? Spouting such caustic nonsense? I know we've always set ourselves apart from the Northerners... but, our own people? Are we truly too proud to take aid from them but so honor-less that we would rob one another? Believe that our brothers and sisters are a bunch of liars? Shame on all of you! Not one of you even considered the children here... The ones who need water the most. I never said I didn't have any water; I said I had a little. So, are we going to tear each other apart in front of our children or behave like we have a *shred* of decency left?" finished saying Karina as the crowd fell silent. They backed away slowly, heads hanging in shame. Though she could not make out the heckler, she figured their head was low, too.

"I didn't want to speak to you all that way–I'm sorry. Today, we need to ensure the children here have something to drink. After that, we can divvy the rest out by need. I won't have anything left for some of you... I promise that tomorrow, I will. I'll find a way, even if that way remains unclear. Maybe the rain will finally fall from the stupid clouds! Whatever the case, come back tomorrow, late. If I have no answers, I'll help you tear open that door myself. Understood?" asked Karina, expecting to hear a wave of voices cry injustice once again.

They all nodded their heads in agreement, some mumbling affirmatively. The little girl, and the other children, came forward with little buckets and pails. She went into the lab, found her last shipment, and came back out.

She bit her tongue every time she poured. Looking into their eyes was hardly any better than seeing how the water slowly lowered in her pitcher with each pour. They could last a while longer without water, but the town was at its breaking point. Worse things than thirst would be born out of conditions like these if something did not change soon.

Not today, though. Thankfully, the last child walked away with enough water for a day. After a few murmurs, a few more people stepped forward with buckets of their own. Pouring what was left of the canister into the pitcher, Karina realized that was it. As the last drop of water drizzled from the edge down the silvery side of the bucket, she watched a wave of defeat wash over everyone else in the room.

A few of them tipped their caps, but soon, all of them left in silence. Soon enough, Karina's head hung in silence, too, as her mind clattered with all manner of ideas, fears, and hopes, all in a vain pursuit of how to make anything better.

The following morning, her head still hung over her work, now in total defeat. Papers, covered in languages she knew and ones she did not, made a halo around her head. They were right... The old woman was right. How could she take care of anyone else? After an entire day and night of work, she had failed to find any sort of solution. This was why no one loved her.

Her reddening face fogged her glasses, casting her vision to a blurry greyness. She set her glasses on the table, eventually settling herself into an all-too-familiar corner. There, no light, green or otherwise, would touch her.

She wept like a fountain. At this rate, she figured all the water would leave her system, and perhaps the town would manage to eke out one more day. When the banging started at the door, she did not answer. They could uproot her, with the rest of the lab equipment, for all she cared. All the red papers really had been the least of her problems. The knocking grew louder still, one strike right after the other, but she remained stone. Eventually, she heard a groan, followed by a shrill squeal of a door busting open. Closing her eyes, she waited for it to all be over until she realized the heavy steps in the distance sounded awfully familiar...

"Karina! My word... What happened? Are you all right?" asked Mr. Brauer, stepping inside to find her, back against the wall, red as could be, and covered in tears. Squinting, she could only vaguely make out his figure, but she lunged towards it, clinging to it for dear life. Unusually, she felt him stifle under her arms although she was far too relieved to really notice. They must all be safe.

"Mr. Brauer! You're alive. Is everyone else, okay?"

"Ms., Karina, it's me... I hope you're not too disappointed," answered the figure, who was apparently Carrion, causing her to blush. Though her tear-stricken face masked it well, his reddening face, despite her relative lack of vision, was not too hard to make out. He pulled his last clean handkerchief free, dabbing her face before helping her put her glasses back on. As her vision readjusted, she locked eyes with two glimmering green dots, realizing it really was the Professor. The Constable and Red were there, too, slinking further to the back. Wiping her face quickly, she tried to smile.

"No! Not at all. Why would you think something like that? There's... Sorry, I've found myself lost for words. It's not been an easy night," said Karina, frantically trying to regain her composure. Her bun nearly drooped down the side of her head, which had, unfortunately enough, become entangled with her glasses. She took her glasses off once more, chuckling in a weak attempt to draw a diversion.

"You know, it might be better to take this down, just this once!" exclaimed Karina, undoing the hair tie that had managed to keep it together until now. Her messy dark hair fell down her face, forcing her to straighten it out before putting her glasses back on–terribly crookedly. Carrion looked backward to Mr. Brauer, who weakly motioned for him to help her. The rail-man swallowed before speaking. Her hair was simply... gorgeous.

How had she managed to fit it in that bun?

"Mind if I help you with those? Can't be in a laboratory when you can't see straight. You really ought to know better," said Carrion cautiously, unsure if witless humor made a crying woman feel any better. He was in luck; she happened to be that sort.

"Oh, well, I would expect that *the Professor* would know of such things," replied Karina, clambering to her feet. Mr. Brauer did not want to rush her, but time was of the essence. His own bluntness, the consequence of brevity, crushed his spirit.

"Karina... This will be a lot to take in. The force did not help us. We found out Dr. Guess had already been killed. There's some organization that wants to poison the Strayer with the stuff you tested. If possible, Red needs to stay here... Where she'll be safest. Winston..." Mr. Brauer struggled to find his words, but Carrion helped him in a way uniquely eloquent for him.

"Is reunited with Amelia. If such a thing is possible, he earned it," finished saying Carrion, beginning to believe the words as they left his mouth. They expected Karina to break out into fresh tears, but she simply shook her head in disbelief. For someone so young, he had experienced so much. Winston could rest now, no longer as a weary soul tugged between two worlds. She would find time to grieve later–this was the only way. Inaction would not cause her to lose anyone else.

"Yes, of course. She will be safe until late tonight. The town will be back to tear this place apart for water. As for Winston... I can't think about that right now. I just *can't*," said Karina simply, sniffling despite her best efforts. She went over to a rack, retrieving the second vial and another unmarked one. Turning back around, she motioned them to follow her. Back at the bar, she sat them down. Pulling up her own stool, she withdrew a small notebook where orders were usually recorded. Realizing they were waiting for her to speak, she began.

"The force has been knocked out of play. Someone mentioned it was boarded up and abandoned. This group must have targeted them first. If they're planning on resuming distribution, the people will be forced to drink it... or die,"

"Then... We have no one to turn to for help. We've already lost," said Mr. Brauer, regretting his choice of words as they flew out of his mouth. Harsh truths were of no use here. Karina shook her head slowly.

"We're not alone, and there's still time. I have a plan to treat the water. It turns out this so-called Serum is a combination of lead, scopolamine powder, and ammonium. The only reason it has a lesser effect in water is that it dilutes; less is consumed with every drink. The burning effect on that brain was the ammonium at work, which, unfortunately, dissolves in water–making it trickier to deal with. The rest of that stuff would kill someone eventually, though, with prolonged consumption. But, I have a way to treat it," declared Karina, brandishing the second vial. Carrion's emeralds lit up with a color that she had deemed lost. It was brief, but she knew her eyes, pained as they were, did not deceive her. Perhaps some hope had found its way to him after all. Scribbling a diagram of the mixture on the page, she showed it to them.

"So, the Councilman's all out of tricks now, eh? Guess we're free of having to listen to him drone on about his marvelous creation. We'll have our chance to put him out of his misery–for good, this time," said Carrion, choking on his words as snot threatened to climb down his nose. His hand had finally blistered over but burned like he still held it over an open flame. He was beginning to suspect it would never heal–hope, like all things, must have its limits.

The Constable wanted to disagree and voice protest, preaching about taking him in, but he could not. The force was no longer around to lock him away. The thing had to be stopped; otherwise, Red would never be safe–she could not be by his side forever. Every attic, every corner, every hallway: none of them would ever feel the same again. Perhaps Herbert had felt his unshakeable gaze, too, stealing his years. Karina knew she could not dissuade him from that path, but she offered her thoughts anyways, expecting them to fall on empty ears.

"Don't do something you'd carry with you to the end of your days. Whatever you feel won't go away,"

"I only wish I had that choice; how sweet that would be. Yet, that may not be my part to play in this grand charade,"

"Carrion, please, listen. You do have a choice. Winston wouldn't have..." said Karina softly before cutting herself off from finishing. The Professor shrugged, turning away from them silently. With a whip of his coat, He shoved his hands in his pockets, then, stormed out the front door. As it slammed shut, Mr. Brauer, Red, and Karina were left to awkwardly stare at each other.

"I... Didn't mean to offend him. I just wanted to help!" cried Karina, polishing the glassware out of sheer nervous habit. Pressing on one far too hard, it shattered, causing her to curse under her breath–more loudly than she had intended. Red, sensing how bothered she was by the ordeal, gave Karina a gentle hug. Sweeping up the broken glass and throwing it away for her, she tried to comfort her further.

"You really can't blame yourself. Carrion's a really difficult sort. He's got a tendency to run off, all about. Art was all set to chase after him and everything,"

"She's right. If it makes you feel any better, he's still out there–I can see his shadow from the window. Some people can be hard to love... I happen to be one of them, too. Give him a moment, and he'll be back inside, I'm sure of it," said Mr. Brauer to a completely indifferent Karina, whose eyes now hovered past his pointing finger, beyond the window, to the shadow. She could not lose it again.

"I'll be back in a moment," declared Karina, collecting herself briefly as she set out through the door. Mr. Brauer let out a muffled warning but decided it was not his place to interfere. He smiled at all the empty beer bottles... There was nothing he wanted to forget anymore. Red smirked, patting him on the back.

"You really think you're going to pick up a pregnant lady by checking out drinks in front of her? I thought you were a gentleman,"

"Oh, I already have a beautiful woman at home who's about to have a great kid of her own. She's a keeper," replied Mr. Brauer as the pair embraced.

Outside, Karina found Carrion leaning near the frame of the window. His face was sullen, with dark rings now visible under his eyes, free from the green light. Fingers darting frantically, he was tearing through and out old pages from a hymnal book, of all things. Little papers flew around, taking flight like doves trying to find their way back from dry land. Eventually, he seemingly settled on a page.

Then, he began to sing... for seemingly the first time. It was horrid yet beautiful, like the overlapping whirring of machines that groaned under their load. A softer, childish quality occasionally poked through but largely remained buried beneath the metallic clinking and clanking that roared on and on. Each word was barely enunciated, but their raw power communicated everything. All the while, the pendant swung like a wild conductor, a pendulum of visceral, emotional release. Yet, she knew the song–it was unmistakable.

"*Twas grace that taught my heart to fear. And grace my fears relieved. How precious did that grace appear. The hour I first...*" sang Carrion before cutting himself off along with the page. Clutching it to his chest for a moment that felt much longer, he pocketed it. She nearly jumped when he addressed her.

"I know you're there. No need to lurk about; I've nothing to hide, not anymore,"

"I... I just came to check on you,"

"Well, are you satisfied?"

"It's not about me. It's about you..."

"I will never be free. Even if my lips say that I'll give hope a chance, I know where I'll go back to for my strength. I know those tools are faithless, but I know them too well to let them go now. When I see him again, *they'll* pull me by my strings, hooks baptized in fear, and I'll kill him. This is my part to play... Fate's made a *pawn* out of me. Winston died just to save another murderer who life owed a bullet," he said bitterly, covering his face in his hands–one so desperately close to healing through blisters and new flesh, the other struggling to find breath beneath the marking seared over it. This grim duality, so terribly evident, cut to her soul.

Step by step, she drew closer to him. Wrapping him under her arms, she hugged him as tightly as she could. His body slowly loosened, and for a moment, he felt like he was back in the sanctuary, which indeed felt like a safe place. So, he did not resist. Not one bit.

Eventually, the pair walked back inside. The former constable, with the subtlety of a rhinoceros, worked to smudge off the crimson imprint left on his cheek. Red, only slightly more convincingly, swept at invisible shards of broken glass that were no longer left on the table. When everyone was settled, Mr. Brauer broke the silence.

"If we make for the plant, right now, we might stop the water from being contaminated to begin with. You have a plan?"

"The filter will pretty much deal with the lead, especially with the size of the particles. Since he'll be poisoning the reserves, it'll have already passed through their filtration system, which means it needs to be sent the other way, recirculated–and then rerouted, again, back to the reserve. As for the ammonium... it, along with anything else, must be distilled. I isolated a few particles from the pure vial you gave me. We need to boil the water and separate it from the foul stuff. I must stress again: the temperature must be *high*. As for the scopolamine... Let's pray that filtration is effective," said Karina, emphasizing each word carefully and raising her hand a good head above her own.

"This sounds too easy. Are you holding back a real challenge?" replied Carrion, scoffing playfully. Either her long-winded explanation was terribly interesting, or it was how she reached so high in the air to prove her point. Her exuberance was beginning to rub off on him like an infection.

"Thank you, Karina. With you both safe here, we'll be able

to get it done. Then everything... will have a chance to regrow," declared Mr. Brauer adamantly. He knew he had the nerve to use the hateful thing in his pocket now–Carrion's poor knocking ability helped him realize that. Red turned away, biting her tongue. She did not want to lose him again for a moment, much less forever.

Yet, with no other clear option, his word would have to be good enough. He would fight for them. Karina wanted desperately to help them more, but she could not think of any way to do so. Perhaps she could cook up something to help them, should they fail to return... Sensing that it was time, the men slowly prepared to leave.

Taking her husband's hand, Red stood on her toes before whispering into his ear.

"Arthur... I'm so proud of you–for who you are. No trophy, prize, or title means anything to you fighting for us. Don't keep me waiting," finished saying Red, choking up. A tear managed to flee her ironclad duct, which he managed to catch with his thumb before it struck the ground.

"I wouldn't dream of it. There's no one else I'd trust to keep our baby safe. I'll be back soon... I promise. The whole world will be waiting," replied Art, both island and eye aligned to take one last look at her belly, where their miracle was. He would gladly die to defend it.

Karina sheepishly smiled at Carrion. Pushing her glasses up slightly, she felt like he might be more resistant to a hug this time. Mustering her courage, she drew close to him and tapped him on the chest–where his heart should be. Placing her hand there, she felt his chest heave up and down, confirming her suspicions.

"There's something good in there, whether you can 'feel' it or not. Don't bother telling me otherwise–you're not that good of a liar," said Karina, giggling lightly as she caught a light smirk flash from him. Her eyes lit up with nearly electric shock as he gently moved her hand aside before wrapping his arms around her. He had to find sanctuary one last time before the end. She did not mind being it.

    "No. No, I'm not."

CHAPTER THIRTY-ONE: THE CISTERN

"It's going to be a long walk there. No carriage to pick up the slack, this time,"

"Guess you will finally be able to burn some fat. That's certainly for the best," replied Carrion as they both chuckled. Walking down the pavement that the plants dared not to cross, they soon saw the church's triumphant spire emerge in the distance. It seemed to pierce the growing, grey clouds that hung in the sky, which playfully drifted as if they had no expectations to meet. While he wished the stubborn things would finally submit and release their tears, he was just happy to see the stormy things at all. Perhaps it was a good omen of things to come... It had to be.

Soon enough, they walked through the market, crushing what little hope he had. The stands were torn apart and scavenged not for coins or food but for water. Broken jars littered the ground, creating a miasma of disparate colors that wanted to tear their feet into equally bright shreds. A variety of coat craftsmen, among others, had boarded their windows as if the apocalypse had arrived. One plank had a particularly ominous message scrawled in big red letters.

"*Outsiders be warned!*" read Carrion, smirking at the irony.

They would have to settle for a foreigner and disgraced cop to save their pissant settlement from extinction. The former constable shook his head before speaking.

"There was a time I felt the same way. You'd think people would get a little less picky when their world starts collapsing around them... But, we'd be wrong,"

"So, it would seem," replied Carrion flatly as the pair continued through the desolation. Eventually, the Cistern, dry as ever, grew on the horizon, only to be dwarfed by something far more magnificent: the Strayer. It was a red-brick, industrial monstrosity: the intake, grated jaws, guzzled the Cistern deep into its belly. Twin smokestacks, hacked up steam, meaning the engine within, a beating heart, droned on. A faded yellow sign reading did little to invite them further.

They approached the entrance, an extension seemingly grafted onto the side of the behemoth, before making their way inside. It was completely abandoned, but it was clear there had been a struggle... The welcome table had been overturned, and bloody handprints marked the tacky wallpaper. A heavy wooden door, leading to the plant, barred their way. Mr. Brauer braced himself to ram it open, but Carrion's growing laughter halted him.

"Did you even try the door first? Or, are you just *so* eager to get this over with that you'll gladly throw yourself at anything?" asked Carrion.

Grunting, Mr. Brauer tried the door, and surely enough, it opened with a pained creak. As they were about to enter, something caught the Professor's widening emeralds: a glass case containing a broad-bladed war rapier, which evidently had been used to officiate the Strayer's birth. Wrapping his ever-itching hand in his handkerchief, he smashed the case open, screaming in pain. Pulling the blade free from its sheath, he tossed the lovely leather scabbard to the ground. Brandishing it, he admired the light that traveled its shiny surface.

"Ah, that'll do nicely. One pull of my strings and this thing will strike true. How nice it is to be reunited with an old friend–

one I hadn't known until now!"

"Have you even held one before? I don't know if carrying it around is..."

"Is wise? Prudent? Probably not, honestly. Though no more wild than you carrying that revolver around, all willy-nilly. That's the joy of realizing what path has been ordained for you–there's no longer a reason to draw strength from fear at all,"

"Better than no weapon," muttered Mr. Brauer as he crept into the darkness past the door. There was no sign of the workers–perhaps they had all been driven away. Groping into the dark, eventually, his hand settled on something that felt like a switch. Carrion's head, atop his frame, seemed to nod downwards in approval, so he yanked the switch down.

Light poured in from a hatch, groaning open, several stories above their heads. Metal ladders climbed across the walls, complemented by rusting red valves and gauges. Somewhere, came a soft chuffing: no doubt, the engine. A large yellow storage tank, the clean water reserve, sat in the center of the room. Strangely enough, wooden girders and supports seemed to frame the space, seemingly from another era altogether. If the brickwork was supported by it, the space was remarkably... delicate.

"He's got to be here somewhere," whispered Mr. Brauer, motioning Carrion to follow him up the ladder. As they made their way to the top, he realized the pipes had been marked with arrows, some pointing in and out of the reserve.

"That green pipe–that's for refiltration. We'll have to get the valve open with that lever," whispered the big man before gesturing at it. Nearby, a little diagram beside the lever indicated that it was intended for three men to operate. One-and-a-half would have to do, should the situation call for it.

A gunshot, followed by a shrill cry–through the door just ahead of them. Pulling his revolver free, Mr. Brauer positioned himself next to the door, ready for action. Carrion stood across from him before putting his ear against the seam to try and make sense of the incoherent noises on the other end.

"Did you... think I'd... something like you?"

"*Fool! Our partnership... eternal,*"

"Quit your sobbing! Did you... think... I'd allow... waltz away?"

"*They... put you down,*"

"Sure. Run along now,"

"The Deputy's here too, apparently," muttered Carrion as Mr. Brauer shook his head in disbelief. Reiner had never cared for him, but how could he sell out the force? After everything they had worked for... Even Beckett was gone—alive or otherwise. Seized with piping hot anger, he flung the door open, aiming the revolver wildly in the general direction of the wailing.

The Councilman, bleeding from his thigh, struggled up a ladder to the roof. Crimson drops slipped down the ladder, leaving a bloodied red trail with his ascent. The Deputy, in his precious uniform, darted behind a crate as Mr. Brauer settled behind one of his own. Carrion, consumed by pure instinct and a severe lack of self-preservation, gave chase to the thing, climbing up the ladder as quickly as his frail arms could carry him.

Reiner laughed heartily. Mr. Brauer felt his chest tighten up as sweat climbed down his colossal forearms to the ground. He had never been a jolly sort—something must have snapped inside him. If he could keep him talking long enough, perhaps he could find a way to reach him and... disarm him. After a dry wheeze, the Deputy shouted.

"So, this is how it's going to end then, huh? Putting a bullet in you like you have rabies? Didn't expect to see your ugly mug again. Couldn't listen, could you? Now, you're gonna make me shoot you. You'd think I would have given you enough spine to look me in the eyes when I do it—even with that fucked-up one you have,"

"The rest of the force, the workers here... What did you do to them?"

"You must have gotten all that blubbering from your dear old mother. They aren't gone, just taking an extended vacation.

Turns out Serum can coax those bastards to stay in their homes for a bit longer, tails between their legs. I tell you, that freak sure could make chemicals. Maybe those fleabag officials will finally listen, and I can finally fix this shithole,"

"So, that's all he offered you? A better place than a convenience store? A uniform that still fits you? That's all it takes for the great James Reiner to bend his knee to a 'freak!' You used to stand for something! Now, you've sold our men out, and for what?"

"They weren't *my* men! I buried them twenty years ago... I didn't like dealing with that thing, but it was a means to an end, my boy, nothing more. Let me teach you one last lesson: if you wait for power to fall into your lap, you're lost. They'll use it to crush you up and grind you into a paste. Then, you're just sticking bricks together so wusses in powdered wigs can build all their fancy fantasies and machinations. Such visionaries! Guess that makes me a simpleton, huh? For trusting in what I can see with my own two eyes?

"No... You can't see beyond yourself. You were willing to throw away the well-being of the entire town just to thwart everyone past some invisible line you drew. And, who are 'they,' exactly? Anyone that has enough moxie to disagree with you? Anyone who thinks differently? You've drawn a circle around yourself," declared Mr. Brauer, muffling his footsteps with his voice as he darted behind a pipe. He was getting closer. The conversation had to keep going.

"I'm trying to save this place from people like Carrion, like *you*! This world's gone to shit. So much desire to carve the whole thing up and begin anew. You see, the world needs someone like me, that still has values, to make sure that never happens. There was a time when men knew better than to stick their noses in every which direction. They'd raise their sons to keep their heads out of their own asses. But now, they're gone... I'm the *last* protector of this place that isn't six feet under. You were supposed to take my place and let me rest finally,"

"And you were supposed to be a good father. All I had to do

for your blessing, that filthy promotion, was put on the shades and be a good boy, doing whatever you asked of me with no questions. I didn't want your approval! I needed your love,"

"You never earned it! That promotion was a pity, nothing more. You really bought into that 'uniform' stuff, huh? If you beg, I'll let you run your greasy fingers over that case again. But, don't you dare lecture me–I'm not your father, and I never loved you! He was a piece of shit, good-for-nothing that left you to a witless woman. You tricked me into thinking you were more than a charity case,"

"You still have a choice. Put down the gun, and I'll see to it you're tried fairly," shouted Mr. Brauer, finding his way past the pipe to another crate. He could hear Reiner's strained breathing coming from the other end. If he did not surrender, he would have to defend his family forcefully. His trigger finger hovered, twitching uncontrollably. He could just make out the profile of the Deputy's revolver near the edge of the box–his hand would be close by. The Deputy, blissfully unaware of Brauer's location, continued to shout all the more.

"Over my dead body! You'll have to kill me first and drag my body out of here. Maybe then you'll have a little trinket to put on your mantle. Red might throw herself at you again just to appease ya. Come on then, face me like a man!"

"If you ever really cared anything for this town, you'll step down. If you have any dignity left, you won't get in my way to save what's left of the water. All his victims would find justice, and you would do your time in a cell… not in the ground. If you ever cared for me, you wouldn't make me gun you down. This is your last warning,"

"I'm not standing down! You have some stones thinking you're some sort of sharpshooter now. Never even held…" yelled the disgraced deputy before being cut off by a bullet that tore through his hand in an instant. His revolver fell to the floor, soaked in red blood. He clutched what was left of his hand to his chest and howled. His prized uniform was as ruined as his hand was. Eyes bulging deliriously, he screamed uncountable profanities before finally twisting a few coherent words together to form a final dagger to stab his accuser with.

"What are you *waiting* for? Pull the trigger and bury me already!"

"I will not hurt you further," firmly stated Mr. Brauer, picking the revolver off the floor before pocketing it. Reiner shook his head wildly, pointing accusingly past the big man to all his invisible enemies, outsiders so terribly vile. He cried injustice, lunging for the oaf's revolver.

"I'll do it myself!" screamed Reiner, struggling to wrestle the gun away to his temple for a moment. Curling his hand into a fist, Mr. Brauer sent it crashing down on his head. In an instant, Reiner crumpled to the ground, knocked out cold. The big man turned away, shaking his head as tears welled up. He lamented over him.

"You abandoned us all... Everyone that ever put their trust in you. Whatever comes next, I'll be there, even if we're separated by bars," finished saying Mr. Brauer weakly, wrapping a tourniquet around the bloodied mess where his hand used to be. Carrion had to be at a higher level, hopefully still alive. Eyes drifting to the ladder, he made his way over to it, beginning his ascent.

Just earlier, Carrion, straining for breath, made it up the ladder to find a sky darkened by bubbling, grey clouds, storming with electric potential. Thunder boomed in the distance, setting a dangerous tempo as he carefully made his way across the cracked tiling that made up the roof. It was far too narrow to traverse at any sort of speed, so each and every step counted. At the edge, the Councilman knelt, leaning on his cane. Across his knees, his thin blade gleamed yellow against the occasional streaks of lightning that zagged across the darkness ahead. His eyes, sickly colorless as ever, glazed over with each passing bout of light that crossed them. The talismans and edges of his bandages jostled against the growing wind, yet he remained deathly still.

"*Too late,*"

"For you, certainly. Already got to the water, eh? It's no matter... Everything's set now,"

"*Set? The future is ever coming. We inflict...*"

"Save your breath. Even if I wanted to spare you, I couldn't. Guess that leaves us a pair of pawns, moving without choice or reason. You love being a good tool, don't you? Come on, then– don't keep me waiting!" screamed Carrion as the sky continued to rumble. Rising, the Councilman threw the cane sheath off the roof, finding a familiar stance. Struggling to find balance on his wounded leg, he leaned crookedly, exchanging the blade from one hand to another. Carrion, mockingly, did the same, all the while waving the rapier wildly in the air.

Stumbling toward him, the Councilman lunged forward, sending the point of the blade hurtling through the air. Seized by pure adrenaline, Carrion awkwardly raised his rapier, redirecting the bloodthirsty edge that sought to take his neck. Seeing an opening, Carrion sent the rapier flying back just as the thing sidestepped past the blade. Swinging his sword, just barely hovering above the floor, towards his opponent's leg, the Councilman felt the steel hiss through the air with little resistance as his opponent leapt back. Punching his bloodied wound and screeching, the Councilman dived forwards, jagged edge championing the charge, only to once again be deflected with ease.

His blade, now stuck between tiles, gave Carrion the perfect opportunity to awkwardly slash him across the ankle, leading the thing to howl more. Tearing the sword free, the Councilman swung it wildly, locking blades with the undisciplined runt before him. Foot slipping violently against the blood pouring from his leg, he lost balance, allowing Carrion to deliver another blow–this time, across the shoulder. As lightning cracked and sizzled on the horizon, the Professor taunted the thing before him, who barely managed to stand.

"Get up! An execution's only fun when the lamb thinks it has a chance against the lion. Besides, you have much more blood to spill," screeched Carrion, raising the rapier far above his head. Barely finding his footing, the thing threw his blade up in a sheer instant as the Professor's blade clattered against it, over and over. With every strike, Carrion felt the thing's guard crumble, iron will and sworn doctrine following in its stead. Eventually, with triumphant glee, he knocked the sword aside, driving his rapier through several of the Councilman's fingers. The sword, the faithless and accursed thing it was, tore itself through tiles in vain before sliding off the roof altogether. The rail-man stood over his prey.

"I lied to myself, don't you see? You did too. Strength from fear carried me to a thankless truth–about who I was, not who I am! How meaningless. Guess your little chant might have something to it, after all: the past's a rotten thing, done and gone. You messed up with the future, though... It's already been decided. No choice we make today can change anything, dust-caked things we are. Escaping our 'purpose,' our part to play, is impossible. The world will keep spinning without us, only releasing us once we've paid our debts. So, now, it is time to pay yours... Don't worry; my time is coming too. Killing you is what I was made for. After that, I'm free from my chains. Hell, I'll be a dove," finished declaring Carrion weakly, raising the blade over the defeated thing before him.

His fingers, sweaty, tightened around the pommel weakly. Thunder, still invisible, boomed ahead. Blood dripped down the jagged edge of the rapier, plopping against the roof tile, eventually cascading down the rest. The pendant, hanging loosely against the wind, swayed in time with his own beating heart as a second of eternity seemed to rattle on indefinitely.

He had broken so many vows. They were gone, demolished by his actions and inactions alike–only a hint of feeling remained in all the swirling, broken parts. Although he could not make sense of the ones he had offered, the ones given to him could not so easily be forgotten.

"*I will never abandon you,*" was what Winston had said a little while before dying. Surely, that promise had been broken... He was gone. He had seen, with his own two eyes, how his body had crumpled against the wall as life left him. In the boy's bloodied stomach, a bullet he had most certainly earned.

Yet, Winston was no liar.

"Mate, are you really considering this still? He's down and out, as it is," said Winston softly, who was, almost certainly, not actually there.

"Why did you do it?"

"Do what?"

"Take a bullet, for me, of all people. You had meaning in your life... I,"

"Carrion, you were my meaning, don't ya get it? I always wanted the best for you. Amelia wasn't around to be loved anymore, but you were hurting and needed help,"

"I don't get it,"

"What's there to get?"

"I never earned your love. I always mistreated you. You should have been glad to see a bullet..."

"Stop. There was nothing you could've done that was gonna make me care for you any less or more,"

"Is that so? What I'm about to do might change your mind,"

"It'd be bad, no question about it. It would set you down a path that would be hard to crawl back up from. When you decide to change, though, I'd be waiting still. But, I don't think you're going to do it,"

"Really? I've already been set into motion. I can't control myself,"

"You might think that, but you can. I'd love to help, but you don't need it anymore, do ya? You're driving this stagecoach on your own,"

"You don't understand! My hands..."

"Well, they look like they work to me. Maybe a little bruised up, but still moving, all things considered,"

"Fate has decreed..."

"You've got the reins, now, mate. No one's going to rip them from your hands. Go on, then–you know what to do now,"

"I *don't* have the strength to do it,"

"Oh, you do. Ya have what you need! Not the rotten stuff that would come from fear but hope. You think there's something brighter out there... good! What are you waiting for? Go find it! I'll leave you here," finished speaking Winston, voice fading away with a chuckle.

"Goodbye, Winston. Go in peace," said Carrion as the pendant settled against his chest. Baring his rancid teeth, he strained to bring the sword down. Sweat climbed down his forearms, wetting his skin, burning red with hatred. Every part of his nature cried out to claim what was his, but he resisted. So, it came down.

To his side. Carrion looked down at the pathetic thing, which snarled and shook its head wildly in disbelief. It did not deserve mercy but neither did he. Putting the sword to his side, he had spared himself, too. Mustering *their* voice one last time, the thing made a bold declaration.

"Such weakness!"

Scampering up, it darted to the edge of the roof to perform one last theatrical act. As it leapt, bandages flapping against the wind to reveal the grisly wounds below, the grey clouds felt tears well up, waiting to be spilled. The thing cackled with the sweet anticipation of the freedom that awaited below.

A large piece of driftwood, a rather gnarly thing, had other plans, however. So easily, the wooden spike ran through the thing's chest, nearly tearing it into two pieces before the rest of the body settled on it. Such power had wrought his ruin. The clouds decided they were tired of playing coy and acted in the one way they knew.

It rained.

Carrion felt each drop plop on his face, climbing down in wet streaks. Scrunching his face with an unusual amount of effort, he was able to smile. His wound felt unusually cool, and for just a moment, it did not sting–it was enough.

He found his way down the ladder to be greeted by Mr. Brauer's booming voice.

"You're alive! The water..."

"Yes. It must be treated, soon,"

"Let's get to redirecting it," replied the big man as the pair made their way to the lever through the empty doorframe. The Deputy was still on the ground, out cold. Pulling his sleeves up, Mr. Brauer grunted in pain, struggling to make it budge at all. Throwing as much of his body weight on the bar as he could, Carrion struggled, but the bar resisted still. Eyes dancing across the room, Mr. Brauer saw an old sledgehammer, rusted a dirty brown, that would do the trick.

Motioning to the pole-man to bring it to him, he lined its crude edge with the lever before slamming it down with as much force as he could muster. It groaned before turning freely. They heard what was left of the reserve rush through the pipe on the other end. Eventually, a thud signaled it had returned to the tank.

"How are we going to heat something that large?" asked Mr. Brauer, unsure of any way to proceed. Carrion shook his head, smirking before replying.

"*We're* not going to do anything,"

"What on earth do you mean?"

"Those wooden beams look mighty flammable. The structure's been built around them, right? It'll collapse with them gone,"

"Professor, you can't be considering this! You'll cook in this place, if you..."

"I certainly do. Brauer, you have a family that needs you... Never leave them again, eh?"

"I refuse to just let you die here,"

"Well, if you want the former deputy behind bars and not burnt to a crisp, you might want to take him with you. He's a bit incapable now,"

"I'm not going to change your mind, am I?"

"No, you're not," said Carrion adamantly, offering his hand to Mr. Brauer to shake.

They were interrupted by the shrill cries of a red pressure gauge spinning wildly. Suddenly, a few pipes, running from the boiler, groaned as they expanded in angry metal blots. Evidently, the lever had been locked in place for a reason. Carrion laughed, shaking his head.

"I guess our little reckoning has come to its end. Go on, then: grab Reiner and get out. There's no more time to debate the finer details,"

"Carrion, I... goodbye,"

"Yes, yes, goodbye, *Arthur*. Do me a favor: don't look back. You have so much to look forward to!" finished saying Carrion weakly as Mr. Brauer's hand met his. They were no longer surprised about the firmness of each other's grips. Nodding solemnly, he darted off, returning with Reiner thrown over his shoulder. Taking one last glance at the large yellow tank that stored the town's hopes, the big man looked, too, at its keeper. The same unkempt hair climbed the sides of his face. His frail arms still stuck out like twigs. Yet, his green eyes burned with something stronger than fire. So, at that moment, there was no one he would have trusted more to save them.

Carrion watched him struggle down the ladder with Reiner wrapped around his back. Soon enough, they were gone, leaving him entirely alone. His marked hand reached deep into his pocket, fishing furiously for what he hoped rested within.

The sheet, crumpled beyond recognition, unfolded in his hand. Finding his prize, he set the paper on the ground after studying it briefly. Reaching once more into his pockets, he pulled a few matches free. There had been a time when he had been overcome with joy at the thought of what he was about to do... That time had passed. He would have settled for a moment in eternity, in his mind or otherwise–one last chance at life.

But now, his lips were wet with spit, and he knew his time was up. So, as each match's red head was struck ablaze, setting beams alight in brilliant blazes of oranges and yellows, Carrion closed his eyes. As smoke filled his nostrils, choking his lungs, he sang like rain still poured overhead. Metal shrieking as it all collapsed around him, he swore he could just make out a voice, through the booming of steam exploding, though certainly not his, crying out.

"And grace will lead me home."

CHAPTER THIRTY-TWO: IN THE ASHES

Mr. Brauer, on his back, lay on the muddy earth, panting. Raindrops pelted his bare face ferociously in some small effort to make up for their absence. The air, however, was little more than ash.

The Strayer had gone up in a horrendous fire. The metal framework had gradually given way, wall by wall, pipe by pipe, until even its jaws had been crushed back to the mushy ground. Though, a dim yellow glint revealed that the reserve had survived–which meant they had too.

People gathered around him, all faces from the town. They swirled around him in half-hearted circles, asking lots of little nothings that entered one ear and left the other. They clenched their caps and hats to their heads so tightly, with such conviction, that he almost wondered if he should do the same. He did not bother: rain was an old friend, now.

Eventually, the fire gave out, surrendering to the showering above. Someone that may have been Mr. Beckett exclaimed something about how Reiner had always been untrustworthy, but he could not be too sure. There was certainly, though, a grand clamor as the body next to his was carried away, kicking and screaming.

"Honey! Oh, my goodness... Are you all right?" asked a woman with a particularly nice jawline and pearly white teeth. She had the sort of hair that leapt over a head like a wildfire, red strands going every which way. He figured her name was Red–it just seemed to fit her, all things considered.

"Karina! He's not responding... Something's wrong with him!" screamed the lady, probably Red, with an admirable level of concern. Another woman, with glasses and a funny bun on her head, ran her fingers past his eyes. It was indeed a proper game, so he played along, allowing his eyes, milky and not, to follow it intently.

"He's in shock. Oh... Carrion... He's..."

His eyes jolted open as the world became real once more. Pulling himself upwards, he made his way toward the wreckage. Red pleaded with him to rest, to catch his breath, but his legs carried him anyways. Past the yellow sign, which had been torn in two, he saw the desolation firsthand.

The tank, surely, had been the only thing to survive. Broken metal shards, scraps of the great industrial corpse before him, littered the ground with defiance. There was only one thing he could do: dig.

So, he did. He dug, crying out every name the pole-man had ever gone by. Karina and Red joined him, screaming in the vain hope that they could be heard. The poor bartender wept, glasses slipping down her face, but her mouth did not stop moving.

They moved to another spot, digging with new energy for a familiar purpose. Surely, he could be beneath the rubble– breathing, alive! His hands bled, cut into bloody streaks by each hateful silvery spike, though he did not mind. Red wrapped herself around him, sending tears streaking down his neck.

Each area brought fresh disappointment. The stupid yellow tank taunted him, daring to still stand amid the rubble. A charred girder, somehow only cracked in two, rested beneath the metal trash. And then, he saw it.

A hand that once had been marked stuck above the rubble.

It had been severely burned, flesh covered in boils and shreds of skin, but it was clean.

The hourglass was gone.

Carrion was found.

Mr. Brauer shouted to the others, running over to the girder. The three of them, mustering what strength they had left, strained to make it budge. Screaming in pain, he threw it to the side, veins pulsing powerfully in his arms. They dug and dug, slowly realizing that Carrion might actually be attached to the hand before them. Biting deep into his tongue, he stuck his fingers to his neck.

There was a faint pulse.

So, their hope had survived, too.

As they wedged him free from his steel prison, his eyes, emerald as ever, flicked open. Weakly, he raised his hand, studying the burn that crawled from his wrist to the tips of his fingers. His terrible teeth formed a wonderful smile, and sweet words followed through them.

"I'm free..."

CHAPTER THIRTY-THREE: FAMILY

The Constable, freshly reinstated as such, studied the pair of tombstones before him, resting above a father and son. Before the son's stone sat a familiar, dusty lantern, burnt out for good. Black clumps of ash were all that remained from the once great flame. He could just swear he still felt warmth emanating from it–though it could just as easily have been the burning anxiousness that came with the weight of having a son of his own.

Red was preoccupied tending to the seed she had found; evidently, the cherry blossoms did not wish to be forgotten so easily. Sakura was not known to be particularly thirsty, and with the rain, unrelenting as ever, overhead, she hoped the little thing would not drown in the mud. Her coat, or "rain-dress," as she now affectionately sold it at her shop, was remarkably comfortable, even when kneeling on damp earth. Though it barely eased the reality that her child had never been real.

"Honey, how's it going over there?"

"Fine. Give it some time, and it'll grow. Just like you," said Red gently as she wrapped her arms around a little boy. She had tailored a precious tiny coat for him, with cufflinks and all. His father was a man of the force, after all. It was simply becoming of him to wear such a thing–and more so, it was cute. He grinned a toothy smile back at her, and his baby-blue eyes widened with glee as he hopped about in the mud in considerable splashes.

"He's already sprouting up! Don't let the boy get too messy if you…"

"I can clean it later. We better get him used to the rain before it's too late,"

"I suppose you're right. Took me nearly four decades… Let's hope Winston fares a bit better than I did," said the Constable warmly, eyes following the boy's bouncing frame intently. When they had found him nearly two years ago, he had been so much smaller, bundled up in a blanket at the doorstep of the force building. Red has just gotten the news… Time had already passed so quickly. Although that pain was only just beginning to fade, they could not be more thankful for the gift before them.

"Thank you… for everything. I only wish I had you longer," whispered the Constable placing his hand on the younger Herbert's grave. Soon enough, his manor would be repurposed into the long-prophesied town hall at the request of his widow. Carrion had helped to find her, albeit begrudgingly. He would arrive soon.

A carriage materialized in the misty shroud of rain that enveloped everything. As it drew closer, the figure in the box, wildly waving the reins in sheer desperation to keep on the road, became clearer: it was Carrion. Gravel crying out, it abruptly stopped, allowing him to step down from the box while dusting his coat off gently. The big man scoffed playfully before speaking.

"Let me guess: *the Fates* held you up, detective?"

"Professor Carrion, mind you, and don't be ridiculous. The precious darling in the back is to blame entirely," said the Professor, sneering with relative indifference at the glowering little man in the cabin behind him. Around the time that the Constable had declined to take Reiner's place as deputy, Beckett had decided he wanted to experience the world in a different medium than paper. The Constable did not have the heart to tell him off, so here he was.

"Oh, look up, already. You've got plenty of time to fill the colossal shoes left for you," added Carrion somewhat sincerely, waving Beckett off dismissively with his hand, which had healed surprisingly well from the burn. Walking closer, he shook the Constable's hand as his emeralds drifted to the pair just ahead of them, prompting him to ask simply.

"How are they?"

"Good, all things considered. Red and I are still looking for our footing. The shop's been good for her. It took her mind off the news, if only for a moment,"

"And Winston?"

"Growing faster than I'd like him to, honestly. One minute he was on all fours, next moment he was waddling around, chasing Foxtrot,"

"I see,"

"Been a while since I last heard from you–what have you been sticking your nose into, dragging Beckett along for? How's Karina?"

"I'm doing fine, thanks for asking! Why would I know how she's doing, Brauer? She's okay. Stanton's is too. All pleasantries aside, I've found something that we need to discuss when you're done... reminiscing on the past," finished saying Carrion carefully, cocking his head at the twin graves. He owed his life to Herbert, which was a nice reminder that the past need not always be a snare.

"Yes, what is it?"

"Herbert knew you because, well, he knew *everyone*. There's something you need to see... Words can't quite do it justice," answered the Professor dramatically. Red and Winston were still playing, so the big man nodded in approval. The pair found their way inside the home. Torn up as it was, it still looked better than when the old man had been alive. The wall where the hourglass had once been was torn to the ground–as it should be. Which reminded him that the last time he had been by, Herbert had been dead...

"You'd think the hourglass carved in the wall would have been a giveaway, but I guess we were too busy to notice... I wanted to raze his house, and you were... Well, I still don't quite know what was bouncing in your big head," said Carrion, rambling as he wedged a small wooden box open. The Constable's island pulsed as it found the contents of it: files labeled with names both foreign and familiar.

"He kept tabs on everyone in this town... and then some. There's my name... top of the heap, no less. Where did he get this kind of information? And why did he want it to begin with?"

"I am unsure. He had one on me too, which explains why I got 'hired' to begin with. Perhaps these were gifts from some other arm of *The Society*? One that liked branding a bit less? Such detailed ordering... Guess he and Dewey were associates, after all," replied the Professor, snickering. The old coot died an enigma, just as he wished–what a life.

"We can discuss this more later. In the meantime, I'm going to finish 'reminiscing,'"

"As you wish. Just don't think too long; you don't have much thought to spare," said Carrion sourly as the pair left the manor. Outside, they were greeted by Winston who barreled towards them rambunctiously. Red followed behind, preparing herself to catch him should he fall backward.

"Carrion, nice to see you again," said Red warmly as she struggled to prevent Winston from faceplanting into the mud below. Carrion smirked, appreciating the determination the boy exhibited–the world was already his oyster, despite being but a few years old.

"Likewise. From the look of the boy, you best keep your eye on him. What a handful he's going to be. 'Uncle' Carrion has got something for him, though," declared the Professor, gesturing to what hung from his neck. Little Winston could just not stop pointing at it–the gleam was so captivating.

It was the pendant. He swung it back and forth as little Winston's eyes followed it intently. The glint of silver managed to shine despite the rain pouring overhead, making it a sun of sorts. The Constable stifled a few words but ultimately settled on speaking up in a delicate manner.

"Carrion, it's very dear to you. I don't think…"

"Nonsense. You see, he's just so taken with it already. I would have to be a truly heartless man to deny him of it. My time with it has passed. Let the boy have his shiny thing," demanded Carrion softly, causing the Constable to nod against his better judgment. Eyes wide in wonder, Winston reached up to take the pendant.

"Now, what do we say?" asked Red, gently prodding the boy.

"Thank you," said Winston, squeaking.

"You are welcome. Now before we settle the unpleasant business before us, is there anything else you need to do?" asked the Professor as the Constable looked at the tombstone one last time.

"Though not always in sight, his work lives on, ever visible to those touched by him," echoed in his mind.

Glancing down at Winston, the Constable patted him on the head, which was already a shaggy mess of hair. He replied as honestly as he could.

"No, I should think not."

EPILOGUE: WASHED NEW

"Here be rain," still misleadingly read a small, crooked sign for a less empty, cheerier place. While it still failed to capture the sheer power of their mistress, the sign was perhaps less egregiously deceitful as the rain came down once again. The town, still before it, was rather bustling with visitors as of late. It, and the people for that matter, had not drifted away in the muck quite yet.

Perhaps the advent of a certain dress shop in the market drove them there; the fashionable rain-dresses, hung before the window, were certainly quite appealing. Wives begged their husbands to brave the elements for them to snag one. Soon enough, the surrounding competition, catching a whiff of the store's success, figured out their coats would be considerably more popular if they weighed a tad less–they were right, as business soon proved.

Thankfully, visitors, foreigners, and even the Northerners found themselves and their coin far more welcome. There had been a funeral a few years back, evidently, for an outsider that died trying to save their water supply. A large man from the force, in a shiny uniform no less, vouched that he had never known someone stronger, from there or otherwise. Though some scoffed at such a sentiment, as new faces continued to pour in with fresh cash, they quickly changed their tune.

The air was wet with new hope. People no longer settled for dreams of some distant town hall–the renovation work on an old manor, donated by some well-to-do widow, made things real enough. The workers were just pleased to work on something less daunting than the Strayer. Its reconstruction had proved remarkably challenging, but the bars made sure they had plenty to drink–which made all the difference. Things would be rebuilt better from the ground up, one cup at a time.

As a carriage prepared to ride off into the darkness of night, a pair of rats, perhaps a father and son, reunited under the moonlight. The older of the two, which faintly remembered being dubbed a type of cheese, had a lovely, sealed envelope dangling from its mouth with a fancy hourglass crest on the cover. As the younger nipped it open, a letter blew out, soaring as it caught a sudden breeze. They were not quite able to make out what it said as the letters were soon claimed by the black.

Not that they would have been able to read it anyways–they were rats, after all. So, unbothered, the pair, with a few squeaks, raced to whatever adventure came next.

A LETTER

Dearest 'Councilman,' or Mr. Trask, as you were once called,

This is a gross overstep. You have ventured too far from the nest this time. Decades of research blundered by your infectious zeal. Did you not learn your place? When the roaring flames danced across your body, did you not know what you were? That mask could never hope to hide your shame. You never let the fire truly cleanse you. Your actions have made a mockery of us.

Your foolishness will not be tolerated. Whatever fervor seized your steps has led you astray to an empty place. Once we repair the damage of your crimes, you will be dealt with accordingly. You will be offered no small mercy this time: no mask to hide behind. What a pathetic thing you are, writhing like a worm in the dirt–so carelessly and casually shaming our Code.

All your butchering has dire consequences. When the town discovers what you are, what we are, they will try to take your head. Be assured; we will take it before they do. Your blade, made blunt by foolish wishes, will be sharpened and passed on to someone more deserving. You are beyond repair, battered beyond recognition, so you will be disposed of accordingly.

How long did that power taste like sweet nectar? Did taking the lives of others make you feel better? All your debaucheries have done nothing to further our mission. Your needless adherence to dead tradition, speaking so foolishly of the present, blinded you to the simplest of lessons.

Blind tradition serves no one, just as some pilgrimage in pursuit of some all-powerful cure. Payment is due now, or in your preferred tongue, sanguis eret sanguis. We will find you to make things right. You have a head start: run along, now.

Warm regards,

Your old friends.

CLOSING: GROWING PAINS

Around five years ago, as of writing this, I was a freshman in a ninth-grade center with a tremendous desire to do something–and writing seemed just right. I had previously dabbled in writing short stories and the like, but I hadn't been able to hang onto any one idea for too long. So, opening a document on a little laptop, which barely stayed charged for more than an hour or two, I set to work to change that. Of course, I had no lofty expectations for it then, nor did I suspect that it would follow me in the coming months, much less years. However, two quarreling men, both deeply insecure, quickly grew into a rather colorful cast–a polygamist and all. I couldn't articulate it at the time, but I knew it was special. So, I hung onto it and, far more importantly, kept writing.

As I continued to grow, the story did too. I was able to put more fancy verbiage to the concepts and things spinning about in my head. Seeing beyond myself, I wrote characters drowning in an absurd world while still treating their feelings and desires as genuine. Most importantly, though, I fought to find the humanity present in every character, no matter how deep within them, and have the tools to communicate it maturely.

I never thought I could write a book. Years later, well in the middle of writing it, I still believed there was some invisible, almost mystical, quality that I lacked to finish it. Yet, I couldn't imagine leaving Carrion, or any of the other less nasty characters for that matter, without a proper ending. Besides, being years deep by that point, I had investment that could not so easily be shaken.

When I first let my dad read the book, it felt like I gave up a piece of myself–all my ideas bare. The next few people, my mom and some close friends, felt no easier. Without her guidance, the editing would have been impossible! I was worried they would find a load of mistakes (they certainly did) or be bewildered by the strange story before them (they were, mostly in a good way). Ultimately, both fears led to editing that refined my book into what I wanted it to be.

I'm so proud of this book, quirks and all. At the end of some five years' worth of work, it's hard to describe the joy that comes with it. Hopefully, this doesn't sound terribly pretentious, but at the ripe age of nineteen, nearly twenty, at the time of release, I'm amazed that I created something that others, younger and older than me, will be able to experience and see through their own eyes.

It has outgrown me… And I love that.

www.ingramcontent.com/pod-product-compliance
Lightning Source LLC
Chambersburg PA
CBHW070321260626
47160CB00003B/911